Book 3 of the Parallel Ops series

THE
GUARDIANS

R.J. ARCHER

NWIDI Press ~ San Ysidro, CA, USA

THE GUARDIANS

This book is a work of fiction.
All names, characters and incidents are either
the product of the author's imagination or are used fictitiously
and any resemblance to any persons, living or dead,
is entirely coincidental.

For more information on the Parallel Ops series, visit:
www.ParallelOps.com.

Library of Congress Control Number: 2001012345

823.0876

"The Guardians" by R.J. Archer

p. cm.
ISBN-10: 0-9779109-8-9 (softcover)
ISBN-13: 978-09779109-84
Science Fiction, general

Published 2012 by NWIDI Press, San Ysidro, CA, 92143

Cover design by Diseño International, La Paz, BCS, Mexico.

Manufactured in the United States of America.

"This work is touted as a 'fictional' account of underwater and other secret places in specific areas of the Caribbean (Andros and the Bahamas) but it is based on a variety of real places and actual events. It is an exciting read for anyone interested in the strange events that have and are taking place in the Bermuda Triangle."

Dr. Greg Little
Author, Explorer and Documentary Maker
www.bit.ly/GregLittleBimini

About the Series

In my first series, *Seeds of Civilization*, I introduced you to Frank, Tony, Linda and Jim—accidental adventurers who joined forces to investigate several of archaeology's many unsolved mysteries. In the *Parallel Ops* series, we catch up with each of the Seeds characters five years into the future. Join Jim (*The Scientists*), Linda (*The Informants*) and Tony (*The Guardians*) as they independently search for that which was lost in the startling conclusion of the Seeds series. And don't miss *The Teachers*, the exciting conclusion to this series and the entire seven-book adventure.

Acknowledgements

Once again I would like to thank my wife, Marty, for her invaluable contribution to this book. She reads (and corrects) every chapter the minute it's finished, she gets invested in the story line and she helps with plot development. But more than that, she keeps me going when I would like to throw in the towel and quit.

I would also like to thank friend Maureen Ryan, of La Paz, and digital artist Jon Hudson, of Georgia, for their critical eyes during the final stages of revision. Their comments and suggestions were greatly appreciated and have been incorporated into the book you are about to read.

A special thanks to Dr. Greg Little for his kind words on the previous page. Since 2003, Dr. Little and his wife, Lora, have been actively searching the Bahamas for hard evidence of a an ancient culture they now believe existed around Bimini, Andros and the Great Bahama Bank. Along with archaeologist Bill Donato, the Littles have discovered megalithic ruins in the area that appear to date back more than 20,000 years!

And I close with a very special thank you to Fred Ray, the man who originally inspired the Tony Nicoletti character. Fred's valuable input has helped me "keep it real" through six novels.

Prologue
(Sunday, March 16, 2008)

Tony Nicoletti looked over his shoulder again to see if he was being followed and when he saw no one, he put his head down and ran as hard as his fifty-four year old body would allow him to move. The Mexican sky was coal black and it was pouring down rain, but he brushed his hair back and laughed. This was the first time he'd been outdoors in more than five years and the rain felt exhilarating.

Headlights on his right quickly brought him back to the reality of the moment. He ducked behind a metal control box and held his breath. Had they found him already?

A white pickup slowed to cross the runway and then sped off into the low fog that was settling over Cancun International Airport.

Tony looked back in the direction he had come and stared at the silhouette of the rusty, run-down hangar that served as the entrance to a secret military complex located far below the ground. Known as MX-2, the facility had been his prison for the past five years, three months and six days and tonight had been his first opportunity to escape. Especially light Sunday night security and a malfunction in the ankle bracelet he'd been forced to wear had allowed him to sneak into the facility's only elevator and make the six-story trip up to ground level undetected. However, the small Sunday crew would also make his absence more conspicuous and he needed to get as far away from MX-2 as he could before he was missed.

Now completely soaked to the skin, Tony scanned his surroundings. The deteriorating weather conditions and the lack of any obvious options in this remote part of the airport made him decide to head to the right, the direction the truck had come. After a distance of only a hundred yards or so, the airport service road pitched down slightly and he could see the lights of several small buildings at the bottom of the short slope. He approached carefully and found an overhang on the nearest building where he could get out of the rain and catch his breath.

Over the noise of the rain pounding on the roof above him, Tony heard a siren in the distance. As the sound approached, his heart raced. Suddenly, the flashing blue lights of a Mexican police car whizzed by the opposite end of the building and continued on into the night.

"A road!" he laughed out loud. Sure enough, the building he was hiding behind was situated on a dark road that ran along the perimeter of the airport. Quietly, he inched his way down the wall, looked both ways and slipped away into the dreary night.

Chapter 1
(Wednesday, April 16, 2008)

Tony Nicoletti was slumped into a tattered booth in the back corner of the dingy bar he'd been calling home for several weeks. He slept upstairs in a spare room, did odd jobs around the bar in exchange for his room and board, and took most of his meals in this very booth. Since his arrival, he had let his dark beard grow out and his normally well-groomed wavy hair was in bad need of a trim. But this morning he'd decided it was time to come out of hiding and go on the offensive.

Across the table, a bubbly girl in her early twenties opened her notebook and smiled.

"I understand you have a story for me, Mr. Smith. Please begin any time you wish."

April Thompson was a reporter for a local newspaper and she'd been contacted by the proprietor of the bar, a woman in her late forties named Carley Quinn.

"Okay, but don't interrupt me until I'm done. A lot of what I'm about to tell you won't make any sense until you've heard the whole story."

Tony sat up in the booth and leaned forward onto his forearms.

"About five and a half years ago, I was a member of a private research group based in Seattle, Washington. We were in the Bahamas investigating some pretty weird stuff when an approaching hurricane made it necessary to move our Learjet out of harm's way. Our leader, a guy named Frank Morton, asked me to accompany the flight crew as they delivered the rest of our team back to their homes in the Virgin Islands and Cancun. We were only gone two days, but while I was away on this fool's errand, Frank went missing, along with an ex-Navy SEAL named Miles Adderly. I knew they had planned to dive a site on the southern coast of Bimini, so as soon as I got back to Andros I spent three days looking for them, but to no avail. Frank and Miles had been screwing around with some special deep diving gear and I suspected that one of them had gotten into trouble, the other had tried to help and both of them had ended up on the bottom, three hundred fifty feet below the surface. Sometime during the third night, I heard Frank's voice in a dream and he assured me that both he and Miles were okay and that I should stop looking for them. I argued, but he insisted I return to Seattle and take care of the business, so I did."

Tony held up his hand to stop the obvious question that was about to burst out of the young woman's mouth. He took a long drink from a glass the bartender had automatically brought.

"I know what you're thinking, but somehow I knew I had really heard from Frank and that he was okay. I can't explain it, but I was absolutely positive.

"Back in Seattle, I took care of the mail that had piled up during our two-week adventure in the Caribbean and then I called the other two members of the team—Jim Barnes, who was still working in a lab at the Navy's AUTEC research facility on Andros Island, and Linda McBride, who I had delivered to Cancun along with her fiancé, Javier. They were both shocked and saddened to learn of Frank's disappearance, of course, but neither was in a position to return to Seattle anytime soon, so I agreed to mind the store until we could meet and decide what to do. I also called my girl friend, Jill, to let her know that my return to her place in the Virgin Islands would be delayed. Jill had been hanging out with us on Andros until the approaching hurricane forced the evacuation I mentioned.

"The very same night that I spoke with Jim and Linda, I had my second visit from Frank. He told me to begin shutting down the Seattle operation and then wait for further instructions. As before, I awoke with absolutely no doubt in my mind that I had somehow communicated with my long-time friend and former Special Forces team mate. You see, back in our younger years, Frank had been an Air Force Pararescueman and I'd been an Army Ranger. During the last months of the Vietnam Conflict Frank and I were both assigned to a joint Army/Air Force black ops team working behind enemy lines in Cambodia and Laos and we'd stayed in touch ever since.

"Anyway, I spent the next two months shutting things down. Although I would have welcomed Frank's input, he chose not to offer it so I did the best I could. I sold his downtown Seattle condo and moved into the apartment he had designed into our headquarters/hangar out at Boeing Field. I sold all the company vehicles except the Dodge Durango Frank had named *Donna*, after his late wife who had been killed in a traffic accident several years earlier. I liquidated as much of the computer equipment and office furniture as I could and I put the recently renovated, state-of-the-art hangar on the market. When the property finally sold, I had to do something with the Learjet, so I did the only thing that made sense to me—I signed the plane over to the Fitzgeralds, our husband and wife flight crew, in exchange for their promise of free transportation whenever I needed it. Together, we flew down to Cancun for Linda's and Javier's wedding the week after Thanksgiving and then the Fitzgeralds moved the plane to a small airport near Miami that they'd found during our investigations in the Bahamas. I divided the cash resulting from the liquidation of our organization three ways, which thrilled Linda and Jim, and I stashed my portion in a numbered bank account in the Cayman Islands. That was more than five years ago, and I still haven't spent a penny of it!"

April had been scribbling notes as fast as she could write so Tony stopped to let her catch up. When she looked up in anticipation, he continued.

"The fateful Bahamas mission had originally kicked off at a secret installation in Cancun, and after the wedding I decided to stop by and visit a Department of Defense agent who was very familiar with our team. We had first met Buzz Edwards on an earlier mission in Nevada and he'd been instrumental in helping Frank acquire the Learjet. It had been Buzz who had summoned our team to Cancun in the first place and it was Buzz who had later orchestrated a clandestine trip into Cuba which almost cost Linda and Javier their lives.

It was Buzz who controlled the Navy SEAL's every move and, as I would later learn, it was Buzz Edwards and those in his inner circle who now want me dead."

"Why do you think they want you dead?" interrupted April.

"When I contacted Edwards, right after the wedding, he arranged to meet me in a bar out on Cancun's hotel strip. After questioning me for more than an hour he apparently decided I knew more than I was telling him about the disappearance of Frank and Miles and, with the simple snap of his fingers, he had me apprehended and put under house arrest in a facility so secret I can't even tell you about it. I finally managed to escape about a month ago and I've been hiding here ever since."

"And what about your friend?" April glanced at her notes. "Frank, I think you called him. Did you ever hear from him again?"

"Oh, yes! After remaining silent for almost five and a half years, he finally contacted me a few nights before I escaped from captivity."

"Really," smiled April. "And what did you two talk about this time?"

"Well, I can't tell you about most of it, but you need to let the world know what Buzz Edwards and his bunch are up to. Frank says they represent a small group of very powerful individuals who have secretly infiltrated the United States and several other important governments around the world. They're trying to find and destroy the *Teachers* and Frank thinks I'm the only one who can stop them."

April raised her eyebrows and stared into Tony's blood-shot eyes. "*The Teachers?*"

"Yes, yes, they're an alien race that's been here for hundreds of thousands of years. They help fledgling civilizations get started and they try to nurse them along. When a civilization ultimately fails, they move on to another emerging group and start over. Our modern civilization represents their thirty-seventh—and final—attempt. If we fail—and we most certainly will if Edwards has his way—the

Teachers will leave Earth forever and the human race will be doomed!'"

April closed her notebook and waved the bartender over. Handing her a five dollar bill, the young woman shook her head and said, "Please bring Mr. Smith another glass of whatever he's used to destroy his brain."

April slid out of the booth and stood up.

"Good day, Mr. Smith, or whatever your real name is. Please give my regards to your invisible friend."

"Hey, wait," pleaded Tony. "Aren't you going to help me expose Edwards and his group?"

"I'm young, Mr. Smith, but I'm not stupid. The secret of your spacemen is safe with me, but please don't ever call me again."

Before Tony could reply, the reporter turned her back and was gone.

Carley returned with another Rum and Coke and set it in front of Tony before she slid into the booth where the reporter had just been sitting.

"I take it she's not interested in your story, huh?"

"Apparently not," frowned Tony. "I guess it's just you and me against the world, kid."

"And they have no idea who they're dealing with," smiled Carley, as she reached across the table and gently patted Tony's hand.

The meeting with the reporter left Tony depressed but even more determined. During his last "talk" with Frank, his friend had indicated that it would be their last "visit" for a while. Frank hadn't offered an explanation, except to say that he was going to be "away" and that he was counting on Tony to protect the secret of the *Teachers* until he returned. When Tony pressed for details, Frank apologized but offered no further explanation. That was thirty-two days ago and there had been no visits since, so Tony assumed he really was on his own. He was determined not to let his friend down, but first he needed a plan.

On a pad he'd borrowed from Carley, Tony jotted down some thoughts, hoping an idea would magically appear:

(1) new identity, (2) get money (3) contact Jill, Linda & Jim (4) keep Edwards away from South Bimini. Tony stared at the pad for a long time, but nothing brilliant popped into his head.

"Tony, are you okay?"

Tony startled awake and sat up. Groggily, he stared around the dimly lit room.

"Uh, yeah, I'm fine. What time is it?"

"It's nearly five," replied Carley. "You've been sleeping for three hours but there hasn't been anybody in the place all afternoon, so I didn't see any need to wake you. However, my landlord will be here in a few minutes and I'd prefer he didn't see my only customer asleep at the table."

Carley smoothed Tony's hair into place as best she could while he yawned and rubbed the sleep out of his eyes.

"Anything I can help with?" she asked, nodding towards the pad on the table.

"I doubt it, but you're welcome to try," replied Tony, sliding the pad over so Carley could read it. "I'm afraid to do anything too public because I'm sure Edwards' people are looking for me and by now they will have checked all my old hangouts. It won't take them long to figure out that if I didn't return to a familiar spot, then I probably went to a convenient one."

Carley tapped the pad with her index finger and said, "Well, I can take care of this first item, but you'll have to trust me if you want to stay completely off the radar. It will cost some money, too – a lot more than I made this afternoon, I'm afraid."

"Which brings us to the second item," said Tony. "I have money—a lot of money—but I don't dare risk accessing the offshore account in case Edwards is watching it."

Just then the front door slammed and Carley turned to see Rob Jefferies, the retired American who owned the building, approaching the far end of the bar.

"Hold on a sec—I might have an idea," smiled Carley as she left to greet her landlord.

A few minutes later, Carley returned with a man in his late forties or early fifties who was dressed in clothes far too nice for the Belize City waterfront.

"Tony, this is Robert Jefferies," said Carley. "Rob, meet Tony Nicoletti."

Tony tried to stand to shake hands, but his leg hit the edge of the table and he flopped back onto the vinyl seat.

"That's okay, Tony, don't get up," smiled Rob as he offered his hand to shake. As he slid into the booth across from Tony, he patted the seat next to him, inviting Carley to join them. "So, I understand you have a little banking issue you'd like to resolve, huh?"

Tony shot a glare at Carley.

"It's okay, Tony. Rob and his wife, Anne, are good people and I'd trust them with my life—in fact I already have, but that's another story. Rob knows all about banking and he might be able to help."

Tony frowned, but since he had nobody else to turn to, he really had no choice.

"Yes, I guess I do. How much has she told you?"

"Only that you have a large sum of money in a numbered offshore account and that you're on the run from Federal agents because you've been talking to aliens in your sleep," laughed Rob. "It sounds like typical Saturday night TV stuff to me, but why don't you fill me in?"

Tony shot Carley another dagger glance and then turned to Rob.

"Let's just stick to the banking issue, okay? Several years ago I was a partner in a privately funded research organization called NWIDI. While on a dive in the Bahamas, the group's principal went missing and was declared legally dead. Unbeknownst to the rest of us, Frank Morton had drawn up a will that left the organization and all its assets to any surviving members of the group. To make a long story short, I ended up with about $18 million, which I deposited in a numbered account in the Cayman Islands. My plan was to make annual withdrawals from the account and retire in the Virgin Islands with a lady friend but I was kidnapped and held prisoner for more than five years by the very same people who had hired us to investigate a matter of national security in the Gulf of Mexico. As far as I know, the money is still there and I'd like to have access to it."

"Of course," nodded Rob. "Well, accessing the account is no big trick, but I assume you're concerned about these agent friends of yours tracking your activities, right?"

"Exactly!" replied Tony. "I don't even have personal identification, much less a bank account or any way to initiate the transaction. Hell, I'd still be sleeping in the alley out back if Carley hadn't offered to let me sleep in the storeroom upstairs in exchange for doing some repairs around the place."

"Well, Carley has a big heart," smiled Rob. "And a good one, too, so I assume she saw something in you that allowed her to overlook the fact that you were just another broke foreigner on the run from agents of the U.S. Government. We get a lot of that here in Belize, you know."

"I knew within the first few minutes that Tony was special," laughed Carley, blushing. "But when he eventually told me the rest of his story, I began to doubt my own instincts."

"Yes, well, I'd really like to hear that story in detail, but let's get this money thing taken care of, first," interrupted Rob. "As it turns out, I have some experience in these matters because I owned a software company back in the States that developed transaction processing applications for banks and credit unions. Most of our customers were regional institutions, but we did have one big client. Have you ever heard of the Bank of America?"

"Of course! Our research group banked with them in Seattle."

"Seattle?" asked Rob. "Now that's a real coincidence! My company was just down the road in Portland, Oregon. Wow, we really have some catching up to do! Listen, if Carley doesn't mind giving up her free labor for a couple of days, why don't you come out to my place while we get this financial thing worked out. And if she doesn't have any better plans for the week-end, we can pick her up Saturday morning and we'll do some diving. In the mean time, she can get started on the ID for you. How does that sound?"

"Great!" exclaimed Tony, "but I'd like to get a haircut and shave this beard off before we take any ID photos and I was serious when I said I was broke. All I have are some clothes Carley picked up for me at a second hand store down the street."

"We can take care of all that on the way back to my boat but to avoid any suspicions, I think your new identity should be that of a local laborer or a dock worker. Carley, will you make sure the new ID reflects that class of person?"

"Sure, but about this week-end. I have to open up here by 10:00 a.m. Saturday morning, so unless you're talking about night diving, I think you'll have to count me out."

Rob put his arm around her shoulders and gave her a hug.

"You let me worry about that, my dear! I have a plan hatching in this head of mine, and I'll drop by Friday afternoon after I have the details worked out. In the mean time, please move forward on that ID for our friend here. We'll get his passport photos taken as soon as we leave the barber shop and drop them off before we head back to my place."

Rob pulled a check book sized wallet out of his sports jacket pocket, thumbed through it and handed Carley two one thousand dollar bills.

"Will that be enough?" he asked casually.

"Enough?" cried Carley, "It should only be about a quarter of this."

When she tried to hand one of the bills back to Rob, he waved her off.

"Tell your friends you want their best quality work. And I'm sure they'll demand a bonus to expedite the process. If there's anything left, buy yourself something nice. Now how about letting us two web-feet from the Pacific Northwest get out of here? We have some work to do!"

After they piled out of the booth, Rob pulled Carley aside and exchanged a few words with her before she smiled and gave Tony a hug. As she headed for the bar, Rob turned to Tony.

"If you have anything upstairs you need you should grab it now because you probably won't be coming back here any time soon."

Chapter 2

By the time Tony and Rob dropped into lounge chairs on the front porch of the cabana, Tony was in a mild state of shock. He had known Rob Jefferies just under four hours and almost every minute had brought a new surprise. The view that now stretched out before the two men was no exception.

"This place is incredible!" exclaimed Tony, stating the obvious. "I had no idea Belize was such a tropical paradise."

"Well, you haven't had a chance to see much of the country from your hideout above Carley's bar. But I must say that Turneffe Atoll, and especially this resort, are at the very top of my list of favorite places in the world. Anne's family is originally from Norway and we spend a couple of months each year over there, but other than that I'm content to stay right here."

"So do you own the whole place?" asked Tony, indicating the row of cabanas along the beach and the main hotel building behind them.

"Me? No! I just own this one cabana, I'm afraid. I did pretty well when I sold my business a few years ago, but not *that* well! I've heard that the European development company that built this place already has several hundred million invested and they continue to make improvements every year. They own this entire twelve acre island and the resort is the only occupant, so privacy is never an issue. The guest facilities line the southern and western beaches and the center of the small island is used for support buildings where we generate our own power and produce our own fresh water. After dinner we'll take you for a walk around so you can see it for yourself."

"You said this is a small island, but when we were approaching on the boat it looked like a really long island. It stretched in both directions as far as I could see," commented Tony.

"What you saw was the western side of the Turneffe Atoll—a thirty-mile-long by ten-mile-wide oval-shaped coral reef. Just inside the reef's protective barrier there's a ring of more than two hundred cays of all sizes and shapes with a huge lagoon in the center. This island actually sits in that lagoon, which is why the water is so calm."

"Amazing," replied Tony. "It's like a whole different world out here."

"And that's precisely why I like it," nodded Rob. "Back in the States the crime, the sky-rocketing costs and the politics were…"

"You're not talking politics already, are you, dear?" asked a slim woman with short blonde hair as she placed a tray on a nearby table and began pouring iced tea into tall frosted glasses filled with ice.

"Tony, this is my wife and life partner, Anne. Anne, Tony."

Tony stood and nodded to the woman.

"My pleasure, Anne. I was just telling your husband what a beautiful place you have here."

"Thank you, Tony, and I hope you enjoy your stay," the woman smiled warmly as she dragged another chair over to join the two men. "I've made up the guest room for you and if there's anything else you need, please don't be afraid to ask."

"Thank you, ma'am," replied Tony. "I appreciate the hospitality both of you have shown me, especially since you don't know anything about me."

"Well, that's not entirely true," smiled Anne as she picked up a folder from the tray and handed it to her husband.

As Rob scanned the pages, he explained.

"Back at Carley's you mentioned Seattle and an organization called NWIDI. When you went upstairs to gather your things, I called Anne and she did a little research for me on the Internet. Later, on our way out here, she texted me with the 'all clear' signal. Otherwise, we would have turned around and taken you right back to Belize City."

"Ah, well, thanks for the vote of confidence and for the caution. I was beginning to think I'd met the most gullible person on Earth," laughed Tony. "So what did you find out?"

Rob flipped back to the first page. "Well, let's see here. The organization you mentioned really did exist. NWIDI was incorporated in October of 2001 in Seattle, Washington by one Frank Morton, now deceased. It says here he was killed in a diving accident in September of 2002, but I think you believe otherwise, correct?"

"I know otherwise! What else does your dossier say?"

"Well, this picture is obviously several years old, but now that you've shaved that beard off, I'd have to say you look like who you claim to be," smiled Rob as he removed a page and handed it to Tony. "Oh, and I have some good news for you! The money you deposited in the offshore bank has accumulated almost a half a million dollars in interest."

"So the money is still there! I was afraid it had been confiscated by my captors."

"Oh yes, your money is still there, all right. All sixteen million dollars, plus the interest. Tomorrow morning we'll start working on a plan to get that turned into something a little more useful, but right now I'm hungry. How about if the three of us walk over to the lodge and see what Chef Gundersen's catch of the day is?"

The lodge's dining room was an elegant, high-ceilinged space clad in beautiful Belizean mahogany—considered some of the best in the world. The food was excellent and the conversation throughout the meal was polite chit-chat about the Pacific Northwest. After leaving Carley's earlier that afternoon, Rob had taken Tony into a fashionable men's store near the marina and bought him a pair of white slacks and a couple of light-weight tropical shirts, along with a supply of socks, shorts and a pair of casual Italian shoes. To anyone in the restaurant, Tony would easily pass as a visiting friend from the States and the dinner conversation certainly wouldn't have betrayed that image.

After dinner, the two men walked Anne back to the cabana and then turned inland for Rob's promised tour of the facilities.

As they walked along a well-lit sidewalk through the mangrove trees, Tony asked the question that had been eating at him all afternoon.

"So, what do you have planned for me, Rob? Back at Carley's you told me I wouldn't be going back there "any time soon" and I doubt if you and your wife want a permanent house guest. Besides, I have something I need to take care of—or at least try to take care of—for Frank. Once Carley gets me some papers and you get my money unlocked, I really should be taking off. I don't mean to sound ungrateful, but Frank is depending on me."

"Understood, but even with a new identity and all that money, you're still going to have transportation issues. If this Edwards is as powerful as you claim, he'll have every airport in the region watched. Besides, I doubt if Carley's contacts can get U.S. identity papers. I think she's just trying to get you local ID so you won't end up in jail if you're stopped by the Belizean police. The info Anne collected said something about a Learjet. Do you still have access to it?"

"Yes," replied Tony, "but I'm positive Edwards has been keeping tabs on it – he was the one who helped Frank get it in the first place. I wouldn't be the least bit surprised to find out it was bugged from the day NWIDI first took delivery. No, the Learjet is out, but even if it wasn't I would need either a U.S. passport or entry visas for every place we landed."

"That's true. Okay, what if you joined the crew of an ocean-going research vessel? As a member of the crew, you'd be granted a temporary entry permit at every port the ship visited. Your entry would be logged, of course, but under a name that could never be linked to the real you. You could travel anywhere you pleased."

"But only if this ship were going where I need to go and, frankly, I don't even know where that is, yet."

"What if you were in control of the ship's itinerary?"

Before Tony could answer, the walkway opened onto a large sandy clearing near the center of the small island and the two men found themselves in the midst of about a dozen concrete block buildings of various sizes. Cables and pipes connected them together in a spider-web that resembled a small factory.

"What the heck..." began Tony.

"This is the support center I mentioned. We have power generation, water purification, a communications center, a laundry and even a small clinic for non-life threatening injuries. It's all here so it wouldn't spoil the view for the guests."

Pointing to the roof on one of the smaller buildings, Tony asked, "What's with the satellite dishes?"

"One is for Internet, the other is for television," explained Rob proudly. "There's also a microwave antenna that links to Belize City's telephone system and a high-powered cell site that serves the entire atoll and connects with Belize Telemedia Limited, the country's largest cell service provider. But the building to your far left is the one I brought you out here to see. After you, my friend."

When they reached the entrance to the white block building, a small plaque to the right said simply, "Building 11 – TWDI Lab."

As Rob inserted a key in the door's lock, he explained. "TWDI stands for Turneffe Wild Dolphin Institute. Anne and I have been involved since we moved here three years ago, but the organization has been in existence for more than ten years. Come on in."

Near the door there were several empty cubicles but Rob walked past them without comment and stopped at a door with a small window in it.

"This is the lab and I need to ask you to be very quiet once we enter. I don't think any of the staff members are here this evening, but there may be some test subjects in for the night." Rob slowly opened the door and pressed his index finger against his lips to remind Tony to be quiet.

The large room contained the normal lab benches complete with scientific paraphernalia and electronics, but the entire back wall seemed to be a single sheet of very thick glass. As Tony approached, he could see that there was water on the other side and the glass appeared to be one side of a large tank.

Tony peered in and suddenly found himself face-to-face with an adult bottlenose dolphin. Startled, he jumped back and yelled.

"That's Emma," whispered Rob. "She's one of our best students. She's also the class clown!"

Rob did something with his hands that looked like signing and the dolphin bobbed its head as if nodding.

"I asked her if she scared you on purpose and she replied... well, you saw her answer!"

"Are you signing to that fish?" asked Tony.

"She's a mammal, not a fish, and yes, she understands about a hundred basic signed concepts. But like I said, she's our star pupil. Here, watch me and then turn and do the same so she can see it."

With his back to the glass, Rob made a three sign gesture as Tony watched. When Tony turned and repeated the gesture, the dolphin immediately cocked its head to the right, as if unconscious.

"You told her 'Good night' and she replied in the only way we can understand. Now wave good bye and let's get out of here so she can get some sleep."

Tony waved and the dolphin ceased its sleep pose. When they were outside the building, Tony was bursting with questions.

"How do you teach them to understand all that stuff? And how big is that tank, anyway? It must be huge!"

"Well, the lecture hall, as we prefer to call it, isn't really that big. There's a large tube in the bottom that connects to a natural cave system under this part of the island. The dolphins come in for lessons but spend most of their time in the lagoon or out in the open water beyond the reef. As for how they learn, well, they're very intelligent creatures—what else can I say?"

"Is that what TWDI is here for?" asked Tony. "Do you teach dolphins sign language and study their ability to learn?"

"No, the sign language is just a necessary evil. Our goal is to understand them, not to make them understand us, but they seem to be the smarter half of the project, so we begin by creating a basis for communication. Currently, Emma and some of her friends are trying to teach us to speak their language."

"And how's that working out for you?" laughed Tony.

"Well, it turns out that the human voice can't make some of the sounds necessary for even the simplest concepts, so things are going pretty slow. The electronics you saw in the lab are being used to develop a computer interface to a sound oscillator that we hope will get us to the next level. Fortunately, the dolphins are very patient and they seem to enjoy—maybe even appreciate—that we're making the effort, as humble as it is. They come back day after day and stay until we sign that we're reached another impasse. We think that in another few months we'll be able to carry on a very basic conversation in their language."

"And then what?" asked Tony, as they headed back down the path towards Rob's cabana.

"Well, the next step will be to take our new-found 'language' into the open sea and make sure Emma and the others haven't just been yanking our chain and teaching us a bunch of four-letter fish words!" laughed Rob. "And for that we're going to need a research vessel. And for that, we're going to need money."

"How much money?" asked Tony, already sensing where this conversation was going.

"Oh, about what you've earned in interest on you offshore account," grinned Rob. "I've had my eye on an eighty-three foot converted shrimp trawler that's currently tied up in Cozumel. It was used as a live-aboard dive boat for a couple of years, but the outfit that owned it went bust and a bank has had it on the market for several months."

"And I bet you think I should buy it and donate it to your dolphin project, right?"

"Oh no, that would be too obvious, Tony. In a couple of days you're going to be posing as a lower-middle class

Belizean dock worker. How would it look if you suddenly bought a $390,000 trawler and donated it to a small non-profit organization? A little suspicious, don't you think?"

Confused, Tony stopped and scratched his head.

"Huh! I was sure you were going to suggest that some of my soon-to-be-available funds should be used to acquire that ship!"

"Oh, I am," smiled Rob. "But the transaction has to be much more complicated than a simple boat purchase. And since TWDI won't need the vessel for some time, it would make a perfect floating base camp to assist your friend Frank. You could pose as a crew member while secretly directing the ship's every move. It would appear to be right at home anywhere there are dolphins and it's already rigged for serious diving work."

While Rob extolled the features of the ship, Tony remained quiet and thought about the proposal. It did seem to be a convenient way to travel and yet stay under Edwards' radar. And the diver support would be a real plus if Tony decided to return to South Bimini and the scene of Frank's "accident."

"Anyway, give it some thought and we can talk about it more in the morning," concluded Rob as they neared the front of Rob's cabana.

"Make it happen," said Tony decisively.

"What?" questioned Rob, caught off guard by Tony's quick response.

"Do whatever you need to do to secure that ship. I need to travel but I also need to stay out of sight and the ship solves both problems. I assume there's a crew, because I don't know the first thing about something this size. I've been around power boats all my life, but this is in a whole different league."

Suddenly excited about the prospect of acquiring the ship for TWDI, Rob nodded vigorously. "Yes, of course there will be a crew! We'll hand-pick them ourselves, although you'll have to play dumb during the process. Just let me know what skills you'll need for your mission and I'll put out the word. We can do our interviews at Carley's place on Friday and I can probably have the vessel here by Saturday afternoon if we get an early start tomorrow."

"What about my money?" asked Tony. "I thought we were going to work on that tomorrow."

"We will, my friend," replied Rob as they climbed the stairs to the front door. "In fact, we'll roll the whole deal into a series of convoluted international transactions that will happen so fast no one will ever figure out where your money went. I've been thinking about it all afternoon and I have a plan that's nothing less than brilliant, if I must say so myself!"

That night, as Tony lay in the guest bedroom of Rob and Anne's beachfront cabana, he reviewed the whirlwind of events that had transpired since this morning when he had been snubbed by the young female reporter. More importantly, he wondered how any of the wheels he had put in motion today would help him fulfill his promise to Frank. As he drifted off to sleep, he was sure he heard Frank's voice faintly say, "Protect the Guardians!"

***

Eight hundred fifty miles away, in the western Bahamas, a meeting was taking place deep beneath the surface of Andros Island.

"Are you sure he can be trusted with this knowledge?"

"Yes, more and more of them are joining us of their own choice and this one, in particular, has proven most sympathetic to our cause. Apparently he has some history with our adversaries and he also has some very resourceful friends who are scattered around the globe. And that's where you come in. As you know, we cannot survive at shallow depths due to the low pressure and our lateral range is also somewhat limited. You, on the other hand, can survive at the surface and can travel relatively long distances."

"So what is this task you ask of us?"

"We need a message delivered to one of these friends. We are currently arranging the time and place, and I will get

that information to you as soon as I have it. I will also provide the message as soon as it is finalized."

"And how do we deliver this message?"

"That technology is already under development and we will provide the engineers with a 'breakthrough' in time to allow you to simply speak to the intended recipient in your own language."

"Incredible! That will certainly help our situation and I'm sure there won't be any reluctance to help you with this project once that news is made known. Shall we meet here again in three risings of the sun?"

"Agreed," replied the metallic sphere.

"Until then," said the old bottlenose dolphin before swimming away through the long underwater passage that led from the Guardian Blue Hole to the open waters of the Atlantic.

Chapter 3

Tony awoke to the aroma of fresh coffee and sizzling bacon and for a moment he didn't know where he was. He'd been having a very pleasant dream about Jill and their time together in the Virgin Islands, but he was sure he wasn't there. Most recently he'd awakened to the smells of Belize City's waterfront and for the five years before that the sanitized and filtered air of the underground facility in Cancun had provided no smells at all. When his eyes focused on the bright print shirt Rob Jefferies had bought him the day before, the events of the last twenty-four hours flooded back into his brain and he jumped out of bed.

After a quick shower and shave, Tony made his way to the kitchen.

"Good morning, Tony!" greeted Anne Jefferies. "I think Rob's out on the back porch hard at work. If you wouldn't mind taking this carafe of coffee out, I'll bring the rest along shortly."

"It sure smells good!" commented Tony as he accepted the carafe and a small tray of cups, cream and sugar. "Which way to the porch?"

As Tony pushed the door open with his shoulder, Rob looked up from his laptop computer and smiled.

"Good morning! I trust you slept well?"

"Very well, thank you. While I've really appreciated Carley's hospitality, that old army cot above her bar is no match for the bed I slept in last night! Thanks again for rescuing me. What are you up to?"

"No good, I'm afraid," smiled Rob. "I just finished putting into play a chain reaction of financial transactions that even I won't be able to trace. Within the hour your money will have disappeared and your Cayman account will be closed."

Tony wrinkled his brow and stammered, "But…"

"Don't worry, Tony. By the end of the day a dozen new numbered accounts will have been opened at various banks around the world and most of your money will be securely—and secretly—back in your control."

"Most of my money?" questioned Tony as Anne pushed a small serving cart through the door and onto the porch.

"Well, you did buy a ship today, you know. That transaction took place indirectly, so as not to be traceable, but the Merchants Bank in Cancun has already acknowledged receipt of $390,000 and the transfer of ownership should occur later today. It seems that the Turneffe Wild Dolphin Institute just completed a very successful fund raising campaign and managed to collect more than enough money to purchase the research vessel MV Dolphin Diver."

"Really!" smiled Tony thinly. "How much more than enough? Will I still be able to afford a Happy Meal at McDonald's when the financial dust settles?"

"Relax, and have some breakfast, Tony. I'll go over all the details after we eat."

Breakfast consisted of eggs, bacon, toast, orange juice and the best coffee Tony had ever tasted.

"All grown locally," replied Anne proudly when Tony complimented her on the meal. "Breakfast is normally the only meal I prepare, so I like to use the freshest ingredients I can get. The coffee is called Gallon Jug and it's grown right here in Belize, over in Orange Walk District."

From somewhere in the house a phone rang and Rob excused himself to answer it.

"Well it's the best coffee I've ever had," said Tony. "I understand we'll be provisioning a ship soon. Can you help me get some of this on board?"

"Of course!" beamed Anne. "And if Rob hasn't already said this, I want you to know how much that ship will mean to the Institute. We give a lot of our own time and money to them, but there's no way we could have ever pulled off a purchase like that. And the staff is so close to a breakthrough—did Rob show you the lab?"

"Yes," laughed Tony. "I met Emma face-to-face, you might say."

"That little stinker! Did she try to scare you?"

"Yes, and she succeeded! I'd really like to learn more about her capabilities sometime, if you wouldn't mind talking slow for this old truck driver."

"It would be my pleasure, Tony. As you may have guessed, Rob's primary interest is computers and software but I was a marine biologist back in the states. I would never have agreed to move so far from home if it hadn't been for the opportunity to work with TWDI and be a small part of their incredible research."

Rob returned to the porch carrying the handset of a wireless phone, which he handed to Anne.

"It's you sister," he said softly.

Anne took the phone and disappeared into the house. Tony sensed something was wrong but he didn't ask in case it was too personal.

"Her sister's husband has cancer," offered Rob. "He's been declining for months and we've been expecting this call. Help me clear away these dishes, will you? We may be making a dash to the airport this afternoon."

While Tony and Rob were loading the dish washer, Anne came into the kitchen with tears running down her cheeks and her hand over her mouth. Rob opened his arms and she crashed into him with a sob. After a long, awkward silence, Anne regained her composure a little.

"Allen died an hour ago," she sobbed. "I need to go stay with June for a while."

"Of course," whispered Rob as he held his wife. "You get packed and I'll make the arrangements. If we hurry you can make the afternoon flight."

Anne nodded and stepped back. She started to apologize to Tony but all that came out was another sob.

"I'm very sorry for your loss, Anne," said Tony. "Rob, how can I help?"

"Ah, well, would you mind heading down to the marina and letting the Captain know that we're going over to the mainland within the hour? We'll meet you there in a few minutes."

"Sure," nodded Tony. "Which way is the marina?

"That way," pointed Rob. "Just ask for Mickey."

Three hours later, Tony and Rob were standing in the Belize City airport watching Anne's American Airlines plane taxi out for the two hour flight to Miami. When the plane was finally out of sight, Rob spoke for the first time in several minutes.

"I certainly don't envy her that trip," he said sadly. "Let's have a drink before we head back."

"Sorry, pal, but even after all your banking magic this morning I still don't have a penny to my name. I guess you'll have to buy—again!"

"I don't mind buying, but as long as we're here, let's take care of your pocket change problem, too. First the bank, then the bar!"

Outside the airport Rob hailed a cab and gave the driver instructions. After some negotiating, the cabbie said "Twenty dollars it is!" and eased his cab away from the curb.

Tony raised his eyebrows at the amount and Rob explained.

"The Belizean dollar is tied to U.S. currency at a rate of two Belizean dollars to one U. S. dollar, so don't be too shocked by the prices here. That Happy Meal you were asking about earlier will set you back $9 here, but that's really only $4.50 U.S. I asked the cabbie to make a quick stop at my bank and then take us down to the Yacht Club for that drink, and $10 U.S. is a fair price for the trip. By the way, when we get to the bank, you should stay in the cab, okay? I'll explain why later."

When Rob returned to the cab he signaled the driver to proceed and then handed Tony an envelope.

"Put that away for now and don't flash it around," whispered Rob, indicating the driver with a flick of his head. "The stop at the Club is on me and we might as well have lunch before we head back to the island."

Rob picked a table in the corner of the large, nearly empty lounge that looked out over Belize Harbor where the Haulover River empties into the Caribbean.

Once they were seated and drinks had been ordered, Tony asked about the secrecy at the bank.

"Well, that's one of the banks where some of your money will end up," explained Rob. "Once you have your new ID, you're going to open an account there so we have a local place to deposit your regular 'wages.' You're not exactly dressed like a dock worker today and I didn't want you showing up on any of their surveillance cameras before we have your new disguise put together in case this Edwards guy is closer than you think."

"Ah, good thinking," agreed Tony. "But if my money isn't here yet, where did I get this?" he asked, patting his shirt pocket.

"Oh, that's just a loan from me to get you by until we get everything in place. There's $2,000 Belizean in there, so don't lose it! Now let's talk about this ship's crew you're going to need. Besides a captain, what other skills are you looking for?"

Tony thought for a minute and then shook his head.

"Wow, I don't know, Rob. I don't even have an operational plan yet. How many people can she carry?"

Rob pulled a sheet of paper out of a thin, leather portfolio he'd brought from the island and laid it in front of Tony.

"She's currently configured like this," he said, tapping his finger on the upper and lower deck floor plans on the page. "There's a large, private cabin forward and the captain's quarters are here, near the bridge. Down below, aft of the engine room, there are six crew rooms, each with a double bunk. So that's, ah, twelve in bunks, two in the owner's cabin and the captain—fifteen, I guess."

Tony studied the plans for a minute before replying.

"Well, I don't know what I'd do with fifteen people but how about if we did this?" Borrowing a pen from a passing waiter, he made some scratches on the drawing. "I'm assuming that you and Anne will occupy the owner's cabin, and I'd like a private room down in the crew area. Even if we turned these two smaller rooms into storage, we'd still have room for six crew members, plus me," he counted out loud. "That should be plenty. We'll need a mechanic to keep the engines running, a dive master to look after the diving gear, a first mate to help the captain and a technician to manage some side-scan sonar I'd like to put aboard. All these folks will have to work as general deck hands when necessary, but I can't think of anything else, can you?"

"Well, I think I'd want to add a cook, too," laughed Rob. "And what about a security type in case we run into trouble at sea?"

"That will be *my* responsibility," stated Tony emphatically. "And one of these storage rooms will become my secure weapons locker!"

"Ah, that's right—you're an ex-Army Ranger, if I remember correctly. Well, it's your call. I have a captain in mind already but we'll need to put the word out for the others, especially the sonar tech."

"Maybe your captain will have some suggestions," said Tony. "Whoever we hire needs to be very discrete or I'll end up back in MX-2—or dead!"

"The final call on each one will be yours, but it's going to be tricky convincing them that you're just a lowly deck hand if they see you in action."

"Once we're at sea the crew is going to have to know that I'm operating under cover, so I want to be sure we end up with a loyal bunch. However, I agree that I need to stay behind the scenes until after the interviews. I figure we'll have our first staff meeting the minute we reach international waters and I'll make up some believable story to justify why I'm posing as a local. That way, the crew will know I'm under cover, even if they never know who I really am."

"So let me get this straight. You're assuming the identity of a Belizean to hide from the U.S. government but you're going to tell the crew that you're a actually a different fictitious person so they won't know that you're really Tony Nicoletti. Is that right?"

Tony thought for a second and then smiled. "Yeah, that's right! Pretty clever, huh?"

"Oh, yeah, it's so clever I'm going to need a script just to keep track of the players," laughed Rob.

After a long and leisurely lunch and more discussions about the crew and provisions, the two men walked the short distance from the Yacht Club to the marina.

"So how does this boat thing work?" Tony asked. "It always seems to be at your immediate disposal, so I assume it's yours, right?"

"Well, yes and no," replied Rob. "When Anne and I first moved here we were back and forth between the island and the mainland almost every day and the resort's boat was old and not very dependable so I bought this one. By the time we'd been here a year, the frequency of our trips had decreased and the resort's boat was on its last legs, so I struck a deal with the resort and Captain Mickey that's worked pretty well for all of us. The resort gets two guaranteed round trips a day that coincide with the airline schedules. Mickey does a sunset booze-cruise six evenings a week and pockets the proceeds and I get the boat anytime I need it as long as my use doesn't interfere with the resort's shuttles or Mickey's cruises. The resort and I share the upkeep and operating expenses, while Mickey makes himself and his helper available from sun up until sun down, six days a week. In a pinch, I can also manage the trip over and back myself but he's much more familiar with the currents and sand bars than I am."

"Interesting arrangement," replied Tony. "So does that mean that you would be able to handle the new ship, if necessary?"

"Not initially, but I love boats and I'm certainly hoping I can tag along and understudy with the ship's new Master if he'll tolerate it."

"Excellent idea!" replied Tony as they reached the catamaran. "I don't like the idea of depending on a single person when so much will be at stake. Everybody needs a backup."

"It doesn't look like Anne will make the maiden voyage, but I'd certainly like to join you on the first leg of your trip. I can help with any initial crew issues and make sure you get off to a good start. Depending on Anne's schedule, I might jump ship along the way and fly back from Miami with her when she's ready to return here."

"That sounds like a plan!" agreed Tony. "And speaking of plans, I'd like to borrow your computer for a couple of hours tonight and begin figuring out what it is I'm going to do. I'll also fill you in on the missing pieces of the Frank Morton story."

"And the *Teachers*," added Rob as the boat eased away from the dock and headed towards the open waters of the Caribbean. "You promised you'd tell me about these mysterious aliens of yours and I'm going to hold you to it."

Once Tony and Rob reached Turneffe Island, Thursday evening passed quickly. Tony studied maps and navigational charts while he brought Rob up to speed on the brief history of NWIDI—from its beginnings with the mysterious Mayan spheres to its sudden end after Frank Morton went missing in deep waters off the southern edge of Bimini Island. Rob was so interested in the story that he suggested they skip dinner at the lodge in favor of a frozen pizza he found in the freezer.

"So you're telling me that the U.S. Navy intentionally falsified navigational charts to hide the fact that there's a megalithic structure on the ocean floor off Bimini?" asked Rob, not believing what he was hearing.

"Well, I saw the chart and I saw the dive boat's depth finder. The chart said the bottom gradually sloped out to a depth of seventy-five feet but the depth finder showed a shear wall that dropped straight down three hundred fifty feet. And the video the dive master took clearly showed a large triangular object protruding from that deep ocean floor."

"That's the video you erased, right?" chided Rob.

"Well, I had to," replied Tony in his own defense. "If that video had gone public every whacko in the world would have descended on South Bimini. Of course, at the time I didn't know I was actually protecting the *Teachers'* secret, but it worked out for the best."

"So is that where you're heading first?" asked Rob. "You've been staring at maps of the Bahamas for two hours."

"No, I don't think so," sighed Tony and he leaned back in his chair and rubbed his tired eyes. "My mission is to keep Edwards and his group away from that site, not lead them right to it. What I think I need to do is create a diversion—maybe a lot of diversions. I think my mission should be to send them chasing after ghosts until they either give up looking for Frank or he provides me with other instructions."

"But you can't very well use yourself as a decoy without blowing your own cover, Tony."

"Yeah, that does complicate things, but something you brought up yesterday got me to thinking," replied Tony. "Remember when you asked me about the Learjet and I told you it was probably bugged? Well, that would mean that Edwards and his buddies know that the day before Frank and Miles went missing that plane flew from Andros Island—Frank's last confirmed location—to St. Thomas and then on to Cancun before returning to Andros."

"Go on," said Rob.

"The truth is that the plane carried only four passengers: Jill Harris, Linda McBride, her fiancé Javier Reyes and me. But for all Edwards knows, Frank and Miles might also have been aboard and one or both could have left the plane at either of the stops along the way. They've probably already looked and not found anything but those two places would still be high on their watch list."

"I suppose so," nodded Rob, "especially Cancun, because they're no doubt looking for you there."

"True, so that's probably not a good choice. But the Virgin Islands have been on my mind a lot lately and I can get there under cover using the Dolphin Diver. As long as I don't draw attention to myself—or the ship—maybe I can create some suspicion that Frank is there and keep the focus off South Bimini until he gets back from where ever he's gone. Besides, I want to check on my friend Jill. We were pretty close and I've worried about her for the last five years. To make matters worse, she has a history with Edwards that goes back before the Caribbean mission."

"But what if you're wrong, Tony. It's been five years since Frank disappeared. What if they aren't looking for him anymore?"

"That's where the plane comes in," smiled Tony. "If I can contact the crew, I'm going to ask them to fly from where ever they are these days down to Andros, on to St. Thomas and then back to their home airport. If the plane is still bugged, the stop in St. Thomas should set off some alarms within Edwards' group and get their attention. When we get there I'll see what kind of misinformation I can cook up to keep them busy a thousand miles away from Bimini."

"This is starting to sound like fun," replied Rob as he opened another round of beers. "Can I throw in a little twist of my own? Give me the phone number and message you want conveyed to the flight crew and I'll pass it on to a friend of mine who lives at the marina in Seattle. I'll ask him to make the call from a pay phone and if this Edwards guy is monitoring the flight crew's calls, he'll think you somehow managed to get back to the Northwest."

After an hour of Internet searches and calls to various small airports in south Florida, Tony finally tracked down Fitz and Susan Fitzgerald. They had moved the Learjet several times during the past five years, but they were now back at the Opa Locka Executive Airport, about eight miles north of Miami International. Tony scribbled down the phone number provided by the evening tower operator, added his message and handed the paper to Rob, who called Seattle.

A few minutes later Rob's cell phone rang and he put it on speaker so both he and Tony could hear the caller.

"So, what did you find out, Jack?" Rob asked. "Were you able to get in touch with the Fiztgeralds?"

"I did!" said the voice in the phone. "The lady, Susan, I think, said they could be wheels up by mid-morning Saturday and would shoot for a 4:00 p.m. touch-down in St. Thomas. They will lay-over there and return to Florida the following day. She was a little confused about the box, but I got an email address from her and told her additional instructions would follow in the morning. Is that okay?"

"That's perfect!" said Tony. "What about the others? Did she have any contact information for Linda or Jim—or Jill Harris?"

"No. In fact she sounded a little surprised when I asked. She said she hadn't heard a word from any of you since the wedding. I assume you know what that means."

After a long silence, the man on the phone said, "Hello?"

"Ah, yes, we're here, Jack," replied Rob. "Thanks very much for venturing out in the rain to make that call. I owe you dinner the next time I'm in Seattle."

After Rob ended the call, he turned to Tony, who had plopped down in a nearby chair.

"What was that about a wedding?"

Flushed, Tony looked up at his new friend.

"That means the Fitzgeralds haven't heard from Jill, Linda or Jim in more than five years."

Chapter 4

Tony tossed and turned all night and twice he was awake for long periods of time thinking about the implications of the news he'd received from the Fiztgeralds. He hadn't contacted them during the past five years because he had been held against his will in a secret underground military installation—so did that mean Edwards had also kidnapped Jill, Linda, Javier and Jim? At the time of Frank's disappearance, Jim was already under a form of self-imposed house arrest at AUTEC, the Navy's research facility on Andros Island, and Jill had returned to her home in the Virgin Islands the day after the wedding. But Javier was a Mexican national and holding him against his will could have serious international consequences. And Linda would struggle against any form of captivity—a struggle Tony already knew could be very painful.

When he heard noises coming from the kitchen, he decided it was time to get up and face the day.

"Morning!" greeted Rob Jefferies. "I'd ask how you slept, but, judging from your eyes, I think I already know the answer. Tough night?"

"You can say that again! Given where I spent the past five years, I'm concerned about the fate of my friends."

"Of course," said Rob as he handed Tony a cup of fresh coffee. "I've put out a few feelers but it will take a day or two to get any response. I have some buddies who are experts in digging up buried data and if there's any trace of your associates, these folks will find it. In the mean time, we have a big day ahead of us, my friend! We need to be at Carley's place by 10:00 a.m. to start interviewing prospective crew members and then we have some banking to do. The Dolphin Diver left Cozumel at sun-up this morning and she should be here about mid-day tomorrow. I've asked the captain who's bringing her down to give us a shake-down cruise tomorrow afternoon and then she's all yours!"

"Well, that *is* exciting, and thanks for making the inquiries about my friends. As soon as I finish this cup of coffee, I'll get cleaned up and we can be on our way."

Rob dashed into the laundry room and came back with a plastic bag stuffed with clothes.

"Here, beginning today you'll need to start dressing your new part, I'm afraid. I borrowed one change of clothes from Mickey's deck hand for today and we'll get you your own wardrobe in town this afternoon. Maybe I'll send you out shopping with Carley after we take care of your banking."

After an unusually rough trip across to the mainland, Tony and Rob took a cab to Carley's bar and arrived about 9:45 a.m.

"Geez, I thought you guys had forgotten about me," she greeted as their eyes struggled to adjust to the dimly lit interior. "Your first two interviews are already here. I put the first one in Tony's old booth and the other one is at the end of the bar. And frankly, I don't like the looks of either one."

"Thanks, Carley. It took a little longer to make the crossing than we expected," replied Rob as he took charge of the situation. "Now here's how I want to do this. I'll conduct the interviews in the booth next to the one you call Tony's. Tony, after I get our first guy moved, you slip into your booth with your back to him. It's so dark in that corner that nobody would recognize you anyway, and with your back to the door they won't be able to see your face. We'll compare notes between interviews, but don't turn and face me at any time, okay?"

"Got it," replied Tony.

When Rob was situated, and had said a few words to the first candidate, Tony slowly ambled across the bar and sat with his back to the other man.

Rob looked at a sheet of soiled paper the man had handed him and began.

"So, you're a marine mechanic, huh? Tell me about your experience, Mr. Crane."

And so it went for almost three hours. After each interview, Rob would talk to the back of Tony's head as they compared impressions and then Rob would jot down a note or two before moving on.

"That's the last one," Rob said when the final interviewee had left the bar. "Come on around here and let's see what we have."

He waved Carley over to join them and she arrived carrying three tall glasses of iced tea.

"A box arrived for you about thirty minutes ago, but I didn't think you wanted to be disturbed," she told Rob as she distributed the drinks and slid in next to Tony. "Hi, big fella," she smiled.

"Hi, yourself," he winked. "So, do we have any keepers, Rob?"

"I think we did pretty good, considering the short notice," he replied as he studied his notes. "I definitely think that last guy, the Indian named, ah, Mejia, would be a good mechanic. He seems sharp, eager and he has experience on a ship the size of the Dolphin Diver. You rated him pretty high, too."

"Agreed, but since I couldn't see him I didn't realize he was Indian," replied Tony. "I thought he said he was a local."

"Not from India, Tony," answered Carley. "He's Garifuna, also known as Black Carib. He's descended from a fierce group of native Amerindians who integrated with African slaves centuries ago and became a unique culture. When the British showed up around here in the 1700s, they deported all the Black Caribs to the island of Roatán but allowed the Red Carib to remain here on the mainland."

"Garifuna," repeated Tony. "I've never heard the word. Well, I'll take fierce over wimpy any day. Sign him up! Who's next?"

"How about dive master?" asked Rob. "There were several qualified candidates. Did any of them stand out from the rest?"

"Yes, I think that Acosta fellow gets my vote. He's worked as both a commercial diver and an instructor and he's experienced with rebreathers—something I really want to learn more about."

"Okay, Acosta it is. I'd like to suggest the Brit as the first mate because my recommendation for captain is also British and I think the common nationality will help them bond quickly."

"He seemed like a decent sort," agreed Carley.

When the two men looked at her and smiled, she quickly added, "Not that it's any of my business, mind you."

"Okay, so we're down to two positions, sonar tech and cook," said Tony. "I understand why you couldn't find any techs on such short notice, but why didn't we interview any cooks. They must be a dime a dozen."

"I've already selected a person for that position, Tony, and I'm afraid my decision is final," smiled Rob broadly. "The box that arrived earlier is a large banner that says, 'Closed for Remodeling' and it's going in that window behind us as soon as we're done here. That is if Carley will agree to sail with the likes of you and me."

"What?" she cried in surprise. "Are you kidding me? Of course I'd love to go, but what about…"

"Closed for remodeling," repeated Rob, jerking his thumb at the front windows. "This place has needed a face-lift for twenty years and I know you can't be making much here. A few weeks at sea will do you good and I'll bet a regular pay check won't hurt, either. I hear our new millionaire owner here pays pretty well."

Carley was beaming from ear to ear when she turned to Tony. "But only if it's okay with you."

Tony pretended to consider his answer for a second. "Well, it will mean turning one of the heads into a powder room. Can we can afford that, Rob?"

Rob laughed and replied, "Actually that's already been done because the Dolphin Diver last worked as a live-aboard dive boat. However, I'm sure Carley will want a private room, so that reduces our maximum crew from six to five. You only mentioned four yesterday, so I didn't think it would matter, but…"

Tony held up his hand to stop Rob in mid-sentence. "I give up!" he laughed. "It would be a pleasure to have Carley along, if she promises to bring some of that great coffee you've been treating me to."

"You must mean Gallon Jug, and it's a deal," said Carley. "Hey, that reminds me, I have something for you!"

She slid out of the booth and disappeared into the kitchen area.

"Thanks," said Rob quietly. "She's a great gal and she's been through some tough times. This adventure will be good for her and I'm glad you don't mind my unilateral decision."

"Are you kidding?" whispered Tony. "I think it's a great idea! I know for a fact that she's a good cook and I owe her a lot for rescuing me off the street when she did."

"I think she's taking a shine to you Tony, but I should warn you that she has a complicated history..."

"Right now I'm only interested in the welfare of my friends and my mission for Frank," interrupted Tony. "Jill hasn't heard from me in five years, so I won't be surprised if she's moved on but until I know for sure I'm not..."

"Shhh, here she comes!" hissed Rob.

Carley slid back into the booth and handed Tony a bundle wrapped in brown paper.

"Sorry it's not gift wrapped, but that's the way things are done on the street," she apologized. "This arrived just a few minutes before you guys did."

Tony slowly unfolded the paper to expose a small stack of documents. One at a time he examined a Belizean passport, a local driver's license and several other pieces of paper all bearing the name of Anthony Wykes.

"They look pretty good, considering the short turn-around time," she commented. "However, I'm afraid it took most of the money you gave me, Rob."

Carley handed Rob a stack of bills apologetically. "I think there's about $700 there, Belizean."

"Hey, I told you to get the best and it looks like you did." Rob pushed the money back across the table. "You hang on to this. I'm sure you'll need this and more before we put to sea. Where is this address, anyway? I've never heard of this street."

Carley smiled proudly. "That's the official name of the alley behind this building and that's the address of the back entrance that used to provide access to the storeroom upstairs. The door has been blocked ever since I've been here, but it's a legitimate address. The old brass numbers over the door were painted over years ago but they're still there in case anybody checks."

"Brilliant!" replied Rob. "Let's put the 'closed' sign up and then Tony and I are going to go open a bank account for him. I have some other errands to run, so I'll bring him back here and you two can go shopping. He'll need a week's worth of work clothes, something to carry them in and whatever personal items he wants. Let's plan to meet back here at 6:00 p.m. and figure out our next move."

Rob had the taxi driver stop a couple of blocks down the hill from the bank and he sent Tony on ahead.

"When you get inside, ask for Mr. Dexter and tell him you've just gone to work for me. Tell him I sent you in to open an account and give him half the money in that envelope I gave you yesterday as an opening deposit. Dexter and I are golfing buddies and I've already told him I'd be sending somebody in, so there shouldn't be any issues. I have a short meeting with the bank president to discuss the Institute's new research vessel so I'll meet you back here. If you get here first, please don't wander off, okay?"

"Yes, Daddy," smiled Tony as he started up the hill.

Tony was standing in the shade of one of the small trees that lined North Front Street nervously glancing left and right when he finally spotted Rob.

"Did everything go okay?" asked Rob.

Tony patted his shirt pocket and replied, "Exactly as planned. You must have some serious influence with the bank because once I told old Dexter that I was working for you, he couldn't do enough to help me."

"Yeah, well, I do have a substantial amount on deposit with them, but so will you by this time tomorrow. The only difference is yours will be in a numbered account and they'll have no idea who the account holder is. The account you opened today is mostly for looks and to make you—Anthony Wykes, that is—appear to be a legitimate individual."

"Well, I hope it works, because I feel very exposed out here on the street. Edwards or one of his hit men could be anywhere. How did your meeting go?"

Rob hailed a taxi and gave the driver the address of Carley's place.

"Oh, my meeting was just a courtesy call, really. The Dolphin Diver is going to be the talk of the town for a few days after it arrives in port and I wanted to give the bank president a chance to brag to his buddies at the Country Club. The next time I need a favor, he'll remember."

"Right," frowned Tony. He had never liked the phony politics that seemed to be a part of the elite life style, but Rob appeared to be right at home with it. Fortunately, Tony would never have to worry about it because his fortune would have to remain a secret for the time being.

Rob dropped Tony at the bar and had already disappeared before Tony discovered that the door was locked. While he was franticly pounding to get Carley's attention, an old man with a cane passed him and laughed.

"Can't you read, mate? They're closed for remodeling!"

Fortunately Carley heard Tony and opened the door.

"Oh, hi!" she said, surprised to see him so soon. "I guess I'd better get you a key. If I'd been in the kitchen, you would have been standing out here a long time."

"And that's not a good thing! I need to stay out of sight as much as possible. I don't know what Rob has planned for tonight, but I hope to be sleeping aboard the ship beginning tomorrow night."

"Too good for the upstairs room, are we?" replied Carley, not quite in fun.

"No, no, it's not that, Carley. I really appreciate the kindness you showed me when I was just another bum off the street. None of what's about to happen would have been possible if you hadn't taken pity on me, and I promise I'll never forget that. If I do, punch me in the nose! It's just that there's a lot at stake and I don't want to become a prisoner again. I keep thinking I'll wake up from a dream any minute and find myself back in MX-2."

Carley rubbed Tony's shoulders gently.

"It's no dream, Tony, but I know what you mean. Yesterday I was really depressed because you'd gone off with Rob and this place seemed even emptier than usual. I was really stressing about how I was going to pay the rent this month and then today Rob springs this remodeling surprise on me. It's funny how things work out."

She stopped suddenly and gave Tony a questioning stare.

"Hey, did you have anything to do with this? Is this remodeling tale just a trick to get me to cook for you?"

"I wish I could say I'm that smart, my dear, but this is all Rob's doing. However, I do think he concocted the remodeling story as a cover so you could close the bar without arousing any suspicion. He hinted at it Wednesday afternoon when he mentioned going diving, remember? I just didn't ever put two and two together until he mentioned it again today."

"He's a good man, that one," replied Carley. "A little naive, but a good man. He and Anne saved my life, and I mean that quite literally."

"Yeah, you mentioned that once before. I'd like to hear that story sometime," said Tony.

"And maybe you will, but right now we have some shopping to do. There's a place a few blocks from here that caters to the waterfront types, so we'll start there. Up the hill the other way, at George Street, there's a Wet Willies—similar to your Walgreens back in the States—where you should be able to find anything else you need. Here, pull this hat down over your face and let's get this done."

Tony settled on denim pants and dark blue t-shirts as his "uniform of the day" but he also picked out three light-blue, long-sleeved shirts and a heavy Navy-style "P" coat in case they ran into bad weather. Carley suggested leather work gloves and a pair of low, steel-toed work boots to go along with the canvas deck shoes he had selected. A set of commercial rain gear, a couple of hats and a belt topped off the shopping spree.

Tony had the clerk pack his purchases into a classic military-style duffle bag—a tall, round canvas bag with a locking top and a shoulder strap for carrying.

"I hope we're going back to the bar first," declared Tony when they were back out on the street. "There's no way I'm carrying this all the way up the hill!"

The shaving supplies Carley had bought him a month ago were nearly exhausted, so he restocked everything at Wet Willies. He also bought a cheap watch and some other miscellaneous toilet articles.

As they were leaving Willies, Tony suddenly darted away from Carley's side and momentarily out of her sight. When he returned, he was carrying a small bouquet of flowers.

"For you," he said, handing her the flowers. "It's not much, but I promise I'll make all this up to you once I know where I stand financially."

Carley smiled and accepted the flowers. "You just did."

Back at the bar, Carley poured two glasses of local serosi wine while Tony emptied his new duffle bag and laid the contents out on a table. Between sips of the sweet, tangy herbal wine, Tony carefully rolled each item and packed them back into the bag.

"What are you doing," laughed Carley. "They were already folded for you."

"Yes, but when you roll clothes, they don't have fold marks later. I hauled one of these things all over Southeast Asia and I was considered something of an expert at getting the maximum amount of crap into a GI duffle bag."

"Quite a distinction," she nodded with a smile. "You've mentioned Viet Nam before. How long were you over there?"

"Well, I was probably in Viet Nam about six months all together, but not all at one time. I was in Southeast Asia a total of two years, eleven months and twenty-one days."

"So where else did you go?" prodded Carley.

"Officially, nowhere. It was all very top secret back then, but I was an Army Ranger and often worked behind enemy lines in Thailand, Laos and Cambodia. That's where I met Frank Morton, my friend who disappeared in the Bahamas. We were part of a small team that went in to rescue downed pilots who had the misfortune of being shot down in countries they weren't technically authorized to fly over."

"Ah, spy stuff!" replied Carley. "Sounds exciting."

"Well, it wasn't. It was rain and mud and bugs and snakes and far too often the pilots we were trying to rescue were already dead by the time we got to them—either dead from the crash or murdered by the local bad guys."

Carley realized that she had touched a nerve. "I'm sorry, I didn't mean to dredge up bad memories. Let's talk about something else."

"No, I'm sorry, Carley. It's just that last night I received news that my friends from NWIDI may have been picked up by the same bunch that grabbed me five years ago and I'm worried about them. It's got me down, that's all."

Standing beside Tony looking down at the now empty table, Carley put her arm around him and leaned her head against his upper arm.

"We'll find them," she whispered.

The long silence was broken by the sound of the front door rattling as Rob let himself in.

"Are you done shopping already?" he asked as he joined the other two.

"I think so," nodded Tony. "The rest of my things are out at your place because you told me I wouldn't be coming back here, but otherwise I think I can dress the part of a ship's hand. There are still some things I want, but they're way out of the budget we had to work with today and probably not items a laborer should be buying anyway. I figured we could slip them into the ship's provisions, when the time comes."

"What do you have in mind," asked Rob.

"I want a computer—you can help with that, I expect—and I want a satellite cell phone like the one Frank used to carry around. I'm also going to need new dive gear, since my stuff is probably still at Jill's place in the Virgin Islands and then there's some things I want to pick up for my room on the boat."

"Well, I need to go back out to the island and pack my own gear, so why don't you tag along? Bring an extra change of clothes, so you can return those we borrowed, and leave the rest of that stuff here. Carley, you're welcome to join us, if Tony doesn't mind sleeping on my couch."

"No thanks," she replied. "I have a lot of loose ends to tie up here before we set sail, so maybe I could get you to drop me at home on your way to the marina. Are we going to be taking anything from here? What about dishes, cooking utensils, stuff like that?"

"If you have some favorite things, go ahead and pack them," said Rob. "But I think the ship will have the basics and we'll add whatever else we need after you've been aboard the Dolphin Diver and assessed her inventory."

"There's nothing here I need," she replied. "Let me get my bag from behind the bar and we can hit the road."

After they left Carley at her apartment on the eastern edge of town, the taxi headed back for the marina with Tony and Rob in the back seat.

Tony yawned widely and said, "Oh, sorry. I guess my lack of sleep last night is catching up with me."

"Well, I think I have some news that will help you sleep tonight, my friend. I'm told that Jim Barnes is still working at AUTEC and he's apparently heading up his own research team there. We couldn't find out exactly what he's working on, but he's apparently made quite a name for himself."

Tony smiled broadly. "That's great news! Please give your friends my thanks. It sounds like Jim may have gone over to the dark side, but at least he's safe. Was there any news about Jill or Linda or Javier?"

Rob shook his head. "I'm afraid not. None of their names have showed up in the media or on any public records since the wedding in November of 2002. It's as if they disappeared off the face of the earth."

"That's exactly what I'm afraid of," frowned Tony.

Chapter 5

Saturday morning Tony was awake bright and early. Although Rob's news of the evening before had left him with mixed feelings, the knowledge that Jim was not only well but was actually flourishing gave Tony hope that his other friends might also be safe. Perhaps they were intentionally staying off the radar or maybe Rob's friends weren't as good as he thought they were. Either way, it was a much happier Tony who followed the smell of freshly brewed coffee into the kitchen.

As usual, Rob was at his laptop on the small, screened-in porch on the back of the cabana.

"Good morning," he greeted without looking up. "Are you feeling better today?"

"More rested, that's for sure," replied Tony. "Do you have an update on the ship? Is it still due in today?"

"Yes, she's right on schedule. I've been busy making the necessary customs arrangements and taking care of port fees this morning and TWDI just rented a slip at the commercial dock under the Queen Street Bridge. It's not the most scenic spot, but it will be handy when we start loading supplies."

"So what's the plan for today?" Tony asked. "Are we still going for that ride this afternoon?"

"You bet we are!" replied an excited Rob. "I thought we'd pick up Carley about 11:00 a.m. and head on over to the dock to wait for the arrival of the Dolphin Diver. After the obligatory meet-and-greet, we'll go aboard and take a look around while the captain and whatever crew he brought with him has a chance to go ashore and do a quick walk-about. When they get back we'll sail up the coast and overnight at sea to find out how she handles. Our new captain, Daniel Braydon, is going to meet us at the dock and go along on the shake down. He wants to take the helm on the way back and have a chance to talk with the old captain, one-on-one. Once we're back at the dock tomorrow, the Mexican crew will fly home and the Dolphin Diver will be all ours."

"Cool," smiled Tony. "If you don't mind, I'd like to start living aboard permanently beginning tonight. I have a lot of planning to do and it will also give me a chance to get familiar with the ship. How soon do you think we'll be able to leave for the Virgin Islands?"

Rob thought for a minute before replying.

"We'll need to confirm that with the Captain, but if everything checks out I'd say we could be underway in a week, maybe less. It will take some time to arrange for provisions and we need to give the new crew about seventy-two hours notice before sailing."

Seeing the disappointment on Tony's face, Rob continued.

"I know you're anxious to get started, but these things take time and you're going to have plenty to do between now and then. By the way, I've listed you as the ship's Quartermaster at the bank, which means you are authorized to make purchases on the TWDI account for supplies. I'll give you the account number later and you can charge whatever you need. Oh, and speaking of funds, your money from the Cayman Islands account has reached all the appointed destinations. Here's a list of the banks, account numbers and access codes. Don't lose that, because you have nearly $18 million scattered around the world and you'll need those numbers to retrieve it. And this envelope contains $100,000 in US currency for miscellaneous expenses. Since you'll be traveling without personal credit cards, I thought some cash might come in handy."

Tony accepted the print-out and envelope and stared at them for a second.

"I really appreciate this, you know. There's no way I could have pulled this off without your help and without the money I wouldn't be able to help Frank and my other friends."

"Hey, don't thank me—I got a ship out of the deal and soon I'll be off on a high seas adventure with you. I think I did pretty well!"

Tony, Rob and Carley arrived at the Queen Street dock to find a white-bearded man sitting on a large trunk beside the empty slip. When he spotted Rob, he got to his feet and smiled.

"Greetings, my friend," he said as he offered Rob his hand. "It's good to see you again."

Tony sized up the captain as Rob greeted the man who could be anywhere from his mid-fifties to his late sixties. His face and hands showed some age but he looked to be more physically fit than someone of his otherwise apparent age. He was dressed in pressed black jeans and wore a white short-sleeved shirt with epaulets on the shoulders. Atop his near shoulder-length head of hair sat a white captain's cap.

"Captain, this is Anthony Wykes," beamed Rob as he made the introductions. "Tony, I'd like you to meet Captain Daniel Braydon, the new Master of the Dolphin Diver."

"It's my pleasure!" greeted Tony. "Do you prefer to be called Daniel or Dan?"

"I prefer to be called Captain," the seaman replied curtly. "Rob tells me that you will be directing her first voyage under the Belizean flag. I hope you understand that while we're at sea I'm in charge and that I expect my orders to be obeyed explicitly."

"Uh, sure," stammered Tony, caught a little off guard by the other man's tone. Recovering quickly, he continued, "However, I reserve the right to blow a hole in her hull and sink her to the bottom. Technically, that would put us back on land, right?"

Tony, spun, hooked his arm through Carley's and walked her briskly down the pier a few yards, leaving Rob and the captain staring at their backs.

"This is going to be fun," he grinned.

Before they reached the far end of the pier, the normal noise of the marine terminal was overpowered by a long blast from a very loud horn and Tony caught his first glimpse of the Dolphin Diver as she entered Belize Harbor.

"Wow, it's bigger than I imagined!" exclaimed Carley as she cupped her hand over her eyes to shield out the mid-day sun.

"It's more than eighty feet long and almost thirty feet wide," offered Tony, recalling the specifications he'd been reviewing the night before. "But it does look ominous floating past those little sail boats, doesn't it? That's going to be home for a while, so I hope it feels just as big once we're aboard."

"This is going to be exciting, Tony, and I can't thank you and Rob enough for inviting me along. The last few years have been a little bumpy for me and the chance to get away from Belize City and those old memories is—literally—a dream come true."

"Well, it's not exactly going to be a vacation, you know. You'll be cooking three meals a day for seven hungry sailors and yourself, so I expect the days will be long and hard."

"I can't wait," beamed Carley. "At least I won't be in this God-forsaken place while I'm doing it."

The two stood at the end of the pier and waited until the Dolphin Diver had made her turn towards the assigned slip before rejoining Rob and his new captain.

Rob was as excited as a kid with a new bicycle and he couldn't wait to get aboard. When the gang plank was finally lowered, he started for the ship but the captain grabbed him by the arm and held him back.

"It's customary to wait for the Captain to invite you aboard," scolded the older man.

Soon a man in his mid-thirties wearing khaki shorts and a white T-shirt appeared at the upper end of the gang plank and shouted to the group on the pier.

"Is one of you Rob Jefferies?"

"Here!" shouted Rob back as he ran up the short incline and shook hands with the man at the top. After a brief conversation, Rob turned and motioned the rest of his group to join him. Back where the pier met the shore, a small group of on-lookers had already gathered to check out the port's latest addition.

One at a time, Rob introduced the captain, Tony and Carley to Miguel, the Mexican skipper who had piloted the Dolphin Diver down from Cozumel.

Miguel led the group along the starboard side of the ship to the rear deck and into the salon area through a large sliding glass door. Tony peeked over the stern, down onto an elaborate diving platform that was an integral part of the ship's design.

"Nice!" he said to himself.

When they were all inside the salon, Miguel introduced his three-man crew and gave the visitors a brief overview of the ship's interior.

Handing each new arrival a photocopied floor plan of the ship's two main levels, he said, "I'll let you familiarize yourselves with the Dolphin Diver while your captain and I go ashore and check in with the Port Authority, Customs and Immigration. Please make yourselves at home and don't hesitate to ask one of my crew if you have any questions. Captain, please lead the way."

Tony, Rob and Carley slowly made their way through the Dolphin Diver's comfortable interior and checked out every square inch of the ship. At the forward end of the salon was the galley, where Carley would be spending a lot of time.

"I love it," she said from behind the built-in serving counter. "It's open, light and right in the middle of everything! I was afraid the galley was going to be a dark windowless cave down in the bowels of the ship!"

To the port side of the galley was a narrow stairway the led down to the crew's quarters, in the aft portion of the ship, behind the engine room. The quarters consisted of six small rooms, each with a set of bunk beds and a small wardrobe. They were arranged three on each side of a short hallway.

"Where are the bathrooms?" asked Tony.

"There are three bathrooms, each with a shower, located upstairs, just forward of the galley," replied the crewman who had met them at the foot of the stairs and introduced himself as Alfie. "They're opposite the Captain's room, which has its own bathroom and shower. There's also a rinse-off shower on the dive platform."

"What's back there?" called Rob, pointing to the metal bulkhead in the aft part of the hallway.

"That's the compressor room," replied Alfie. "The dive platform is directly above the compressors and your tanks can be refilled right on the platform. As you probably know, the Dolphin Diver was last used as a live-aboard dive boat, and this arrangement eliminated the need for us to haul tanks up and down the narrow stairs."

"You said 'us'," noted Tony. "I take it you worked aboard this ship recently, then?"

"Si, *Señor*, for the last year. This way, please."

The crewman led them back up to the main deck and then down an adjacent set of stairs into the engine room, which was located amid-ship.

The engine room seemed unusually large and its stainless steel sparkled like a restaurant's kitchen. Two large power plants, located about six feet apart in the center of the room, were surrounded by other machines and various control panels. Against the forward bulkhead stood a long, well-equipped work bench and a large metal locker.

"Wow," said Rob. "This is quite a set-up."

"Thank you," smiled Alfie. "I was the ship's engineer and I spent a lot of time in here."

Tony moved around the room, examining various devices before addressing the crewman.

"I think I know the answer to this question already, but I'm going to ask anyway. Is there anything you would add to this room if money were no object?"

Alfie thought for a moment and then shook his head.

"No, *Señor*, not that I can think of. If you plan to make long voyages, you will need to stock more consumables such as air filters, generator belts and lubricants, but otherwise this boat is very well equipped."

"I thought so," smiled Tony. "Now how about getting us out of this heat?"

The group went back up the stairs to the main deck where they were met by another crewman.

"Edgar will take you forward," called Alfie. "I still have some things to do down here before we go back out to sea."

Tony, Rob and Carley were led forward down another narrow hallway. They passed three bathroom doors on their left, one marked 'Women' and two marked 'Men.'

Edgar tapped the wall on their right and said, "This is the Captain's quarters and it's only accessible from the bridge."

At the end of the hallway, stairs led up a half flight to the elevated bridge. Miguel and Captain Braydon were examining some instruments on the left and stopped their discussion to welcome the group.

"So how does she look so far?" Miguel asked with a smile.

"Beautiful!" replied Rob as he drooled over the instrumentation on the bridge. "And it looks like you've saved the best for last!"

"Please take your time and look around. The stairway immediately behind you leads down to the main stateroom and the shorter one beyond leads to my quarters. The crew is going ashore for a couple of hours, but you can make yourselves at home in the salon if you wish. After all, she's yours, now."

After a quick peak in the captain's double-sized room, the three visitors headed down to the large stateroom located forward of the engine room and directly below the bridge.

"Now this is nice," whistled Rob as he reached the bottom of the stairs. "Anne is going to love this and there's even room for my computers!"

The trapezoid-shaped stateroom had a queen-sized bed against the port wall, a large wardrobe against the forward wall and an office desk and chair tucked away on the starboard side next to the stairs. A couple of high-back chairs separated by a small table completed the room.

Tony and Carley took turns offering Rob "decorating tips" before the three finally made their way back up the stairs and down the hallway past the bathrooms. On their way to the salon, they passed a door that led out to the port side rail. Tony stepped outside to check out the view and the other two followed him.

"So what do you think?" asked Rob. "Did I spend your money wisely?"

"Oh, absolutely!" replied Tony. "There are a few things I'd like to change, but she'll make a perfect home base until Frank returns from wherever he's off to. Let's go up on top and check out the sun deck."

The roof that covered the middle two thirds of the main cabin also served as an outside deck and bulk storage area. An inflatable zodiac boat was tied against one rail and several fifty-five gallon drums were lashed to the opposite side. About midway down the starboard side was a small boom and hoist unit that the third crewman was using to lower Captain Braydon's steamer trunk onto the starboard deck just outside a door to the bridge.

"I wondered how they were going to do that," smiled Tony. "I'm guessing that's also how we'll load provisions. Did you notice the door in the galley that leads out onto that same deck?"

Forward of the upper deck was a large vertical tubular frame that supported the exhaust tubes from the engines, a variety of antennas, lights and flags and a small observation platform.

"The crow's nest!" smiled Tony. "I already have some plans for that."

Rob pointed to three men in dark suites that had just separated from the growing crowed on shore. The three seemed to be headed towards the ship with a purpose.

"That will be Belizean Customs," explained Rob. "I'd better go down and meet them."

A few minutes later the Mexican captain returned with temporary visas for his crew and they scampered down the gang plank like kids in a toy store. He, however, escorted Captain Braydon to the bridge to begin an orientation.

Three hours later, the Mexican crew was back from their brief shore leave and the Dolphin Diver prepared to make her first voyage with her new owner aboard. Rob, still fascinated by the elaborate bridge, was hanging out with Miguel and Captain Braydon. On the rear deck, Tony and Carley felt the engines come to life as the ship backed slowly out of the slip, reversed direction and moved toward open water. From shore, many in the growing crowd were waving, so Tony waved back.

"I feel like a celebrity," he laughed. "But what's the big attraction? This can't be the biggest ship that's ever showed up here."

"No, of course not," explained Carley, "but the word is out that this ship belongs to TWDI, which is a local organization. There's a lot of home town pride back there."

"Well I hope all that interest stays focused on the Dolphin Diver and doesn't spill over onto the crew. The last thing I need is to have some nosey reporter digging into my identity. I mean, what if…"

"The reporter you met with on Wednesday!" exclaimed Carley. "My God, what if she recognizes you? She's seen you up close, Tony, and she knows about Frank and the *Teachers*!"

In an instant, Tony was off the deck and into the salon.

"I doubt if anybody could recognize me now that I've cleaned up," he replied, "but you have a point. I should probably limit my shore time until we leave Belize for good."

"And there goes your fifteen minutes of fame!" smiled Carley.

The shake-down cruise up the coast of Belize had gone very well and the Dolphin Diver was anchored in Corozal Bay, about fifteen miles south of the Mexican border. Carley had helped Edgar prepare a light meal of sandwiches and fruit and then the eight temporary shipmates had hung out in the salon to listen to Captain Braydon tell sea stories, something he apparently enjoyed doing a great deal.

The captain had traveled extensively and his stories were the stuff of folklore, but by 9:00 p.m. some of his listeners were yawning and he graciously suggested that it was time to call it a day.

Rob had offered Captain Braydon his stateroom for the night, so he and Tony were bunking in the two forward crew rooms. Carley had taken the center room on the starboard side and the Mexican crew members had spread out in the remaining three rooms.

Tony had just turned off his reading light and closed his eyes when there was a loud thump on the side of the ship, followed by indistinguishable shouting. Tony's first thought was that Edwards had somehow located him and he was off his bunk and into the hallway in a matter of seconds.

"What's going on?" he asked as Rob opened his door.

"I don't know, but it doesn't sound good. Maybe it's just a routine customs boarding. Or maybe we're closer to Mexican waters than we thought."

Rob scrambled up the stairs and stopped at the top to listen.

"We're being boarded!" he whispered back down to Tony and Alfie, who was now also in the hallway.

Soon Edgar and Mario joined the others and Tony passed along Rob's alert.

Before the words were hardly out of his mouth, the three Mexicans disappeared back into their rooms and returned carrying large-caliber handguns.

"Pirates!" exclaimed Edgar when he saw Tony's look of surprise. "Do you have a weapon?"

When Tony shook his head, Edgar handed him his own gun and dashed back into his cabin for another.

Meanwhile, Alfie had convinced Rob to come back down the stairs.

"You should lock yourself in your cabin, *Señor*, and don't open the door for anyone."

Quietly, Mario crept up the stairs and he had just reached the top when a thunderous boom came from outside, on the port side of the ship. A second later it was followed by another and Tony instantly recognized the sounds as those of a shotgun, probably one with a shortened barrel. Seconds later they heard the sound of a high-powered speed boat disappearing into the distance.

The three Mexicans raced up the stairs and left Tony and Rob momentarily staring at each other.

"Carley!" shouted Tony. "Where's Carley?"

Chapter 6

Before Rob could answer, he was hit in the back with an opening door and turned to find himself face to face with a startled Carley.

"What's going on?" she asked as she slid the stereo headphones off her head and down around her neck. "What are you two up to?"

"Didn't you hear anything?" hissed Tony. "We think pirates may be trying to board the ship! Get back in your room and lock the door!"

"I will not," she replied defiantly, noticing the gun in Tony's hand for the first time. "Where's everybody else?"

"Upstairs," replied Rob. "We were just heading up to see what's going on, but Tony's right. You need to get back inside until we find out what's happening."

"Look, guys, we might as well get something straight right now. I didn't run a waterfront bar for the last ten years by hiding in a closet every time there was a little trouble. I know Tony did a tour in Southeast Asia, but I'd wager that I've been in more bar fights then the two of you put together. Now let's get up there in case they need our help."

When Tony, Rob and Carley reached the top of the stairs, they could see the rest of their shipmates along the port rail shining flashlights into the water.

"Is everybody okay?" asked Tony as he took a mental roll call.

"Yes, but we think one of them might be in the water," replied Miguel. "They never actually got aboard and after your captain fired on their speedboat, he heard a splash just before they took off."

"So that was your shotgun," said Tony as he squeezed past the others to get beside the captain. "It sounded a lot like a Mossberg 500 Series with a shortened barrel."

"I see you know your firearms, Mr. Wykes," smiled the captain. "It's actually a twelve-gauge 590A1 with a fourteen inch barrel. I like it because it packs nicely into my sea trunk."

"Well, it's an excellent choice, although I prefer a longer barrel for better accuracy. I lugged one across a large portion of Southeast Asia many years ago. When we get back to port I'd like to hear your recommendations regarding ship's safety before we head for open water next week."

"Certainly," replied the captain. "I'm sure this won't be our first encounter with unfriendlies and I believe in being prepared. I'm glad to hear that you feel the same way."

After more than an hour of scanning the waters around the ship, the crew finally gave up their search and returned to their quarters. Miguel's three crew members were the best armed, so they offered to take turns standing watch throughout the night. Before Tony went to sleep he drew up an extensive list of security upgrades he planned to make before the Dolphin Diver set sail for the Virgin Islands.

***

In a windowless office in Washington, D.C., Buzz Edwards slammed a packet of papers down on his desk and ran his fingers through his short hair.

"Why haven't you found him?" Edwards asked the man sitting in front of his desk. "What's wrong with you and your team, anyway?"

The other man stared at his shoes, knowing that Edwards didn't really expect him to answer. He was just going through the same ranting routine he'd been going through on a weekly basis for the past five years.

"He's out there somewhere, Mueller, and we're going to get him back. Miles Adderly knows too much about our operation to be loose and unaccounted for. We have to find him, do you understand?"

"Yes, sir, I do but the more we look for him, the more it appears he drowned, along with Frank Morton, just as the media originally reported. We know that two rebreather rigs were missing from Adderly's place on Andros Island and we have statements from the crew of the Coast Guard chopper that gave them a lift to Bimini. They were never seen again, so it seems obvious that…"

"Then I want a body, some bones—something!" shouted Edwards. "If he's dead, there should be evidence and we're not going to stop looking until we have it. And what about this last item?" scowled, Edwards, tapping the packet of papers.

Erik Mueller nodded. He hadn't wanted to include any information about the Learjet in his weekly report because he knew it would fuel his boss's theory that Frank Morton and Miles Adderly were still alive, but he was afraid to leave the information out for fear that Edwards would find out through other channels. If that happened, Mueller had no doubt that he would suffer a long and painful demise courtesy of Buzz Edwards.

"Well, it could just be a routine flight. We've been monitoring that plane's movements for a long time and we've never seen the Fitzgeralds do anything even remotely suspicious. They operate a successful charter business and it's reasonable to assume that at least once in five years they'd book a passenger to St. Thomas."

"Reasonable to assume?" shouted Edwards again. "We're not assuming anything when it comes to the whereabouts of Miles Adderly. I've had it with this attitude. You get your butt down there and find out why that aircraft stopped at Andros on its way to St. Thomas and you find out who was on board. And don't come back here until you have some answers."

"Yes, sir!" replied Mueller as he stood to leave. "But we have people…"

"Erik, I'm dead serious about this. From this moment on, this is your personal problem, do I make myself clear?"

As Mueller sat in the boarding lounge waiting for the departure of his flight to St. Thomas, his anger grew. He was off on an impossible mission to find a man who was probably dead and his own future—and possibly his life—was on the line. And none of this would be happening if Tony Nicoletti hadn't escaped from MX-2 that rainy Sunday night a month ago. Edwards had been on the verge of calling off the useless search for Miles Adderly when Nicoletti slipped away and disappeared into thin air. And for that, Mueller hated Tony Nicoletti almost as much as he feared Buzz Edwards.

***

The following week passed quickly and Tony stayed much busier than he had imagined. In addition to the security measures he had added, there were provisions to acquire and some remodeling to do. Carley spent every day on board but she returned home each afternoon, and this gave Tony time to develop a plan of action. It also gave him time to get to know Captain Braydon a little better.

Friday evening found the two men sitting on the back deck enjoying a glass of local wine and watching the lights of Belize City.

"Well, Captain, what's your assessment? Are we ready to take on the open sea and make our way east to the Virgin Islands?"

"Aye, Tony, I think the ship is up to the challenge. I just hope the crew is equally prepared."

"Yes, me, too," replied Tony. "I'm sorry we're going to be one hand short for a while, but I just couldn't find a sonar technician here in Belize that I thought would fit in with the rest of the crew. They all seem to take to you, by the way."

"I can work with most anybody, as long as they do their job and stay out of trouble," commented the captain as he took a long drag on his ornate, ivory-stemmed pipe. "And that's why I'm still against having a woman on board. That situation can only lead to trouble."

"Now, Captain, we've discussed this every night this week," laughed Tony. "Carley is a member of the crew and that's all there is to it. Besides, you love her cooking and you can't deny that."

***

Saturday morning Tony awoke at sunrise and was sipping coffee in the salon when the first crewman arrived at

8:30 a.m. Cesar Acosta was carrying two large duffle bags, similar to the one Tony had purchased on his shopping spree with Carley. Tony went out through the large sliding glass door at the rear of the salon and offered the ship's new divemaster a hand.

"Let me help you with that," he smiled as the other man struggled his way onto the aft deck.

"Gracias," mumbled Cesar as he handed Tony one of the bags. "I mean, 'Thanks.' I guess it's going to take me some time to get used to using English again. That bag is all dive gear, so if you don't mind lowering it over the rail, I'll go down on the dive platform and get it stowed. Can I just leave this other one here for now?"

"Of course," replied Tony. "We're going to have a quick meeting inside once everybody's on board, so come on in and help yourself to some coffee when you're done."

Carley was the next to arrive but since most of her stuff was already on board, she only had a small carry-on. When she stepped into the salon, she stopped, looked around and took a deep breath.

"Well, here we go!" she smiled.

"Nervous?" teased Tony, knowing that Carley was feeling more excitement and anticipation than fear. For some reason, she was very happy to be leaving Belize.

As Carley made her way down to her cabin to stow her last bag, Tony spotted Rigo Mejia, the dark-skinned Caribbean (Garifuna, Tony reminded himself), approaching the foot of the ramp that led up to the ship. Since he appeared to be laboring under the load he was carrying, Tony rushed out to help him onto the boat.

"Ah, thank you, my friend," smiled Mejia broadly as he handed Tony a heavy tool box and stepped aboard.

"You know, we have a pretty good selection of tools onboard already," grimaced Tony as he accepted the toolbox.

"Yes, but they're not *my* tools. These are my friends and they go everywhere with me. Together, we will keep this ship running A-1."

"Suit yourself," replied Tony. "As soon as the First Mate gets here we're going to have a short meeting and then you can stow your stuff below. Come on into the salon and have some coffee—it's Gallon Jug."

"I feel at home already," smiled the short, thin twenty-five-year-old.

Tony turned back to scan the dock for the last member of the crew and almost knocked him into the water.

"Wow!" Tony exclaimed. "I didn't hear you come up the gangway!"

"I didn't," replied the curly-haired man that Tony recognized as Nicholas Banks. "I've been on the bridge with Captain Braydon for more than an hour but when I saw the other blokes come aboard I thought it best to come back and check in. I understand there will be a meeting soon?"

"That's correct. Join the others in the salon and I'll go round up the owner and the captain."

Tony made his way along the starboard rail and entered the bridge through one of its two side doors.

"We're ready, Captain." he called as he ducked down the stairs that led to Rob's stateroom. He reached out to knock but before his knuckles touched the door Rob pulled it open and Tony almost fell into the room.

When Tony and Rob reached the main deck, the captain was waiting for them and they made their way down the corridor into the salon single-file with the captain leading and Tony bringing up the rear. To Carley's surprise, the three new crewmen stood, almost at attention, when the captain entered the salon.

"Please be seated," said Captain Braydon. "As you already know, my name is Captain Daniel Braydon, and I'll be the Master of the Dolphin Diver on our upcoming voyage together. To my left is Rob Jefferies, who represents the vessel's owners. Mr. Jefferies will be quartered in the forward stateroom below the bridge and is serving as Executive Officer. He will be assisting Mr. Banks and me with certain bridge duties.

"To my far left is Anthony Wykes. Mr. Wykes will be serving as a member of the crew but he has a special role that I'll let him explain. Mr. Wykes."

Tony stepped forward slightly and smiled at the crew.

"Thank you, Captain. But before I start, I think I should clear up something that even you don't know. I was going to wait until we were at sea to tell you all this, but I decided I should do it now, in case any of you want to change your mind about this trip and go ashore before we depart."

Tony expected the look of surprise on the three male crewmen's faces, but when he glanced sideways to check the captain's reaction, all he saw was the same stern, emotionless expression as usual.

"First of all, my name isn't really Anthony Wykes. That's the name on my documents, but it's not my real name. Just call me Tony.

"Secondly, while I'll be working with you as a member of the crew, I've actually chartered the Dolphin Diver for the next few weeks and I'll be directing her course. As you can probably tell, I'm an American and a few years ago I was a member of a team that made some incredible discoveries. There are those in my government—and in several other governments around the world—who want to know what I know and the Dolphin Diver's mission will be to keep this international coalition busy looking in the wrong place until they either give up or I get different instructions. I'm sorry, but I can't provide any more details and that's why I'm giving you this opportunity to go ashore."

Tony looked around the salon for reaction.

"So, are we taking on the CIA or something?" frowned ship's engineer Mejia.

"No, I promise you that our adversary is not a lawful agency, although some of its members may hold legitimate positions in various governments. It's essentially a rogue group of individuals who seek to control the course of history by secretly and quietly manipulating international events. We're the good guys here, I promise."

"I'm a lover, not a fighter," added divemaster Acosta. "I'm not afraid of a fair fight, but when you start talking about going up against an international group—unlawful or not—that sounds pretty dangerous. That's not what any of us signed on for."

"You're absolutely correct, Cesar, and that's why I moved this briefing up—so you would have an opportunity to withdraw your application and go ashore now. Our original salary offer was better than you're used to getting, but let me sweeten the pot a little more. Those who stay until we make port in the Caribbean will be given a second opportunity to withdraw from the crew with full pay for the time you've served and a plane ticket home. If you still decide to stay onboard, I'll bump your original offer by twenty-five percent for the duration of our mission. How does that sound?"

"Well, that certainly makes things more interesting, but I'm not interested in becoming a criminal and all we have is your word that we're really the good guys. We don't even know where we're headed," replied Acosta.

"Mr. Jefferies knows my background in detail and, except for the part about my identity, the Captain knows all about the mission and the risks involved. I'll have to let their presence here vouch for my truthfulness. As for the exact destination, I'll share that with those of you who stay as soon as we get underway."

Once again, Tony scanned the room.

"Any more questions?"

"When do we leave, mate?" smiled First Mate Banks. "I could do with a little adventure."

Acosta and the ship's engineer, Mejia, smiled thinly and nodded.

Tony turned to the captain and asked, "Well, Captain, when *do* we leave?"

"Stow your gear and prepare to cast off in one hour!" barked the captain in a commanding voice. "Mr. Banks, please report to the bridge in fifteen minutes."

After the captain disappeared in the direction of the bridge, Tony escorted Rob, Carley and the crew below deck.

Standing in the hallway outside the crew rooms, he continued his briefing.

"Since you have all decided to stay, I guess I can let you in on our destination now, rather than later. The Dolphin Diver is headed for the British Virgin Islands and a port called Road Town. Our journey will take us almost due east and our only planned stop will be at Kingston, Jamaica, to take on fuel and provisions. I could have packed enough stuff onboard to make the trip without a stop, but it would have made the ship feel pretty cramped.

"Speaking of the Dolphin Diver, I've made some changes since she arrived a week ago. First of all, those two small rooms in the back have been turned into store rooms. The one on the port side is mine and it's locked. However, the one on the starboard side is available to anyone who needs to stash anything bulky. Please respect each other's property.

"I've had the upper bunks removed in the front two rooms and they're now single occupancy—the one on the port side is mine and the other one is for the lady. That leaves the middle two rooms for the three of you. You can work out who bunks where, but we'll be picking up one more crewman when we reach our first port, so you'll all have a roommate, sooner or later. I've tried to make your rooms a little more functional by adding a wardrobe and a small desk.

"I've also installed an audible and visible alarm device in each room that's connected to a ship-wide emergency warning system. I actually bought it from a local contractor who installs fire alarm systems in schools, so it may look familiar. However, this is to be used in any ship-wide emergency, not just fires.

"You'll also notice that each bunk has been equipped with a personal sound system and a pair of noise-blocking headphones. If the emergency warning system goes off, it will be fed into those headphones, so you won't miss anything."

Tony smiled at Carley but he didn't mention the incident on the shakedown cruise when she missed the whole pirate boarding due to her iPod.

"And, last but not least, Carley is the ship's cook but she's not your mother and she's not your maid. Please clean up after yourself and get to the salon on time if you want to eat. If you're on duty—either on the bridge or in the crow's nest—your meal will be brought to you so you don't have to leave your station.

"And speaking of the crow's nest, I've added a few creature comforts there, too. Every member of the crew except Carley and the Captain will take part in a rotating look-out schedule when we're at sea, so I suggest you go up and check out the accommodations when you have a minute.

"Okay, that's it for now. Get your personal items stowed and then let's get this tub out to sea!"

Carley went up to the galley to prepare a light brunch and Tony followed Rob forward to the stateroom for a quick meeting.

"So how do you think it went?" Tony asked after Rob closed the door.

"Well, they all seemed to take it pretty well. They're young and adventurous and I think your international intrigue bit hooked them."

"And the Captain?"

"He's a tough one to read, isn't he?" replied Rob. "I suspect you and I will be hearing from him privately in the very near future. He's too proper to speak out in front of his crew, but I'm sure he'll let us know if he's unhappy about the mission."

"Yeah, I'm sure he will, but let's extend the salary increase to him, too, just in case he's having any doubts," smiled Tony looking around the large stateroom. "So how was your first night aboard?"

"Not bad! It takes a while to get used to the rocking, but this is a pretty nice setup. I feel guilty taking up all this space by myself."

"Well, hopefully Anne will be able to join us soon," replied Tony. "How are things going with her sister?"

Rob pointed to a sophisticated-looking device on his small desk and said, "We talked last night by short wave.

I brought this radio from the house and her sister has a similar unit that we used a lot when we first moved to Belize, before Vonage was available. Her sister is still a wreck, but time will take care of that. When we make port in Road Town, we're going to decide whether I fly up to Miami to meet her or she flies down to meet me. She's never been to the Virgin Islands and she's excited to see the Dolphin Diver, so we may pick up a new crew member shortly after we arrive in Road Town."

"Cool," replied Tony, still focused on the short-wave radio. "Hey, could Anne contact your friend in Seattle and ask him to check in with my flight crew again? I'd like to know how their flight to St. Thomas went."

"Sure. And once he's made contact, he can report back to Anne and she can pass the info on to us at sea. That way we can stay in contact and still remain anonymous."

"That's exactly what I'm hoping for," mumbled Tony, lost in thought.

***

"What sort of box?" asked Erik Mueller as he pumped the U.S. Customs agent for information. "How big was it? How much did it weigh?"

"Listen, Mr. ah, Mueller," replied the agent as he glanced at the other man's passport, "I'm sorry your shipment wasn't delivered to your hotel, but I've already told you more than I should have and since it arrived on a private charter jet there's no way I can track it. I suggest you file a claim with the shipper. Now, if you'll excuse me, I..."

"What's the problem, Jimmy?" asked a slim black woman who appeared through a door behind the counter.

"Mr. Mueller was expecting a box to be delivered several days ago and it's apparently lost. It was brought down from the Bahamas by a private carrier, so we must have cleared it here but it never made it to his hotel. I was just explaining that..."

"You must mean that big ol' thing that's been taking up space out back. We don't run a warehouse operation here, Mr. Mueller. Follow me, please."

And with that, Mueller's day improved significantly. His informants on Andros had seen a large box being unloaded and then reloaded onto the Learjet now operated by the Fitzgeralds but in the five days he'd been on St. Thomas he hadn't been able to determine the current location of that container. It now appeared that it had never left the Customs office!

The woman led him across a disorganized loading dock to a wooden crate about three feet square and six feet tall.

"Does that look like your shipment?" asked the woman.

"Well, I'm not really sure," Mueller lied. "You see, the fellow that packed the merchandise was involved in a terrible car accident the same day he shipped it and I haven't been able to get much information."

As he approached, he saw a shipping tag wired to the crate and when he read it he smiled broadly.

"This is it!" he exclaimed. "This is my boss' name— Buzz Edwards."

The Customs supervisor looked at the tag and frowned.

"But this says 'From Buzz Edwards' and 'To Buzz Edwards' and you're not Buzz Edwards. I'm afraid I can't release it to you, Mr. Mueller."

"He couldn't make the trip from the mainland and he sent me down instead," Mueller lied again. "Listen, we can call him and he can tell you directly."

An hour later, and after Edwards had sent several signed faxes to the St. Thomas Customs office, Mueller finally had legal custody of the box but his persistence had worn thin on the supervisor.

"The paperwork describes the contents as Communications Equipment, Mr. Mueller. I'm afraid I'm going to have to examine this equipment before I can let you take it."

Carefully, the supervisor and her agent tilted the crate over and laid it on its back. Using a small crowbar, they loosened the lid and removed it.

"Just what's going on here!" shouted the supervisor as she snatched her radio off her hip and called airport security.

Inside, the crate was padded and lined with cloth. There was even a small pillow attached to one end, giving the box the appearance of a homemade coffin. However, if the crate had ever contained a body, it was now long gone.

Chapter 7

From his position in the crow's nest, Tony watched the Belizean coastline fade into the distance and wondered what the next few days and weeks would bring. He still wasn't convinced that his "confuse and distract" plan would work or that it was even the right strategy. Was he putting the crew of the Dolphin Diver in harm's way for no good reason? And what about his own safety? Somehow, he was going to have to attract the attention of Edwards and his henchmen without being recognized and recaptured.

With five crew members taking part in the look-out rotation, each would be on duty four hours each day, except for divemaster Cesar Acosta, who was pulling two shifts per day since he currently had no other duties. Tony had elected to take the first watch of the day to set a good example. He also wanted to make sure his redesigned crow's nest worked as good in practice as he had envisioned.

Since either the captain or the first mate would always be on the bridge with their attention focused forward, Tony had designed the lookout station on top of the ship to face aft and provide unobstructed views to either side. The chair Tony now occupied had originally been designed to secure sports fishermen while they fought four hundred pound marlin and swordfish. The restraining harness rivaled those used by NASCAR and the chair itself tilted, reclined and rotated into a hundred different positions. The right arm of the chair had been enhanced with a console to control the powerful search lights mounted on the small roof and the entire station could be enclosed with clear plastic side curtains in case of bad weather. A long, weather-proof container directly in front of the look-out chair contained a pair of Navy surplus spotting binoculars and a Winchester 308-magnum rifle fitted with a high-powered scope. While the captain's shotgun had been effective in dealing with pirates at close range, the 308 had a kill range of more than eight hundred meters.

The two-way radio in Tony's shirt pocket crackled and then Carley's voice said, "How's it going up there, cowboy?"

Tony retrieved the small device and pressed the talk button.

"So far, so good. How's everybody doing down there?"

"A couple of early risers have been up to the galley for coffee, but it's still pretty quiet. Do you want anything before I start preparing breakfast?"

"No, I grabbed a thermos of coffee before we left port but you could save me one of those pastries until I get off? And would you ask Rob to come up here after he's finished eating?"

"Will do," replied Carley. "See you later."

Tony glanced at his watch. It was just coming up on 7:00 a.m. and the sun was now fully above the horizon behind him. He inserted the earpieces of his new iPod and tapped the play button. It had taken him an entire day to load the tiny gadget and learn how to use it, but it was going to be a real comfort during his daily 6:00 a.m. to 10:00 a.m. look-out watches. As the first beats of a Chicago tune played, Tony eased back into the chair and began a slow scan of the horizon to see if anyone had followed them on their pre-dawn departure from Belize City.

Ninety minutes later, Tony was staring intently through the large Navy binoculars when Rob tapped him on the arm and startled him. He jumped and snapped his head around.

"Sorry," apologized Rob when he realized Tony hadn't heard him approach. "Is there something out there?"

Tony lowered the binoculars, removed the iPod ear buds and furrowed his brow.

"Well, I'm not sure. I picked up a slight glint behind us and off to the starboard side a few minutes ago but it's too far away to make out anything. It's probably nothing, but it seems to be matching our course and speed exactly. Do you think somebody tailed us out of port?"

"I think you're just paranoid, my friend, but we could always have the captain change course if you'd like."

"No, not just yet. I'll keep an eye on it and we can make a decision at the end of my shift. In the mean time, don't say anything about it, okay? I don't want to spook the crew on our first day at sea."

"I agree!" replied Rob. "Carley said you wanted to see me. Was it about that?"

"No, I'd like your advice on something else. Is there any way for me to contact Jim—or the others, for that matter—without giving away my position or the position of anyone involved in the communication? Obviously, I don't want Edwards and his bunch to find me, but I also don't want to jeopardize anyone else's safety."

"Hmm, let me think on that for a bit, okay? There should be a way to use a combination of the radio and the Internet to fool even the best of them."

"That would be great. I have no way to contact Jill, Linda or Javier, but I do know where to reach Jim. In fact I found an email address for him while I was doing some digging back at your place." Tony handed Rob a piece of paper. "Here's his contact info and the message I'd like to get to him. He needs to know about the danger Edwards presents and maybe he'll have some way to pass the word on to the others."

"I'll see what I can do," smiled Rob. "Anything you need up here?"

"No, I'm good. I'll see you down in the salon about ten. Don't let my relief leave me up here all day."

The next hour and a half passed slowly but eventually Nickolas, the ship's first mate, crawled up the ladder to the roof of the cabin to take Tony's spot. After offering some pointers to the young man, Tony made his way down to the salon for some fresh coffee and to see what—if anything—Rob had come up with.

"How'd it go?" he asked Rob as he poured a cup of black coffee.

"Excellent!" replied Rob. "I radioed your message to Anne, who used her sister's laptop to create a Gmail account, send your message and then quickly delete the account. In addition, she used a VPN account to mask her location. It's not likely that anyone would have intercepted your message among the millions in cyberspace, but even if they had it would have appeared to originate in Europe. The Gmail account was my idea, but Anne came up with the VPN trick."

"Well, I have no idea what either a Gmail or a VPN are, but I'm glad you were able to deliver my message. I'm concerned about my friends' safety. Is this Gmail thing something we could do again, if necessary?"

"I don't know why not. She'll just create a new account each time you have a message to deliver. Of course, there's no way to receive a reply from Jim, because by the time he receives and reads you message the email account will have been deleted."

"That's okay. I don't need to hear from him. I just wanted to get the warning out about Edwards without compromising our position and it looks like you and Anne have accomplished that. I'm going down to my cabin to take a shower and study some maps. I'll see you at lunch."

The rest of the first day at sea passed quietly and Tony turned in about 10:00 p.m. much more optimistic than he had been when they had pulled away from the dock in Belize City. The crew seemed to be meshing well and Carley seemed happy in her role as ship's cook. Rob was spending most of his time on the bridge and the captain actually seemed to enjoy having an understudy to tutor. Everything seemed to be going well, for a change.

A knock on his cabin door accompanied by a female voice yelling "Rise and shine, Tony!" startled him awake the next morning. Tony glanced at his watch. It was 5:55 a.m. He scrambled into his clothes and slid the latch back for Carley.

"Good morning!" he yawned as he stepped into the hallway and locked his door behind him.

"Good morning, sleepy head," smiled Carley. "How are you this fine Sunday morning?"

"Well, I'd be late for duty if you hadn't pounded on my door. What are you doing up so early?"

"I've always been an early riser," she replied, "so I'm taking advantage of the quiet time before everybody else is up to plan my menus for the day and get organized. You'd better scram or Cesar will have you on report!'

Tony had assigned Cesar the two-to-six shifts, both morning and afternoon. As Tony reached the top of the ladder, he saw Cesar staring at the horizon off the port stern.

"What have you got?" yelled Tony from the top of the ladder to avoid scaring the young Mexican.

"There's a ship following us," he replied without lowering the large binoculars. "I first spotted her at dawn, but she's probably been out there all night."

"And all day yesterday," added Tony. "I noticed it on my first watch yesterday morning but I couldn't be sure it was another vessel so I didn't mention it. It must have backed off during the day, because nobody else mentioned it, including you on your day shift yesterday."

"That's true, and I'm pretty sure I would have seen it. I assumed we would be followed for a while, so I've been looking for another ship and there she is. What are we going to do?"

"Nothing, for now," replied Tony, "except keep an eye on it. If it approaches, we'll take more aggressive action but I don't want to tip our hand if it's just a harmless sightseer. I'll take over. You go get yourself some breakfast and sleep. You're back on duty in ten hours, you know."

As Tony settled into the lookout's chair, he once again began to doubt the usefulness of his mission.

***

Erik Mueller paced the small holding cell in the St. Thomas Customs Office. By intimidating a junior customs agent, he had learned that the NWIDI Learjet had delivered a large crate to St. Thomas. He had then convinced a supervisor that he was the intended recipient of the box and talked them into turning it over to him. But that's where his luck had run out because when they had opened the crate for a routine inspection, the empty crate appeared to have been used to smuggle a human (or at least a human body) into the U.S. Virgin Islands and now the U.S. Customs Service was very interested in what Mueller was up to. Of course, Mueller had never seen the box before and had no idea what would be under the lid when the agents pried it off. He was just trying to appease his boss, Buzz Edwards, by getting any information he could about the mysterious flight of the private jet formerly used by the NWIDI team.

"Nicoletti!" he yelled out loud. "I'll get you for this!"

If Tony Nicoletti hadn't escaped from the secret MX-2 facility in Cancun, Mueller would have never been sent to St. Thomas and he wouldn't be in this cell right now. He promised himself he was going to get even with Nicoletti one day, and the sooner the better.

"Mr. Mueller?" asked a uniformed agent as he approached the cell door.

"Yes, I'm Erik Mueller."

Opening the door, the agent said simply, "Follow me, please," and led Mueller down a series of hallways to a conference room where the Customs supervisor was waiting.

"Well, I don't know who your friends are," she frowned, "but it looks like we're going to turn you lose in spite of your very suspicious activity. Apparently your friend Mr. Edwards has some well placed connections in Washington D.C. because my orders came directly from our Headquarters up there."

Mueller smiled, which seemed to irritate the supervisor even more.

"However," she continued, smiling herself for the first time, "one of the conditions of your release is that you are not to leave this island until I have personally completed a thorough investigation. And I intend to be *very* thorough, Mr. Mueller."

Mueller's smile turned to a scowl but he kept his mouth shut. If this woman thought she was going to tell him what to do, she had another think coming.

"And just to make sure you don't forget the terms of your release, I'm going to hold on to your passport until I file my report," added the supervisor, her smile growing even larger. "That didn't come from my superiors; it's just a little extra insurance for me."

Mueller had had enough. "I get it! Don't leave this stupid little rock you call an island until you say so. Can I go now?"

The supervisor turned to one of her agents and nodded. As Mueller was led out of the room, she called to him in a mockingly sweet voice.

"We'll be watching you, Erik!"

Outside, the sun was glaringly hot and Mueller was beginning to hate this place more by the minute, but he expected Edwards would work more of his pseudo-political magic and have his passport back to him in a matter of hours. In the meantime, he'd been sent here to find Tony Nicoletti and he was now convinced more than ever that the man must be nearby. And if the crate recently impounded by Customs really had held a body, dead or alive, perhaps he could hand his boss either Frank Morton or Miles Adderly and pull himself up several rungs on the organizational ladder of the Six.

Mueller took a minute to calm down and then smiled before hailing a taxi back to his hotel.

***

"The plan is proceeding on schedule and your messenger must leave today in order to reach the destination at the appointed time. Once the messenger arrives, the message should be broadcast to the local population so it can be transferred to the recipient at the earliest opportunity," stated the sphere.

"And so it shall be," replied the dolphin.

***

Except for Captain Braydon, the entire crew was assembled in the salon of the Dolphin Diver.

"So here's the deal," began Tony. "A ship has been following ever since we left port yesterday morning. The Captain has reduced our cruising speed several times to see if our shadow would overtake us, but each time they've matched our speed and course exactly so we have to assume that their presence is no accident. Tonight we're going to make a slight course change suggested by Captain Braydon but I want you all to be very alert until we figure out who's following us and why. We've already been challenged once by pirates and we have to assume that a ship of this size and type will attract some unwanted attention on the open seas.

"Tonight I'm going to stand watch as an assistant from dusk until dawn. That will put an extra set of eyes on the water in case these guys attempt to board us. If nothing happens overnight, we'll arrive at the Swan Islands just after sunrise and, with the permission of the Honduran Navy, we'll anchor just off shore and do some diving. I'm hoping our stalkers out there will think we're just another live aboard dive operation and lose interest in us. If not, we'll have the Hondurans nearby if we need them."

"Well, it certainly didn't take long for this trip to get interesting," commented Cesar. "I don't mind some unscheduled diving, but I've never heard of the Swan Islands."

"Nor had I," interjected First Mate Nickolas Banks, "but according to the Captain they were once owned by the United States which built a weather station there in the late 1920s and maintained it, in one form or another, until 1972 when the islands were turned over to the Honduran government. The biggest island is only about two and a half miles long but it has a dirt airstrip on it. That's where the weather station was. Some of the original buildings have apparently been patched up and are now used by a small contingent of the Honduran Navy that monitors the surrounding waters for drug traffic. We'll only be about ninety miles from Honduras when we anchor tomorrow morning."

"And we won't be staying long," added Tony. "We'll put a couple of divers in the water and if our friends don't leave soon we'll try to convince the Navy to run them off.

I'm hoping this will only add one extra day to our original four-day first leg. That would put us into Jamaica late Wednesday and we could still make the British Virgin Islands, by a week from tomorrow. Is everyone okay with that?"

No one seemed to object, so Tony dismissed the meeting but motioned for Cesar to stay.

"I'll get someone to take your watch tonight so you can get some rest. I don't know how long we'll have to keep up the appearance of a dive charter, but you'll probably get plenty of diving tomorrow and I need you rested. Besides Rob, Carley and me, are there any other divers on board?"

"Yes, the First Mate told me that he's been diving a few times but he's not certified. Rigo has never been diving and I don't know about the Captain, but he doesn't seem like the type, if you know what I mean."

Tony smiled. "I know exactly what you mean. I'll need a couple hours of sleep if I'm going to stand watch all night, but I'd definitely like to take advantage of this unscheduled stop to get some fin time. I was a military diver and a pretty active sport diver up until about five years ago, but I haven't been in the water since then."

"A military diver, huh?" frowned Cesar. "That means you have all the bad habits we try not to let sport divers develop. Where did you do your diving?"

"Southeast Asia, mostly," replied Tony. "I was involved in recovering downed pilots during the Vietnam Conflict. After that I did a lot of recreational diving throughout the Caribbean, most recently in the Virgin Islands."

"Sounds like you're serious about diving—why the five year break?"

"Uh, I just couldn't get away to go diving," stammered Tony. He smiled as he realized how accurate his attempted cover-up actually was. "I'd like to get up to speed on rebreathers once I log some time underwater, but that can wait until we get to Tortola."

During the night, the Captain gradually shifted the Dolphin Diver's course slightly south to approach Great Swan

Island from the west. Tony maintained a position on the aft deck and let the regular watch occupy the chair he had installed on the deck above the salon. Under his zip-up sweatshirt, Tony carried a nine millimeter Berretta automatic similar to the one he had used in the Army except that this one was fitted with a special fifteen round magazine.

About midnight the Captain called Tony on the walkie-talkie to let him know that contact had been made with the Honduran Naval detachment in the Swan Islands and that the Dolphin Diver had been given clearance to approach the island and anchor off the western end where the navy maintained a pier. When they had asked if the "other vessel" would be joining them, Captain Braydon had simply played dumb and replied that the Dolphin Diver was traveling alone.

At 3:40 a.m. at loud thump on the hull of the ship startled everyone and Tony raced to the starboard rail with his weapon drawn. With the ship at a dead stop, a careful examination of the surrounding waters finally revealed a large mahogany log floating nearby. With a sigh of relief, Tony ordered the boat back to cruising speed and by the time they approached the tiny island Tony had all the firearms stored in a cylindrical steel storage locker he had designed to look like a cylindrical water purification unit.

By 8:30 a.m. Cesar Acosta was making his first dive with Rob and Carley, and Nick Banks was preparing to make the next dive with Acosta. The Captain had gone ashore to pay a courtesy call on Great Swan Island's ranking Naval officer and Tony was sound asleep, exhausted from a night of walking the ship's decks.

The sound of a nearby gunshot jolted him awake and brought him to a sitting position instantly.

Chapter 8

Tony's feet hit the floor with a thud. He snatched his keys off the nightstand and burst out into the lower deck hallway. Glancing both ways, he scanned the lower deck and started for the weapons locker but the sound of a second gunshot stopped him in his tracks. He scrambled up the ladder into the main salon where he could see Rob, Carley, Rigo Mejía, the Captain and a uniformed person leaning over the rail on the aft deck. They appeared to be waving at someone in the water below.

"What's going on?" he puffed as he reached the back of the ship.

"Shark!" cried Carley, pointing to the water behind the boat. "Cesar and Nickolas are out there."

To his right, Tony saw the uniformed man—probably Honduran navy—raise his arm and aim a handgun.

"Alto!" he yelled at the man. "Are you crazy?"

Using just his hands, Tony slid down the handrails of the ladder to the dive platform on the level below. He kicked off his sandals, grabbed a spear gun off a rack and splashed into the water. Below the surface, he could see two divers holding onto the yellow patch he had painted on the anchor line. They were doing their three minute decompression stop at fifteen feet!

As he made his way towards Cesar and Nickolas, one of them started waving wildly and Tony spun to find himself just inches from an approaching reef shark. Grasping the spear gun in both hands, he slammed the point of the spear into the soft underbelly of the predator as hard as he could and hung on. The shark snapped sharply right and then left, trying to free itself from the spear. Tony hung on as long as he could but he could only hold his breath for about two minutes these days and eventually he had to let go of the spear. As soon as he did, the shark headed down and he raced to the surface for air.

Gasping, he grabbed onto the dive ladder and filled his lungs as quickly as he could before diving back down the anchor line. When he reached the divers, he gave them the "thumbs up" signal, meaning go to the surface immediately. Cesar pointed to his wrist and signaled "one minute" but Tony was already running out of breath and couldn't stay to argue. He signaled one more time and then kicked his way to the surface as fast as he could. Glancing over his shoulder, he saw the two divers slowly moving up the line.

Tony was furious as he climbed onto the dive platform.

"Who is that idiot with the gun?" he yelled up to the Captain on the deck above.

"Commander Espinoza at your service," called down the uniformed man in perfect English. "Or, if you prefer, Commander Idiot."

"Do you have any idea how dangerous it is to shoot into the water when there are divers down?" yelled Tony, not amused by the man's remarks.

"Do you have any idea how dangerous it is to dive in these waters?" he replied. "I lost a sailor just last week because he decided to risk a swim in this very bay. When your good Captain here told me what you were up to, we rushed back over here as fast as we could, just in time to find your two divers in a pretty bad situation. Another couple of minutes and they would have been dead, I'm afraid. I'm sorry it didn't occur to me to jump into the water and engage in hand-to-hand combat with the shark, but I did what I could."

Tony had started to cool down a bit so rather than argue with the Honduran, he turned his attentions to helping his crewmates out of the water.

"And what's with you?" he barked at Cesar. "When there's an angry shark in the neighborhood and I signal 'get out of the water' I expect you to do it!"

"Normally, we'd have been to the surface like a cork," nodded Cesar, "but there were some extenuating circumstances you weren't aware of, Tony. Besides, I'm the dive master on this vessel and unless I've been fired, we'll do things my way in the water."

"What circumstances?" snapped Tony.

"Well, our new diver got a little disoriented when the shark showed up and before I could grab him he was at ninety feet and plunging. If we had shot to the surface without decompressing, we'd both be dead or dying right now. If you're going to dive with me, you need to understand that once we're in the water my dive computer is the law. Otherwise, I'm off at the next port."

"We'll discuss that later," replied Tony gruffly. "Is he okay?"

Nickolas Banks was lying on his back on the dive platform and he hadn't moved.

"He's fine," frowned Cesar. "Considering this was his first dive ever, I think he did remarkably well. Help me get him inside, will you?"

Tony and Cesar helped Nickolas up the ladder to the main deck and settled him onto one of the couches in the salon. Banks still hadn't said a word and Tony was worried about the man going into shock but Cesar checked his vital signs with the technical skills of a doctor and Carley brought a blanket to cover him.

"He'll be fine," smiled Cesar, "although he may not want to go diving again for a while."

From the couch, Banks mumbled something and tried to sit up.

Carley bent down to listen and then laughed out loud.

"He asked if his next lesson would be this difficult!"

Banks' comment relaxed the crew a bit and Tony approached the Captain and his Honduran comrade.

"Listen, Commander, I think I owe you an apology. It's just that I've been in the water when bullets were flying and I've seen them do some pretty bizarre things. I realize that you were trying to protect the divers, but…"

"No apology necessary," interrupted the Honduran. "Any man who dives into the ocean to take on an already angry shark with just a spear gun can yell at me all he wants to." Offering his hand, he continued, "As I said, Commander Espinoza, at your service."

"Ah, Anthony Wykes," lied Tony, stumbling over his fake name. "I'm sorry we didn't make adequate inquiries before diving in this area, but we were anxious to get into the water after two days at sea. We'll be more careful next time."

"A wise decision," replied Espinoza. "The sharks in this area are especially aggressive and we don't know why. I have a marine biologist assigned to my team, but he hasn't come up with any answers yet. And now we have a shark out there somewhere with a spear in his belly. You know that we have laws about fishing without a license, don't you?"

Espinoza smiled just enough to let Tony know he was kidding and then turned serious again.

"Your Captain has told me a little about your long voyage and it looks like you've already picked up an unwanted companion. I'd like you to stay tied up here until we can check out this other vessel—and no diving, please! You and the rest of the crew are welcome to come ashore but I would recommend leaving a security detail onboard. I assume you're equipped to defend yourselves on the open seas between here and the British Virgin Islands, correct?"

Tony nodded. "We can take care of ourselves, but thank you for asking. We'd like to get back on course and on schedule as soon as possible, so I think we'll pass on the shore leave. Any idea how long your inquiry will take?"

"I have our patrol boat headed out to intercept that other vessel right now and they should make contact in about two hours. If they're harmless we'll give them a stern warning and send them on their way."

"And if they're not harmless?" asked Tony.

"Well, in that case, we'll blow them out of the water," grinned the Commander. "In either case, you should be on your way by morning, Mr. Wykes. We'll get back to you soon."

As soon as the Honduran was off the boat, Tony called a crew meeting in the salon. Since the ship was at anchor, every crew member attended.

"Okay, everybody, listen up. First I want to say that I was out of line earlier when I challenged Cesar about his decisions in the water. He's the dive master and he makes all the calls when we're in the water. Period.

"Secondly, if I ever see one of you shooting into the water when there are divers in the water, I will personally tie you to the anchor and throw you over the side. Like I told the Commander earlier, I've seen too many people injured, some of them fatally, by bullets that took bizarre trajectories in the water. Understood?"

There were nods, but no one said a word.

"Okay, let's talk about the vessel that's apparently following us. Commander Espinoza has offered to take care of that problem, but we should expect to pick up other tails if this one is turned away. Those bad guys I told you about are powerful and if that's who is following us now they will have another boat on us at the next major port. There's nothing we can do about that. However, if they try to interfere with us in any way, we will defend ourselves. Toward that end, I have a cache of interesting weapons in my private storeroom down below. I'm going to run down a list and if you've ever had experience with any of the items, please raise your hand.

"M9 semi-automatic pistol?" Tony was surprised to see every hand raised, including Carley's.

"Rifle, high caliber, with scope?" This time every hand except First Mate Banks' went up and Tony raised his eyebrows.

"Shotgun, pump action, 20 gauge?" This time only Captain Braydon, Rob and Carley raised their hands.

"Assault rifle, M-4 or M-16 military style?" Now it was only Rob and Carley with their hands up.

"Grenade launcher, M203 rifle-mounted?" Only Carley's hand went up and Tony stared at her with a look of surprise. Everybody else on the crew was also looking at her and grinning.

"Hey, can't a girl like guns, too?" she shrugged before looking down to avoid the smirks.

Tony turned his attention to Rob.

"Army National Guard," offered Rob to Tony's unasked question. "Lieutenant Colonel, retired."

"It appears that we have our own guerilla army," smiled Tony.

Carley raised her hand again but looked up when there were several chuckles from her crewmates.

"Oh, sorry, that wasn't a question, was it?"

Tony ignored her and continued his briefing.

"When we get back out into international waters, I'm going to make some firearms assignments and then we're going to do a little target practice so you're all familiar with your weapons. Does anybody have a problem with that?"

Again, Carley raised her hand and this time the chuckles became outright laughter.

"I was just kidding about the grenade launcher, Tony. I've never actually fired one myself."

Tony scowled and snapped, "Listen, folks, you need to take your own safety—and that of your crewmates—seriously. This is a beautiful vessel but it's not very fast and we're not going to be able to outrun anybody who really wants to catch us. That means that if we're challenged, we'll have to stand and fight. I spent a lot of time and considerable money making sure we're equipped for that eventuality, but our success will ultimately depend on you."

The tone in the salon turned serious again and several nodded agreement.

"That's better," admonished Tony. "Now I was up all night and I'm beat. I'm going to go below and get some sleep, but I urge you to take this ship's security seriously. Nick's watch is about to start but, under the circumstances, I'm going to excuse him. Carley, would you take his shift, please? We'll have lunch a little late today and hopefully Mr. Banks will be well enough to resume his regular duties tomorrow."

"Me?" asked a surprised Carley. "You want me to take a watch?"

"Yes," nodded Tony. "We're a little short-handed and seeing as you have so much experience with firearms, you seem like the perfect substitute. Any problem with that?"

"No, absolutely not!" replied an obviously excited Carley. "I'd love to do something for a few hours—other than be the ship's *Mom*."

"And with your permission—and Carley's, of course—I'd be happy to take over lunch duties for the day," offered Rob. "I make a killer cob salad, if I must say so myself."

"Okay, so be it," agreed Tony. "In that case lunch is back to the regular time. And if I'm still asleep at noon please wake me up. I definitely don't want to miss this!"

The crew dispersed to their regular duties, leaving just Tony and Carley in the salon.

"What was that all about?" he asked when they were alone.

"What? I really am happy to get out of the kitchen, so to speak."

"You know what I mean," replied Tony. "All that weapons stuff. If you were trying to get a laugh at my expense, it wasn't the right time, Carley."

She tilted her head sideways slightly. "I'm sorry about the grenade launcher thing, but the rest is all true. Depending on just how good you really are, I may be the most qualified weapons handler on this ship."

"Then why didn't you say something before now?" challenged Tony.

"Because nobody asked," returned Carley just as defiantly. "I was asked to be the cook, and I agreed. But I'm equally willing—and prepared—to be a soldier, if that's what you need. All you had to do was ask. Now show me this fancy look-out tower you built for us."

Carley turned and headed out the back of the salon towards the ladder leading to the roof with a very confused Tony close behind.

*   *   *

Back at his hotel, Erik Mueller removed a bottle of Vodka from his suitcase and filled a tall glass. So far, his time on St. Thomas had not gone well, but he intended to make the rest of his stay in the Virgin Islands much more enjoyable and he was going to start by nabbing Tony Nicoletti and having a little "chat" with him before sending him back to Cancun's MX-2 facility. And if Nicoletti's pal, Frank Morton, turned up, maybe Mueller could score double points by bagging them both!

Mueller knew his job was going to be tricky with the U.S. Customs Service on his tail, but he'd outsmarted agents a lot better than these government lackeys.

He took a thick manila folder out of his brief case and laid it open on the small hotel room table. The file contained everything the Six knew about NWIDI and its team members. There were biographies, family histories, military service records and more. Mueller had read every word at least once, but he vowed to do it one more time before morning. Tomorrow he would turn the island upside down and find whatever—or whoever—had been in the coffin-shaped box that had caused him so much grief during the past few hours.

***

Once Carley was belted into the look-out chair high atop the ship, Tony sat down against the rail and crossed his arms behind his head.

"Okay, let's have it," he said.

Carley lowered the binoculars and replied, "Let's have what?"

"Your back story, my dear. How did you happen to come in contact with the U.S. Military's entire small arms arsenal? Come on, Carley, you know more about me than almost anybody else on Earth. If I'm going to trust you, you have to let me in on your secret."

"I should never have raised my hand," she grumbled. "I should have just let it slide."

"Come on, kid, this is Tony. Remember me, the guy who escaped from a secret underground complex and ended up on your door step? How much worse can it get?"

"A lot worse, I'm afraid. You're not going to like this story, Tony—it's better left untold."

"Good, bad or ugly, I need to know your history if I'm going to trust you as a team member and comrade," insisted Tony.

Carley sighed and leaned back in the look-out chair.

"How much do you know about the recent history of Guatemala?"

"A little," frowned Tony. "They went through a pretty grizzly civil war, but that was more than ten years ago."

"Twelve years ago," corrected Carley, "and the U.S. Government provided most of the weapons and all of the training to the Guatemalan military in their war against the opposition forces that had united under the URNG guerrillas."

"Is that how you became so familiar with U.S. weapons?" interrupted Tony. "Were you in Guatemala during the war?"

"Yes, and with the help of the United States the Guatemalan political and military machine systematically destroyed four-hundred fifty Mayan villages and more than 200,000 indigenous people—mostly Maya—before the U.N. stepped in and brought an end to the war. But there were others brutally murdered, too—students, workers, professionals and opposition leaders."

"Well, a lot of us were misled about that one, Carley. You can't beat yourself up about being on the wrong side when all the information painted such a horrible picture of the guerrillas. Some of the intelligence photos I saw showed mass graves full of hundreds of bodies. We were led to believe they were government soldiers murdered by the URNG but they turned out to be innocent people killed by the government in their genocide against certain ethnic groups."

"Oh, I wasn't on the *wrong* side!" snapped Carley. "I fought with the URNG for more than three years and the U.S. weapons I used were ones I took off the bodies of dead Guatemalan soldiers and their murderous U.S. allies."

Tony was silent for a long time.

"See, I said you wouldn't like the story," Carley finally said. "I'm sorry, but you just wouldn't leave it alone. Unlike the news that was being reported in the United States media, the stories we were hearing in Belize were much different. After my husband died, I decided I had to do something so I caught a bus to San Ignacio, about eighty miles east of Belize City, and walked across the border into Guatemala. I hooked up with a small band of opposition forces almost immediately and due to my background in nursing I was moved inland and then south to the front lines in the rugged mountains north of Baja Verapaz."

"I didn't know you were a nurse," said Tony softly.

"Well technically I'm not. I was about half way through nursing school when I went to Guatemala, but I learned more in the two years I worked in the field hospitals then I would have learned in a hundred years at school."

"I thought you said you were there three and a half years."

"I was but after our hospital was destroyed, we all fled into the jungle and I became just another fighter. Earlier, when I said I had experience with grenade launchers, I guess I was just being morbid. My experience was as a target, rather than a shooter, and I was taken prisoner on two different occasions. Those were difficult times and I still have enemies in Guatemala. Some of those who I fought against have now risen through the ranks and are powerful people in the government. By the time the war was over and I was back in Belize I was pretty screwed up from all I'd seen and done. When I first met Rob and Anne, I was living in the alley behind the bar. That's how I knew about the door back there that we used as the address on your papers."

"I'm sorry, Carley, I had no idea what you'd been through. But I do know what it's like to fight in a war that makes no sense—one that should never have happened. And I know what it's like to patch soldiers up so they can go right back out and fight again."

"Vietnam?" asked Carley.

"And other places," nodded Tony. "So many innocent people died for nothing and the ones who deserved to die lived long and prospered, to paraphrase my friend Spock."

"Who?"

"Spock, but it doesn't matter. I'm sorry I made you dredge up old memories but I respect what you did and the reasons why you did it, even if you might have done it to some of my comrades. And I'm glad we're on the same team this time."

"Me, too," whispered Carley.

As they both sat there, quietly lost in their own memories, a distant explosion rocked the tranquil tropical setting.

As Carley grabbed for the binoculars, Tony smiled.

"Thanks, Commander Idiot," he mumbled to himself.

Chapter 9

After finishing his own lunch, Tony took a serving of Rob's cob salad up to Carley at the lookout post on top of the Dolphin Diver.

"So, how was it?" she asked, accepting the plate with a smile.

"It was good, but not as good as your cooking," replied Tony. "If I had to pick one to be a cook and one to be a lookout, I'm afraid you'd be right back down in the kitchen."

"Bummer! I was hoping I'd get to spend a little more time out here in the sunshine. By the time I prepare, serve and clean up after three meals, I've missed most of the day. I'm kind of enjoying being out in the sun for a change."

"Well, if you're serious about that, I'll see what I can do to rearrange the schedule. I'd rather have you in the kitchen for breakfast and lunch because I think those are the two most important meals of the day, but how would you feel about swapping your evening meal duties for a shift up here? I could probably talk Rob into taking over supper once in a while and there might be others who would like to show off their culinary skills, too."

"That would be perfect! My kitchen day would end about 2:00 p.m. and I'd be available for one of the afternoon, evening or night shifts."

"Yeah, but probably just Acosta's shift from 2:00 p.m. to 6:00 p.m. or Rob's from 6:00 p.m. to 10:00 p.m. Anything later than that would give you a short night before beginning your morning breakfast routine."

"Well, whatever you decide is fine," replied Carley, "I would love to pull a shift up here every now and then, even if it's not every day. So what do you think the chances are that we'll get underway tomorrow morning?"

"Assuming that explosion we heard this morning was our shadow ship headed to the bottom of the ocean I'd say they are pretty good. I expect…"

Tony was interrupted by a voice calling from a distance. Taking the binoculars, he scanned the shoreline and spotted Commander Espinoza headed down the long pier towards a small inflatable dingy tied up at the far end.

"As I was saying," continued Tony, pointing towards the pier, "I expect we'll be hearing from the Honduran Navy anytime, and here he comes right now."

When Commander Espinoza arrived, the crew, except for Carley, assembled in the salon.

"I have some good news and some bad news," began the Commander. "The good news is that the ship which has been following you will no longer be a problem."

"You actually blew it up?" asked a surprised Tony.

"No, and I'm afraid that's the bad news. Rather than allow us to board her, the crew apparently destroyed the vessel. There was a huge explosion as my patrol boat was approaching and before my men could get close, the ship had already slipped below the surface so we have no idea where it was from."

"What about the crew?" asked Captain Braydon. "Surely one of them can be convinced to talk."

"As far as we can tell, there were no survivors," frowned the Commander. "At least there were no bodies in the water when my men got to the site."

"Isn't it possible that they got away in a smaller boat without your men spotting them?" asked an increasingly skeptical Tony.

"No, it isn't," insisted the Honduran. "My patrol boat was between them and this island and the next closest land is more than one hundred miles away across open water. Someone would have to be a fool to attempt that trip and even if they had, my men would have spotted them with the high-powered optics we have onboard our patrol boat. Either the crew vanished with their boat or there was never a crew aboard in the first place."

"Are you suggesting it might have been remote-controlled?" asked Tony.

"It's a possibility we have to consider," nodded the Commander. "Either that or the crew was loyal enough to die for their employer."

Tony turned to his ship's engineer. "Rigo, what do you think? Could a vessel like this one be configured so it could be operated remotely?"

"I suppose anything is possible," replied Rigo, "but it would be a very expensive project. All the control systems would have to be redesigned and the remote operator would have to get real-time feedback from the boat to keep it on course and avoid running aground."

"Yes, but given all that, it could be done, right? The necessary data could be passed back and forth via satellite, for example, and theoretically the boat could be operated from anywhere on Earth."

"Excuse me," interrupted the Honduran commander, "but why would anyone with those kinds of resources be interested in your dive boat and its relatively small crew?"

Before anyone had a chance to blow the ship's cover, Rob stepped in.

"I can probably answer that, Commander. While our ship is technically a live aboard dive vessel, it's actually owned by a small research company in Belize that's on the verge of a major break-through in dolphin research. I'm not at liberty to discuss any details, but if their work pans out they will own a new technology that would be very attractive to any major military power. They've tried to keep their work secret, but they're a small organization and apparently something has leaked out."

"I see," nodded the commander. "And do you have any of this new technology onboard now?"

"No, absolutely not," replied Rob. "This is a crew training mission and nothing more, but someone must think the research is further along than it really is."

"It would seem so. Since a ship, and possibly its entire crew, has been lost, I'm going to have to file a report about the incident and I'll need some information from you Mr. Jefferies. Could I trouble you to come ashore with me now? That way you can be on your way at sun up and, hopefully, put this unpleasant experience behind you."

Rob looked to Tony, who nodded, and within minutes Rob and the Honduran commander were headed towards the pier in the dinghy.

What's all that talk about dolphin research?" asked the ship's dive master, Cesar Acosta. "I thought our mission was to get you to BVI."

"It is, Cesar, but what Rob said is also true. The real owner of this vessel is a small research company that has been working with dolphins for many years and they're getting very close to a scientific breakthrough that will stun the world. Those of you who stay on through our visit to BVI and make the return voyage to Belize will have the opportunity to be part of history, I promise you."

"So what's this breakthrough all about?" asked Rigo Mejía.

"I think that information should come from Rob, if he's willing to discuss it," replied Tony. "However, I can tell you that it's so amazing I just might sign on as a deck hand after I finish my other business so I can watch the research evolve. Now, since it sounds like we'll be getting underway tomorrow morning, how about if everybody gets back to work and prepares to depart at sun up?"

An hour later, Tony was deep in thought at his desk when there was a knock on his cabin door, followed by Carley's voice"

"Tony, do you have a minute?"

"It's open!" he called.

Carley opened the door but didn't cross the threshold.

"Sorry to bother you. I was just wondering what the meeting with the Honduran Navy was all about. The rest of the crew seems to be all pumped up about something, but I couldn't find Rob to ask him what's going on."

"It's no bother, kid! Rob's gone ashore for a little while but come on in and I'll bring you up to date. How was your first watch?"

When Tony had finished briefing Carley, she asked the same question Rigo had.

"So what's this dolphin research all about?"

Tony gave her the same answer he had given Rigo, including his comment about signing on as a deck hand after his mission in the British Virgin Islands was finished.

"Well, that would certainly be nice," smiled Carley. "At least we'd see you in Belize City whenever the ship is in port."

"You don't think you'd be interested in becoming a permanent member of the crew?"

"No, this will be interesting for a while, but I already feel a little claustrophobic. I need my daily walk-abouts in the trees to keep me sane."

"I guess I'm just the opposite. I've loved boats since I was a kid and I could make the Dolphin Diver my permanent home without any trouble at all. On the other hand, a small island somewhere wouldn't be bad either. Maybe it's just being near the water that I crave."

"Well, if that small island has some trees on it, let me know and maybe I'll stop by sometime," smiled Carley. "I need to get supper started, so I'll leave you alone. Thanks for the update."

After the door had closed, Tony leaned back in his chair and clasped his hands behind his head. His comment about living on a small island had dredged up memories of his days on St. John Island with Jill and those memories reminded him that he hadn't heard anything about the inquiries Rob had made regarding Jim and Linda. He made a note to himself and taped it inside his desk before raising the drop-down writing surface and locking it in place.

***

Mueller awoke with a start as the maid outside his hotel room called, "Maid service!" for the third time.

"Come back later," he yelled back angrily.

He had fallen asleep at his table sometime after 2:00 a.m. without finishing his re-read of the thick NWIDI file and now it was apparently morning and time to get back to work. He stumbled into the bathroom to brush his teeth and tried to remember what—if anything—he'd learned during the previous evening's reading. He had organized the file by person, beginning with Tony Nicoletti and followed by Frank Morton, Linda McBride (now Linda Reyes) and finally Jim Barnes. He'd only gotten part way through the Morton section, but he'd read enough to be reminded of the bond between Nicoletti and Morton that extended back many years to when they were both in the military in Southeast Asia. Contrary to his boss, Mueller still considered it possible that Morton had died in the diving accident five years earlier. However, if Morton were still alive, Mueller was sure that Morton and Nicoletti would try to hook up again, now that Nicoletti had escaped from MX-2. He also knew that they would be a formidable adversary if that ever happened. His best chance would be to find one or the other before they found each other. And once he had the first one, the second one would find *him* in no time.

Of course, he had no real evidence that either Nicoletti or Morton were in the Virgin Islands—or even headed that way. All he had was the mysterious coffin-like box that the former NWIDI Learjet had delivered to St. Thomas, USVI, after making an unexplained stop in the Bahamas. And he couldn't back-track the shipment to Andros Island because he was under orders to remain on St. Thomas until the local U.S. Customs office finished its investigation and returned his passport.

By the time Mueller stepped out of the shower, he had made up his mind to spend the day doing some old fashioned detective work by taking to the streets of downtown Charlotte Amalie. If there weren't too many cruise ships in, he might even spot Nicoletti or Morton on the street. If the crowds were heavy in the morning, he'd stop into some of the more popular bars and cafés and show their pictures around. Maybe somebody knew one or both of them as regulars and, at the very least, he'd be creating a network of eyes to help him watch the city. Before leaving his room, Mueller grabbed a stack of business cards he carried for just this purpose. Although he had never actually been to New York City, the cards proclaimed that he was Detective Erik Miller and listed a phone number consistent with one of NYPD's Brooklyn precincts. However, the number was actually permanently forwarded to his cell phone.

As luck would have it, there were four cruise ships tied up at the Havensight piers by the time Mueller reached that end of town and the "cruisers" were everywhere so he caught a taxi back to the east end of the island and stopped at a small café in the American Yacht Harbor strip mall for breakfast. The long, two-story commercial center was an odd mixture of restaurants, store-fronts and office spaces fronted by a beautiful marina crowded with yachts and sailboats. It was also just a short walk to the ferry that ran between East End, on St. Thomas and Cruz Bay, on St. John. The ferry is the only public transportation between the two islands and runs every hour, more or less. As Mueller sipped his coffee, he wondered if Tony Nicoletti had ever sat in this restaurant waiting for the ferry on his way over to see his friend Jill Harris. He showed Nicoletti's picture to the waitress, but she shook her head and dashed off to help another table.

Based on the thick folder back in his room, Mueller knew that the Six had already tried unsuccessfully to locate Jill on St. John but they had never put feet on the ground until now. Since he had Tony's picture to help jog memories, he decided to leave St. Thomas to the cruisers for the day and wander over to St. John. By 5:00 p.m. the cruise ships would be gone and things would get back to normal again on St. Thomas.

During the twenty minute trip across Pillsbury Sound, Mueller leaned against the port rail and gazed at the turquoise water and stunningly beautiful islands. From some limited reading he'd done in his hotel room, he knew that most of the islands he could see were British territory. Only St. Thomas, St. John and several small cays belonged to the United States. Everything else north and east of St. John made up the British Virgin Islands. An article in one of the hotel room magazines made BVI sound like the perfect vacation destination but he had no interest in the place. For now, his interests were here, where Tony Nicoletti had once been and where he might again be.

When the boat arrived in the tiny settlement of Cruz Bay, Mueller began a casual inventory of the bars and restaurants near the ferry dock. His third stop was at Purser's, a double-decked store and nautical-themed pub overlooking the harbor. It didn't strike him as the type of place Nicoletti would frequent, but he asked anyway, showing the picture.

"I'm supposed to meet a friend of mine here on the island this morning but somehow I managed to lose the piece of paper he sent me with the name of the place on it. Does this guy happen to look familiar?"

The bartender studied the picture for a minute and then shook his head.

"I'm afraid not," he said, handing the picture back.

Just then, a bubbly waitress dressed in what was probably supposed to be a pirate-like outfit zipped up to the bar and handed the bartender an order ticket.

"Hey, Suzy, you ever see this guy around here?" he asked motioning for Mueller to show her the picture. And then to Mueller, "Suzy's been on the island longer than anybody I know."

The attractive woman of indeterminate age slapped the bartender on the arm playfully and then took the photo.

After studying it for a few seconds, her face lit up.

"He's a lot more clean-cut in this picture than I remember him, but I swear that's the Sicilian."

"Who?" asked both Mueller and the bartender in unison.

"The Sicilian, ah, Tony something or other but everybody just called him the Sicilian. He hasn't been around for a long time, though. Is he a friend of yours?"

"Ah, yes," stumbled Mueller. "His name is actually Tony Nicoletti and I haven't seen him in a while, either. We were supposed to meet here on St. John today but I've misplaced the name of the meeting place so I'm going door-to-door hoping to find him or somebody who knows him. Why did everybody call him the Sicilian?"

"I have no idea," replied the waitress. "I don't think I ever heard his last name because the one you just said doesn't sound familiar. And I doubt if he'd pick this place to meet. Back in those days I worked up at the *Paradiso* and your friend was a regular big spender. He always had his lady with him and when they walked in he'd loudly announce that the next round of drinks was 'on the Sicilian.' Hey, maybe that's why they called him the Sicilian!"

"Yeah, maybe," frowned Mueller. "Where is this place you mentioned?"

"The Paradiso? It's up the street to your left at Mongoose Junction but you won't find him there, either, because they don't open until 5:00 p.m."

Accepting the photo back from the waitress, he asked "Is there any place around here that you think might be up to his lunch standards?"

"Well, you might try the Terrace, up at Caneel Bay, but I never actually saw him during the day. He lived somewhere on the other end of the island, I think, and stopped in at the Paradiso on his way back from day trips over to St. Thomas. Maybe you should just hang out down by the ferry dock and let him find you."

"I may have to do that but I'd like to look for him a bit more. His girl friend's name was Jill and she was in real estate here the last I knew. Is St. John Property Management still in business?"

"Yes, I think so" answered the bartender. "They're also up at Mongoose Junction but at the opposite end from the restaurant."

"Well, maybe I'll check there. He has to be here somewhere!" Mueller laughed.

After saying "Thanks" to both, he left casually, as if on holiday. Once out on the street, he quickly made his way to Mongoose Junction, an eclectic collection of shops, restaurants and galleries under a common roof with pleasant gardens and plenty of outdoor dining. He located the Paradiso for future reference and then set out to find the real estate company.

"Good morning," he said as he closed the door to the office behind himself and adjusted to the air conditioned interior. The hill up from the ferry dock looked gentle but the walk had taken its toll on Mueller and the woman sitting at the desk noticed.

"It's going to be another hot one," she said, smiling. "How may I help you today?"

"Well, I'm supposed to meet an old friend of mine here on St. John today but, unfortunately, I've misplaced the paper that has the restaurant name written on it. I stopped here because the last time I saw him—which has been more than five years, now—he was dating a lady who worked here. Do you happen to know if Jill Harris is still on the island?"

Mueller knew, of course, that she wasn't, but he was hoping to get some detail that would lead him to Nicoletti.

"Jill Harris? No, she's no longer in the Virgin Islands. She left about three years ago and I believe she went back to Las Vegas. She seems to be pretty popular lately."

"What do you mean?"

"Well, after not hearing her name for a long, long time I received a call about a week ago asking about her and now you're here."

"That was probably my friend," he smiled. Inside, he was cheering because he might actually be closing in on Nicoletti.

"I doubt it," replied the woman, shaking her head. "The call I received was from a woman."

"A woman?" he asked as his second of euphoria crashed. "Any idea who?"

"No, sorry. I didn't ask. I told her the same thing I just told you and she hung up rather abruptly."

"That's okay, I was just curious. It was probably one of Jill's old friends or something. As I mentioned, I'm actually trying to hook up with Tony and I just thought she might know where he would be likely to meet someone coming over on the ferry."

The woman smiled and said, "You might try the ferry dock. Or is that too obvious?"

Mueller smiled back. "I know that sounds logical, but I'm sure the letter Tony sent me had the name of a restaurant or bar on it. He's going to think I stood him up but I have no way to contact him because all his contact information was on that piece of paper."

"Well, I'm sorry I can't help with that, but if you need a second for lunch, I'd be happy to introduce you to one of St. John's best kept secrets."

Never one to pass up an unexpected opportunity, Mueller smiled his most charming smile.

"I'd be delighted."

***

The Dolphin Diver weighed anchor at 6:30 a.m. and soon had the small patch of land called Swan Island behind her. Captain Braydon charted a course to the northeast that would take the vessel to Kingston, Jamaica, some 470 miles away, and the crew fell back into their old routine. All except Tony. He had let the Honduran commander go on about a remote controlled boat and he'd even fueled the conversation by suggesting a satellite link. However, Tony had his own ideas about what had happened to the crew of the exploded ship—he believed they might have slipped away in a small mini-sub carried for just such a situation. From his lookout station high atop the Dolphin Diver, Tony scanned the nearby water with his high-powered binoculars. He didn't like the idea that something sinister might be lurking below them.

Chapter 10

As his shift wore on, Tony became more and more depressed. This was just the fourth day at sea and they were already a day and a half behind schedule. Less than three hundred miles into their sixteen hundred mile voyage they had their first encounter with an unfriendly, survived a close call with a shark and been scrutinized by the Honduran Navy. And to top it all off, Tony still had this nagging concern about whether he was even doing the right thing. Frank had asked him (albeit in a dream) to protect the Guardians, whoever they were, but there had been no other guidance or instruction. Was the purchase of this vessel and the voyage now underway going to make the secret any safer? Tony just didn't know and it was eating him up.

"Hey, sailor, ready for some breakfast?" asked Carley, as her head came into view. She placed Tony's breakfast on the deck and climbed the last few rungs of the ladder onto the upper level of the Dolphin Diver where Tony had built his state-of-the-art look-out station.

"Yeah, sure," mumbled Tony, glancing at his watch. "Is it only 7:30 a.m.?"

"That's right," nodded Carley as she opened the Tupperware container she used to haul food up to the lookouts. "How's your coffee?"

Tony swirled his thermos and nodded. "It's fine. How are things going down below?"

"Oh, fine, I guess. Rob has everybody all jazzed up about the dolphin research project and that's all they can talk about, but at least it gives them something to think about besides eating. Did I understand the Captain to say that it will be two and a half days before we make landfall again?"

"That sounds about right. Assuming we don't run into any more snags, we should reach Kingston, Jamaica, about mid-afternoon on Thursday but unless we need supplies I don't plan on stopping any longer than it takes to top off the fuel tank."

"Some luxury cruise this is turning out to be," pouted Carley. "I hear Kingston is a pretty jumping place at night."

"Yes, and pretty dangerous, too. Sorry, but this isn't a vacation trip. The sooner we get to the Virgin Islands, the better."

Carley came around to face Tony and made eye contact.

"And then what, Tony? You didn't have a plan when we left Belize and I'll bet you don't have one now. But even if you do, what difference is a day—or even a whole bunch of days—going to make after five years? What's the rush?"

Tony's shoulders sagged and he sighed heavily. "You just don't get it, do you?"

"No, I guess I don't. If someone were waiting for us in Road Town or if some event were going to take place, then I could understand being in a hurry. But if you still don't have a plan then you need to be out here, under the stars where you can think things through. Once we're in the British Virgin Islands you're going to feel the pressure to do something—anything—and it won't necessarily be the right thing. Personally, I think you'd be better off adrift at sea than storming into port all charged up without a plan. But, hey, that's just me. I'll see you when your shift is over."

And with that, Carley disappeared down the ladder and left Tony with his thoughts.

***

At lunch, Erik Mueller learned that his companion, Jeri Addison, was originally from Milwaukee, Wisconsin. She had moved to the islands twelve years ago and had owned St. John Property Management for the past seven years. She was also quite a talker!

During one of her infrequent quiet moments, Mueller managed to slip in a question about Jill.

"I understand Jill lived on the other end of the island, is that right?"

"Yes, she was taking care of a place for a client of mine," nodded Jeri between bites of salad. "It's a small house, and very secluded. Except when her friend was here, Jill stayed very much to herself. But when Tony was around, well that was another matter!"

"Yes, so I've heard. Could I talk you into showing me that house after lunch?" asked Mueller. "I realize she's no longer there, but I'm curious, anyway."

The real estate agent thought for a minute and then replied, "I'll tell you what. If you'll let me check on another property along the way, I'll drive you by Jill's old house and then we'll come back along the north shore. Maybe we'll even have time for a quick swim in one of the secluded bays out that way."

"I'm staying over on St. Thomas and I didn't bring my swim suit with me," replied Mueller, as he handed the waiter his credit card.

"That won't be a problem at the beach I have in mind," smiled his new friend.

Jeri Addison drove her small, red sports car along the winding road like a seasoned race driver. At one point she navigated a hair-pin turn so fast that he thought for sure they were going to fly right off the cliff. As she turned into a blind driveway and slid the car to a stop, Mueller relaxed his white-knuckle grip on the side of his seat.

"I'll just be a minute," Jeri said. "You're welcome to come along, but I'm just going to do a quick walk-through. Maybe you'd prefer to check out the beautiful grounds, instead.

Mueller elected to stay behind and stretch his legs. The house was set towards the back of the deep lot and the front yard was heavily wooded and beautifully landscaped but it seemed like a strange setting, here on what he knew was an island paradise. When Jeri, returned, he asked her about it.

"The owners are from Canada and they wanted to preserve a little of the "north country" feel so they left every original tree standing out front. But let me show you the view from the other side."

Jeri led Mueller around the side of the one-story house and out onto a large deck that commanded a view of what must have been the most beautiful bay in the world. In the distance, Mueller could see the end of a large island and beyond that several smaller ones.

"Wow!" was all that would come out.

"Yeah, pretty nice, huh? Everything you see out there is in the British Virgin Islands and you actually need a passport to go over there. The water in between is the Sir Francis Drake Channel. There was a time when it was filled with tall ships and many of them pirate ships. Shall we go check out Jill's old place?"

Ten minutes later Jeri brought her little car to a stop in front of a large gate constructed from what looked like old ship planks. After fishing around in her purse she finally produced a garage door opener and clicked the large button. Slowly the gates opened inward, revealing a lot very similar to the one they had just left. While they waited for the gate to come to a stop, Jeri explained.

"Lots of trees here, too, but the difference is that this house doesn't have an ocean view from the back. Instead, there's a large rock cliff in back that makes the place unapproachable from that side. That's why Jill liked it, I guess, but I never understood that. It's like she was afraid somebody was going to sneak up on her. When she lived here she had two large Rottweiler dogs that roamed the grounds and they'd tear your leg off if she didn't chain them up before opening the gate."

Mueller climbed out of the car and assessed the scene.

"Okay if I look around a bit?"

"Sure," replied Jeri. "Take your time. I'm going inside to make sure everything is as it should be. Come on inside when you're done out here."

Mueller knew it was a long shot, but if Tony Nicoletti had returned to the islands in that coffin-like box, he would need a place to hide and what better place than a house he knew to be easily defendable. In fact, Mueller reasoned, Nicoletti might still have a key to the place!

After walking the entire front grounds, Mueller circled around back. Jeri had not understated the size of the cliff that rose nearly straight up just a few yards behind the house. The high chain-link fence that ran down both sides of the property was anchored securely to the rock face of the cliff, sealing the house inside.

As he entered through the open back door, Jeri was just coming back into the kitchen.

"It's a fortress, all right," he commented. "Is everything okay in here?"

"Everything looks fine! There's an alarm system that rings into my office, so I didn't think anyone had been inside. I just wanted to make sure the utilities were still on and that we weren't having any rodent problems. It's been empty since Jill left."

"Don't the owners ever come for a visit?" questioned Mueller. "It's a beautiful place, even without the view."

"They're old and they're having health issues, so they don't travel anymore. Their children are all doctors, or something like that, and own their own properties in Hawaii, so they never visit, either. It's a real shame. I expect we'll be trying to sell this place for them by year's end."

All this information strengthened Mueller's belief that if Tony had returned to the islands he might also return to this place. He walked the house making some mental notes and then returned to the kitchen where Jeri had remained.

"Well, I've seen all I need to," he said. "Shall we go?"

"You betcha!" smiled Jeri. "Next stop—the beach."

⁕ ⁕ ⁕

Tony sulked for the next two and a half hours and when his shift in the lookout station was over he went straight to his room. He was angry, but not at Carley. He was angry with himself because he knew what she had said was true. He had no plan and he wasn't getting any closer to coming up with one. As he started second-guessing himself, he seriously considered altering the ship's itinerary and heading straight to South Bimini Island, the site of Frank's disappearance. At least there he would have something to guard!

Tony had been on a dive off the south coast of Bimini with Frank, Jill and a British divemaster named Ian when they had made some pretty weird discoveries. Among other things, they had discovered a three hundred fifty foot shear wall where the local navigational charts indicated the water to be only seventy-five feet deep. For another thing, they had discovered several large rectangular openings in the wall that seemed to be venting cold, fresh water. And then there was the video Ian had made while using his rebreather gear. He had volunteered to descend to the bottom of the wall and in the brief minutes he was there he had captured pictures of a triangular opening in the sea bottom that was definitely *not* a naturally-occurring feature. Maybe instead of heading to the British Virgin Islands he should be heading to South Bimini to stand watch over the anomaly that he felt sure had lured Frank and Miles Adderly back for that last, fateful dive.

His solitude was interrupted by a knock on his door and Rob Jefferies' voice outside.

"Tony, are you in there? I have some news from Anne via the short-wave radio that I think you're going to want to hear."

Tony jumped to his feet and opened the door.

"Come in, come in! Any news would be good news right now—what do you have?"

"Well, I just got off the radio with Anne and she has news from your flight crew. She spoke by telephone with someone named Susan."

"Yes, Susan Fitzgerald," interrupted Tony. "What did she have to say?"

"Well, this sounds a little weird, so I had Anne repeat the whole story—Susan told her that she had been contacted by Linda who says that there's an assassin headed to Seattle to kill you. Does that make any sense?"

"An assassin?" laughed Tony. "Why would anybody... unless it's Edwards and his bunch. But why Seattle? And how does Linda know about this? For that matter, where is Linda? I haven't heard from her in more than five years!"

"I thought I remembered you telling me that, so I asked Anne to follow up with this Susan lady and see what she could find out. It's pretty weird, though, huh?"

"Yes, it certainly is!' exclaimed Tony."Apparently the package I had transported to St. Thomas didn't fool anybody."

"Yes, but the good news is that if they're looking for you in Seattle, they sure don't know you're here. And that means they didn't track you to Belize, either."

"Good point," replied Tony, "but then how do you explain that boat that was following us? They had to be up to something or they wouldn't have sunk it right in front of the Honduran Navy."

"Maybe it really was an accident," offered Rob.

"I don't believe that for a minute, but I also don't have a better explanation right now. When do you expect to hear from Anne again?"

"About this time tomorrow," replied Rob."Would you like to talk to her, too?"

"Tony shook his head. "No, I don't want to infringe on your private time, but would you mind if I made you a short list of questions?"

The news about Linda lifted Tony's spirits significantly and he joined the rest of the crew—except for Captain Braydon and Nicolas Banks—in the ship's salon for lunch. Carley was surprised to see him, but said nothing. Before the meal was quite over, Tony made a group announcement.

"It's been brought to my attention that I didn't build any R & R time into this trip, so I think we'll lay over one night in Jamaica. But I need every single person's word that you'll be careful and sensible while you're ashore. I don't want to have to rescue anyone from the jail—or the morgue."

Faces brightened all around the room, especially Carley's.

"Since I want everybody to enjoy this short break, I'll remain onboard for security," he continued.

Carley's smile quickly faded and she turned her back on the group to focus on her kitchen clean-up.

Cesar Acosta offered that he'd been to Kingston several years earlier and suddenly he was the center of attention with the other male crew members all asking him questions at once.

Tony made his way to Carley's side and said, "Hey, what's up? I thought you'd be happy about the shore leave."

"I am, but why do you always have to be the one to take up the slack? I was hoping we could go dancing or have conch fritters along the water front or something like that."

"And so you shall," interrupted the Captain as he came down the hall that led from the bridge. "I've been to Kingston too many times in my life and there's nothing there I wish to see—or that I wish to have see me."

The Captain winked and Tony nodded his acceptance of the other man's offer.

"There, you see? All better! Now get this mess cleaned up and get up on that Lookout deck. Nickolas is waiting for some relief."

"What? Am I on a watch shift today?" Carley was beaming from ear to ear.

"Just for today, you're taking Cesar's shift, he's taking Rob's and Rob is handling dinner duties again. You said you wanted to get outside, so you're on duty at 2:00 p.m. sharp!"

Tony was surprised at how much the news of the Kingston layover changed the mood aboard the ship. Not that the mood had been particularly bad before, but now the crew had something to look forward to in the short-term—something more immediate than arriving at their journey's end several days from now. Lesson learned, thought Tony.

Rob surprised everyone for the second time with an evening meal of pan-seared fresh fish finished with a dill sauce and served with steamed rice and baby carrots. When the dishes were done, he and Tony retreated to the aft deck to watch the sunset and enjoy a cold beer.

"You seem to be doing better," commented Rob as he leaned on the rail overlooking the dive platform.

"Better than what?" asked Tony.

"Well, better than this morning, for one thing."

"Your news about Linda helped a lot," nodded Tony. "Now I know she's alive and well. At least she's well enough to worry about me getting assassinated. And my earlier email reply from Jim means that all three of us survived the past five years."

"Yeah, I imagine that quite a load has been lifted. So are you going to try to hook up with them?"

"Maybe, but not right away. I have my own thing to do for Frank and, for all I know, they do, too. But if somebody really is trying to kill me, it's not safe for us to all be in one place right now. Jim's obviously working out in the open, but he's also under the watchful eye of the U.S. Navy. Linda and Javier could be on the run or living under assumed names—or both. I don't want to blow anybody's cover and I certainly don't want them to blow mine!"

"Well, as long as we can keep this short wave link working, you may not need to meet in person. Shall I have Anne try to reach Jim, too, and let him know what's happening?"

"No, let's wait on that for now. When we get to Road Town I'll make some inquiries and make sure Edwards didn't somehow get to Jim. I apparently have a contract out on me and Jim gets to play scientist in plain view. It doesn't make sense."

"But like you said," countered Rob, "he's under the watchful eye of the Navy. He may be so well protected that he isn't in any real danger."

"Or he may be a prisoner of the Navy, rather than a guest. After all, we were led to believe that Buzz Edwards worked for the Department of Defense before he took me prisoner for five years."

"True," agreed Rob. "So what's the plan now? Are we still heading for the Virgin Islands?

"I've been asking myself that all day, Rob, and I'm still not sure I know the right answer but until a better idea emerges, I'm sticking to the original plan. I believe—although I'm not positive—that the place Frank asked me to protect is exactly the same spot where he and Miles Adderly disappeared. Since we're just one lightly-armed ship, we'd never be able to defend that spot for very long, especially if the U.S Navy turns out to be on the other side of the battle. I think a better plan is to create a diversion to keep the bad guys from even thinking about the South Bimini site. They can send as many thugs as they want to the wrong spot as long as they don't send any to the right spot."

"Sounds logical," nodded Rob. "But that puts the bulls-eye right on us, doesn't it? Won't it be up to us to draw their attention away from Bimini?"

"Not if I can help it. I want their sights on me, not the Dolphin Diver or her crew. If I can use a virtual version of me that's what I'll do, but if I have to stand up and shout 'Hey! Over here!' then that's what I'll do. And if I have to go to Bimini and defend the site myself, well, then I hope Cesar has me rebreather-trained before I have to go."

***

Mueller awoke the next morning to the sound of his hotel room shower. It took him a minute to reconstruct the previous night and remember that Jeri Addison had insisted that she bring him back to St. Thomas in her sports car on the last west-bound ferry of the night. After closing the bar at 3:00 a.m. they had stumbled back to his room but that, unfortunately, was where his memory of the evening ended.

"Good morning," he said as Jeri stepped out of the bathroom wrapped in a large towel.

"You're alive!" she said in mock surprise. "I tried to wake you before I got into the shower but I finally decided you were either unconscious or dead so I gave up."

"Sorry," apologized Mueller. "So what's your hurry? Come back to bed."

"I can't! I have to get back to St John as fast as I can. My security company called me a few minutes ago to tell me that the silent alarm went off at the house where I took you yesterday."

"The first one or Jill's house?" Mueller was now fully awake and sitting up in bed.

"It's the one where Jill used to live. It's possible I didn't close one of the doors tight and the wind blew it open or maybe the alarm just malfunctioned, but the keys are still in my car, so I need to get back over there before they smash their way in."

Mueller was already pulling his pants on.

"I'm coming with you!" he shouted. But silently, he screamed, "I've got you Nicoletti!"

Chapter 11

By the time Mueller and his new friend Jeri Addison rolled off the ferry on St. John more than two and a half hours had passed since the call from Jeri's alarm company. Swearing and passing on the wrong side of the road, she finally maneuvered her sports car around the vehicles in front of her and raced up the hill and away from the tiny ferry landing and its congestion. Once on the open road, she drove even faster than she had the day before but this time Mueller was as eager to reach their destination as his companion.

As the St. John scenery flashed by Mueller considered his options once they reached the house. His companion knew nothing of his real interest in Tony Nicoletti, of course, and sliding to a stop in the gravel driveway would surely alert anyone inside the house.

"You know," he finally said, "if there is somebody in the house, we probably shouldn't rush in there and confront them. What if they're armed?"

"You don't strike me as a man who'd be afraid of a little action," laughed the woman, "but if you want to stay outside, I'll call you when the coast is clear."

Mueller shot a glare to his left, but Jeri's eyes were riveted to the road and she didn't even notice. He decided to let the comment slide—for now. The woman had been a lot more appealing the night before when he'd had too much to drink. Today she was just a means to an end.

As the car careened around the sharpest of the hairpin turns, both passengers saw the plume of black smoke at the same time.

"Oh, my God, no!" screamed Jeri. "That can't be the house!"

But as they rounded the final bend in the road, it became apparent that it was the house Jill had lived in. A police motorcycle with lights flashing was blocking the road and a pickup-turned-fire truck was part way through the gate.

"My God, Arnold, what happened?" Jeri asked the policeman who had signaled for her to stop her car. "I was over on St. Thomas when I got the call about the alarm."

"Yes, ma'am, I know," smiled the coal black policeman, who couldn't have been more than 25 years old. "I was just on routine patrol this morning and I smelled smoke as I passed this property, so I stopped to check it out. I knew the place was empty, and smoke didn't seem like a good thing so I called the fire department. Clarence and James came right up but by the time they got here, smoke was pouring out of the place. It seemed to be coming from the back, ma'am—maybe the kitchen?"

"Can I go in?" begged a frantic Jeri.

The policeman said something into a walkie-talkie and then nodded.

"They have the fire out, but Clarence says to watch your step. He'll meet you at the front door."

Without saying a word to Mueller, Jeri flung open her car door and bolted for the gate. Mueller started to get out and follow, but the policeman shook his head.

"Just the lady, I'm afraid. She's the legal representative of the owners and Clarence needs to ask her some questions but I'm afraid everyone else has to stay back until they determine the cause of the fire. Sorry, sir."

Mueller shrugged and leaned against the car to wait.

"So tell me, officer," he said with his friendliest smile, "did you see anyone around here this morning? Are they thinking it might be arson or something?"

"No, sir, I didn't see anyone but I didn't actually enter the property until the fire crew got here. We don't have a fire investigator here on St. John, so Clarence and James will make an initial assessment and if they think something looks fishy they'll have someone come over from St. Thomas."

"So I take it you don't have many fires here on St. John," asked Mueller, pretending to be interested.

The black man smiled broadly. "No sir! This is the first one in three years, I believe. Folks are pretty careful over here.

James is just a volunteer and Clarence spends most of his time checking out sprinkler systems and washing the fire truck!"

Mueller laughed and offered the other man a bottle of water he had grabbed from the hotel room as they ran out the door.

"You're going to need this, my man. You may have a long day ahead of you."

The young policeman accepted the bottle gratefully and glanced at the label.

"I take it you're just visiting the islands?" he asked.

"That's right," nodded Mueller. "I was supposed to meet an old friend of mine for lunch yesterday, but he never showed. While I was poking around trying to find him I ran into the lady and, well, you know…"

"Yes, sir, I do!" smiled the young man again. "Who is this friend of yours—maybe I can help."

"Oh, wow, that would be great!" exclaimed Mueller in mock surprise.

Unable to remember exactly what lie he'd told Jeri the night before, he just made up a story as he went.

"He's an old Army buddy and I haven't seen him in twenty years. His name is Tony Nicoletti and I understand he's pretty well known here on St. John. In fact, the lady I arrived with told me he used to date the woman who last lived in this very house! Quite a coincidence, huh?"

"It sure is! I've heard the name but I don't believe I ever met the gentleman. I moved here from St. Croix about eighteen months ago but I think I know all the current residents. And this place has been empty ever since I arrived. I'll keep my ears open, though. If I hear anything I'll let Ms. Addison know and she can pass the info along to you."

Mueller reached into his shirt pocket and pulled out one of his fake NYPD business cards.

"Actually, I'm heading back to New York in a couple of days," lied Mueller, "so would you mind calling the number on this card instead? "

"Wow, a detective with NYPD! It's a pleasure to meet you, Mr. Mueller. And I will certainly call you if I hear anything." The man nodded toward the gate. "Here comes the lady and she doesn't look happy."

The policeman was right—Jeri Addison looked very upset as she approached the car.

"Jump in," she barked. "I have to get back to my office as soon as possible and get on the phone with the insurance company. Sorry to kiss and run, but I'm going to be tied up for several days with this."

"I understand," nodded Mueller, grateful for the unexpected termination to their brief relationship. "Do they have any idea what caused the fire?"

After an unusually long silence, she replied. "They think it was smoker's carelessness."

"But nobody lives there and you were the last person in the house with a cigarette yesterday when… oh!"

"Yeah, oh! If they find out it was my cigarette, it will seriously damage my business. And if the insurance company denies the claim, I'll be financially ruined, too. Needless to say, I have to focus on this so where can I drop you?"

"Ah, the ferry dock, I guess," replied Mueller. "I think I've learned all I can here so I'll probably poke around on St. Thomas for a day or two and then I guess I'll head home."

Jeri Addison was silent the rest of the trip back to Cruz Bay and when Mueller closed the door of her car she sped away without so much as a "Good bye."

"Good riddance," thought Mueller as he made his way to the small white building where ferry tickets were sold.

For the next two days and nights Erik Mueller canvassed the island of St. Thomas hoping that some trace of Tony Nicoletti or Frank Morton would show up. He distributed a number of his fake business cards and asked to be called if anyone matching Tony Nicoletti's description turned up. With each card, his explanation of why a detective from NYPD was looking for the illusive Nicoletti changed slightly, but it didn't matter since these people had no apparent connection to each other.

**

The past two and one-half days had been uneventful—almost boring—aboard the Dolphin Diver and all hands were on deck to watch the lights of Kingston harbor come into view. Most of the crew members were anxious to get ashore but Tony was beginning to have second thoughts about allowing the overnight layover.

Originally founded in 1692, Kingston had its share of ups and downs due to earthquakes and fires and the historic downtown area suffered from cycles of political and gang violence due to the rampant drug trafficking activities on the island. During a pre-arrival briefing a few hours earlier, Cesar had described his last visit to Kingston when he had witnessed a murder in a waterfront bar.

As agreed, Captain Braydon would be staying aboard the vessel while the others went ashore and Tony had no doubt that the old sailor could—and would, if necessary—protect the Dolphin Diver. But Tony had much less confidence in his own abilities to protect his crew once they left the boat.

The Captain eased the eighty-foot craft into the assigned slip and shut down the engines. Using his walkie-talkie, he contacted Tony who was on the main deck preparing to lower the gang plank down to the floating dock.

"I have to make the customary stops at the Port Authority, Customs and Immigration," he said. "You will all have to sit tight until I get back."

"Roger that," replied Tony. No other comment seemed necessary.

When Captain Braydon returned, the group divided more or less along social lines. Crewmen Nicolas Banks, Cesar Acosta and Rigo Mejía headed for a nearby night spot popular with seamen while Rob, Carley and Tony caught a cab uptown to the New Kingston area for dinner at a more upscale place.

"Wow!" commented Carley, as she slid into the large, curved booth towards the rear of the main dining room. "This sure puts my place back home to shame."

"Well, the Captain did say it was the nicest public place in Kingston," replied Rob as he gazed around the large room, "but I don't think Belize City is ready for something like this yet. Besides, you don't have to go back to the bar, you know. We'd love to have you sign on with the Dolphin Diver when we begin our research voyages."

A busboy arrived with bottles of purified water followed closely by the wine steward with some recommendations.

After they ordered a bottle of wine, Rob revisited the subject of Carley's position on the boat.

"Rob, I'm really grateful for all you've done for me and this trip has already been a wonderful experience, but I don't think I want to live at sea—always on the move and never having any roots. I guess I'm just more of the white picket fence type of gal."

"I can understand that, I guess," frowned Rob, "but if you ever change your mind, there will always be a place for you aboard the Diver. And of course the Pirates Cove back in Belize is yours for as long as you want it—after we finish the remodel, that is."

Rob and Carley continued to chat about the future until their waiter brought the dinner menus. After the interruption, Carley realized that Tony hadn't said a word since entering the restaurant and seemed to be lost in thought."

"Still working on that plan?" she asked.

Finally realizing that she was talking to him, he looked up and frowned.

"Yes, I guess I am," he apologized. "Sorry."

"Forget about it for tonight, Tony," admonished Carley. "Enjoy the evening because tomorrow you'll be back at sea and then you'll have plenty of time to come up with a plan. Maybe getting away from it for a few hours is just what your brain needs."

"Yes, maybe you're right," Tony smiled as he noticed the menu for the first time. "So what's for dinner?"

The food was delicious and called for a second bottle of wine. When the dessert cart was brought to the table, both Carley and Rob gave in to temptation but Tony resisted and ordered black coffee.

Tony had been much more himself during dinner and when Carley mentioned dancing he surprised her by insisting on the first dance.

While they were waiting for the bill, the maitre d' came to the table and discreetly asked, "Are either of you gentlemen Mr. Wykes?"

When both Tony and Rob shook their heads, Carley nudged Tony to remind him that Wykes was his shipboard alias.

"Er, yes, I am," he stuttered. "I'm Anthony Wykes. Is there a problem?"

"You have a telephone call at the desk, sir. This way, please."

Tony slid out of the booth and turned to shrug at his companions before following the man out of sight. At a podium near the entrance to the dining room, the man handed Tony a telephone handset and then stepped away to give Tony privacy.

"Hello?" Tony asked.

"Tony, this is Captain Braydon. I hate to interrupt your evening, but I think you should return to the boat as soon as possible. The young mates have gotten themselves into a bit of trouble and I can't leave to assist them."

After accepting more than enough money to cover the restaurant charges plus a generous tip for himself, the maitre d' summoned a taxi and gave the driver instructions. He had apparently sensed the urgency in Tony's voice and passed that on to the driver, because the ride back to the harbor rivaled a thrill ride at Disneyland.

Captain Braydon was waiting at the bottom of the gangway when the taxi screeched to a stop.

Fearing the worst, Tony flung open the door and bolted to the Captain.

"What's happened? Are they alright?"

"They are fine," replied the captain calmly as Rob and Carley joined Tony. "They just got into a little scrape at a bar down the street and the local police won't release them to anyone except their captain. If you wouldn't mind taking my watch for a few minutes, I'll go retrieve them and bring them right back."

Tony nodded and the Captain walked casually towards the street and the waterfront bars.

Rob and Carley climbed the gangway to the ships main deck but Tony held his position on the dock. After what seemed like an eternity, Tony spotted the silhouettes of a small group headed his way and he soon recognized the captain by his bushy white beard.

Banks, Acosta and Mejía had obviously had too much to drink and were laughing loudly among themselves, so Tony didn't even acknowledge them. Instead, he directed his question to the captain.

"What happened?"

"Just a little bar brawl, that's all. I haven't been able to get too much out of our boys, but according to the police these three got into it with another group. There weren't any serious injuries, and I offered to cover the damages in exchange for the immediate release of our crew. We can't very well sail this thing in open waters without them, so it seemed like a reasonable trade."

"Of course, Captain, it was an excellent trade. Get these clowns aboard and to their rooms and I'll deal with them tomorrow once we're in open water. Do I need to go down there with some cash?"

"No, I've already taken care of it and we can settle up later. Right now I suggest we go aboard and hoist the gangway just in case the other bunch decides they haven't had enough fun."

Tony was the last one up the gangway and he took charge of raising and securing it. "I guess I'll take the night watch," he said to himself angrily.

When he stepped into the ship's main salon, he was surprised to see Nicholas Banks, Cesar Acosta and Rigo Mejía sitting side by side looking very sober and very serious.

"What the hell's going on?" demanded Tony.

***

Late Friday evening, a sharp rap on his hotel room door startled Mueller awake. He had fallen asleep watching television again and his neck screamed in pain as he sat up straight in his chair.

"Erik Mueller, this is the police. Please open the door immediately."

Mueller quickly scanned the room for an escape path but found none—not unless he wanted to jump six stories to the ground.

"Erik Mueller! Please open the door!" shouted the voice again.

Mueller scanned the room again, this time looking for contraband or anything that might give away his real identity. When he spotted his Smith and Wesson 38-Special on the night stand he quickly locked it into his brief case. He made his way to the door and opened it without releasing the safety chain.

"What is it?" he asked. "I was sleeping."

The door slammed against the chain and the voice repeated, "Open this door, Mr. Mueller, or we will open it for you."

Seeing little in the way of options, and sure he had nothing to fear, Mueller closed the door, unhitched the chain and opened the door after stepping to the side.

The door flew open and two large uniformed men stormed into the room. One of the men flipped on the overhead light and they both visually searched the room. Satisfied that he was alone, one of the men approached Mueller and motioned for him to turn around.

"Assume the position—hands against the wall with your feet apart. Erik Mueller, you are under arrest for impersonating a New York City police officer."

A stunned Mueller listened while his rights were being read and his hands were being handcuffed behind his back. When the two men led him from his room, a third officer was waiting outside.

"No one enters this room until you hear otherwise from me," barked the man who had summoned Mueller to the door.

"Yes, Sergeant!" snapped the third man as he pulled the door shut and planted himself squarely in front of it.

At the local police station, Mueller was led to an interrogation room and seated at a table with his hands still secured behind him.

"Wait here!" he was told.

After several minutes, the door opened and he was surprised to see the female U.S. Customs agent enter alone and close the door behind her.

She leaned on the back of the chair opposite Mueller and smiled broadly.

"I told you we'd be watching you, Mr. Mueller. And I also told you not to leave this island until I gave you my permission, so what's this I hear about you heading back to New York soon?"

"I don't know what you're talking about," muttered Mueller.

"Well that's not what my cousin Arnold tells, me, Mr. Mueller. He says you are planning to leave St. Thomas soon—maybe even tomorrow. Is that true?"

"Who?" demanded Mueller.

"My cousin Arnold. I believe you met him at the scene of a fire over on St John a couple of days ago. And I believe you told him you were…" The woman consulted some notes. "heading back to New York in a couple of days. Is that correct Mr. Mueller?"

"No, of course not. I was just making conversation. How can I leave St. Thomas when you have my passport?"

"Well, that's exactly what I would like to know. And I'd also like to know why you're impersonating a New York City police officer. You see, I called a friend at NYPD and there's no record of a Detective Erik Mueller anywhere in the department. Can you explain that, Mr. Mueller?"

Chapter 12

Tony scanned the faces of his three crewmen, waiting for an answer. Just minutes earlier they had been escorted aboard acting like a bunch of drunks. Now they seemed perfectly normal.

"Well," he demanded, "is somebody going to tell me what's going on?"

The three men stared at the floor for several long seconds before Nicolas Banks finally raised his head and looked Tony in the eyes.

"We were just having a few drinks, trying to figure out how to spend our evening ashore. In the booth next to us, four guys who obviously had a big head start on us were talking louder than necessary and we couldn't help overhearing. It didn't take us long to realize they had been aboard the ship the Honduran Navy sank while we were on Great Swan Island so…"

"Wait a minute!" interrupted Tony. "The Hondurans told us all hands were lost at sea when the ship went down."

"Well, with apologies to the Honduran Navy, these four were definitely not lost at sea," said Banks. "From what we overheard, they had been under orders to scuttle the ship if it was approached by the authorities but they seemed worried about the consequences. They never actually said how they ended up here in Kingston but they were clearly waiting for transportation off the island."

"They were probably running drugs," interjected Cesar Acosta.

"Probably," nodded Tony. "But what about the fight? What started that?"

Rigo Mejía, the smallest member of the crew, beamed proudly.

"Oh, that was my idea! They were getting pretty drunk and their conversation had shifted away from their dilemma, so we decided it was time for us to move on, too."

"So a fist fight was your way of saying goodbye?" frowned Tony.

"No, that was our way of getting our hands on some real information," smiled Mejía as he pulled a wallet out of his sweatshirt pocket and offered it to Tony. "We thought you might be able to track one of the crewmen back to the ship's owner. The guy who owns this seemed to be the leader of the group."

Tony accepted the wallet with a look of surprise. "So there wasn't really a fight?"

"Oh, there was *definitely* a fight," smiled Banks, rubbing his jaw, "but it was just a distraction so Rigo could pick a pocket."

Tony was already thumbing through the well-worn leather wallet, but he nodded his approval.

"Well done, guys. I'll get to work on this immediately and see what I can turn up. I think you'd better stay off the waterfront for the rest of the night, but you could take a cab uptown and enjoy the rest of your evening—I doubt if you'd run into your friends up there and I'd be happy to pick up the tab."

"Actually, I'd rather order in pizza and wait to see what you find out, if you don't mind," replied Banks.

A quick vote among the crewmen made it unanimous and Tony gave his three crewmen a big smile. He took the wallet down to his cabin to begin tracking the identity of a sailor named Jerrod Bellamy.

About thirty minutes later Rob knocked on his door to let him know the pizzas had arrived.

"I'm still stuffed from dinner and couldn't eat another bite," said Tony, "The pizza is a small consolation for giving up their shore leave."

"That was pretty clever of them, huh?" he asked as he sat on the edge of Tony's bed to peer over his shoulder. "What have you turned up about our new friend?"

"Not much, so far," replied Tony without looking up from his laptop. "The name turns out to be fairly uncommon because I only found about one hundred fifty hits on Google but they are mostly Facebook and MySpace pages of younger men. This guy just turned thirty-eight, if his driver's license is real."

"Driver's license? Where's it from?"

"The District of Columbia, but like I said, I'm not sure it's real. What would somebody from D.C. be doing in the middle of the Caribbean with orders to scuttle a boat if it were approached by the authorities?"

"Well, it sounds like Cesar hit the nail on the head upstairs," replied Rob. "They're probably part of a sophisticated drug-running operation and losing the ship—and its cargo—might be a better option than getting caught red-handed. Without the cargo, there's no evidence and without the evidence there aren't any convictions."

"Yeah, I've read about that practice. It sure seems like a waste of boat and drugs, but I guess they can always grow or manufacture more of whatever they're smuggling. This guy, however, just doesn't fit the profile of your typical, low-level drug smuggler. Not if he's a U.S. citizen that lives in—whoa!"

"What?" asked Rob.

"Well, I just mapped the address on this driver's license and it's in the very upscale Chevy Chase area of D.C. And look here," said Tony, pointing at his laptop screen. "This house is on the same block and it's for sale for more than a million dollars!"

"Hmmm, you're right. This guy is sounding less and less like a two-bit punk and more and more like an operative of some kind, if he's really Jerrod Bellamy."

Tony leaned back and rubbed his chin.

"We need to find out if Mr. Bellamy is still in D.C. minus his wallet or if he's really hanging out on the Kingston waterfront. I suppose I could just walk down the pier to the payphone and call him, but if this really is his license, he'll probably have a call tracer installed on his telephone line and he'd know the call originated in Jamaica. We can't risk tipping our hand yet."

"Do you want me to ask Anne to check him out when I call her tonight?"

Tony turned in his chair and faced Rob.

"Listen, I know these have been some tough days for Anne and I appreciate what she's already done, but if she could get this guy's number from information and check him out, it would be a big help. Maybe you could also ask if she's had time to work on those questions I gave you a few days ago. I'm curious if she's been able to contact Susan Fitzgerald about setting up some way for Linda, Jim and me to communicate more freely. I hate to ask, but..."

"Tony, don't give it a second thought! I'm sure Anne will be happy to help."

***

For the second time in less than a week, Erik Mueller found himself in a detention cell at the St. Thomas Customs office. The hard-nosed female Customs agent was having him held as a flight risk pending her investigation into his involvement in human trafficking. Okay, so maybe the Customs agent had a reason to be suspicious, but it was too late to retract his story. He had even been forced to involve his boss, Buzz Edwards, in his lie in order to secure the release of the coffin-like box.

The female Customs agent entered the room containing the detention cell followed by a uniformed policeman.

"That's him," she said as they approached. "I can't keep him here overnight and I'm not letting him loose again until I find out what he's up to."

"I can only hold him for seventy-two hours without filing formal charges, Selma, so you'd better get busy. I'll take him from here. You know how to reach me."

Mueller soon found himself being led out of the Customs office in handcuffs. He tried to protest, but the burly policeman didn't even acknowledge his presence when Mueller spoke. Instead, he stuffed Mueller into the back seat of a marked patrol car, climbed into the driver's seat and sped away.

At the station, Mueller was processed and locked into one of eight cells in the jailhouse. From his position in the first of four cells on the left side of the large concrete room, his ears told him that he wasn't alone but he couldn't see any other prisoners.

"I want to talk to my lawyer!" yelled Mueller to no one in particular.

"If he's in here, you're in big trouble, brother!" someone called back in a thick Caribbean accent.

***

Tony documented all the information he had collected from the wallet and turned it over to Rob to pass along to Anne. While it remained to be seen whether or not the wallet had been "borrowed" from its true owner, the contents of the wallet seemed to be genuine and consistent. A dues receipt in the name of Jerrod Bellamy matched a real country club in the Chevy Chase area and a wrinkled ticket stub in the money compartment matched the name of a movie theatre in a mall not far from the address on the driver's license.

When Rob went forward to contact Anne on the short-wave radio, Tony changed out of his dinner clothes in favor of something more casual and headed up to the main salon with the wallet. The guys were eager for any news about the sailors they had encountered earlier, so Tony brought them up to date.

Holding up the wallet, he said, "I've scanned everything in here, so I think it's time to return Mr. Bellamy's wallet. When he sobers up he'll discover that it's missing and he'll no doubt remember the bar fight. If this turns up there, he'll be much less suspicious and less inclined to come looking for the three of you."

"Can I go with you?" asked Carley, who had already changed and was tidying up in the galley.

"Sure thing! You and Rob had your evenings cut short, too, but this may turn out to be worth it," he replied, indicating the wallet.

After getting directions to the tavern, Tony and Carley walked down the pier towards the waterfront under a clear, warm night sky.

"Well, this isn't exactly the dancing I had hoped for," sighed Carley, "but a walk under the stars is almost as good. And if you hadn't changed your mind about spending the night in Kingston you wouldn't be on the trail of this Bellamy guy. I think you owe me big time!"

"Yes, I guess I do," laughed Tony. "I'm sorry you're so uncomfortable aboard the Dolphin Diver, but in three or four days we'll be tied to a pier in Road Town and you can spend as much time on dry land as you want."

"I didn't realize being in close quarters for just a few days would affect me this way, either," replied Carley. "I don't know what it is—everybody aboard the Dolphin Diver is great and they all seem to appreciate my cooking, but the hours just drag by even when I'm outside on guard duty. There's something about knowing I can't leave the ship that really gets to me."

"Well, it will soon be over. This way," indicated Tony as they reached the end of the pier and stepped onto solid land.

"So, have you come up with a plan yet?" asked Carley, changing the subject.

"Not exactly, but I'm trying to come up with a way to contact Linda and Jim, my old NWIDI teammates. Maybe if the three of us put our heads together, something will jump out at us."

"Yeah, maybe," replied Carley under her breath. "That's the place over there."

The Dirty Duck had a medium-sized crowd of seamen and local girls but Tony spotted a booth against the far wall and led Carley to it. While they waited for service, Tony studied the interior of the establishment. Caesar had drawn Tony a diagram indicating which booth the other sailors had been sitting in and Tony had intended to slide into the booth, pretend to find the wallet, hand it over to the bartender and leave after a quick drink. Unfortunately, the booth was currently occupied by two couples who were studying menus and didn't look like they would be leaving soon.

After the waitress brought a draft beer for each of them, Tony nodded towards the booth.

"I guess we could hang around and wait them out," he said quietly, "but I'd really rather be back on the boat. Any ideas?"

"Well, you could go to the bathroom and pretend to find it in there. It would be pretty safe to assume that the wallet's owner went in there at least once, right?"

"Yes, but if he had his wallet out to pay after visiting the bathroom, he might get suspicious."

"Yes, I guess that's true, but…"

"Uh, oh," interrupted Tony. "Don't turn around, but I think Bellamy just came in and he doesn't look happy. He's talking to the people in his booth and they're looking around on the seats."

"If he doesn't find it there he's going to suspect our guys. Give it to me, quickly."

"What?" whispered Tony. "What are you going to do?"

"There isn't much time. Give it to me and follow me to the front door."

Reluctantly, Tony slid the wallet across the table covered by his large hand. Carley slid out of the booth and started across the large room.

Tony tugged on her arm and hissed "What are you doing?" but she headed straight for the front door without replying.

The door was in the corner of the tavern at the end of the long bar and the two stools at the end were vacant. As Tony reached for the door handle, he saw something slip to the floor and connect with the end of Carley's shoe.

"What the heck was that?" she exclaimed loudly. "Was that a rat?"

The word "rat" attracted the attention of several nearby customers, including one at the bar. Carley appeared to be scanning the dark floor behind the door and then shouted, "There it is! What is that?"

Taking his cue from Carley, Tony leaned into the corner and picked up the wallet she had just kicked.

"It's nothing, dear," he said holding the wallet high enough for everyone within earshot to hear. It's just some poor bloke's wallet."

Tony handed his "discovery" to the bartender who had come to see what all the commotion was about. Glancing to his left, he could see that Bellamy had also seen the wallet and was headed towards the bar in a rush. Tony opened the door and followed Carley out confident that the bartender and Bellamy would sort things out.

Once on the sidewalk, Tony looked quickly up and down the street and spotted an ice cream shop a couple doors down.

"This way," he said, leading Carley firmly by the arm. "We need to get off the street."

They hurried through the door and sat at a small metal table near the back of the shop. While the shopkeeper was taking their order, Tony saw Bellamy pass the window and continue on down the street.

"He's gone," announced Tony with a sigh of relief. "That was pretty clever, back there."

"I have my moments," smiled Carley, "but so do you. Taking refuge in an ice cream shop was a brilliant idea—I hope you brought lots of money!"

An hour later, Tony and Carley entered the ship's salon to find the whole crew, including Captain Braydon, huddled around one of the tables.

"What's up?" asked Tony as he approached.

"Take a look at this, you guys," replied Rob, waving them over. "Anne was able to track down Jerrod Bellamy."

On the table, Rob had spread out several sheets of paper Anne had just emailed him. Tony's eyes went immediately to the one on the far right.

"That's him!" he shouted. "That's the guy we saw in the bar!"

"What? He was there when you returned the wallet?" asked Rob.

"Yes. No. Well, sort of, but that's him. The picture on the driver's license shows a clean-shaven business-type, but that's definitely him in your photo—bushy beard, unruly hair and all."

"Tony's right," Carley said as she squeezed her way up to the table. "He came in after we arrived and he was looking all over for his missing wallet."

"So you didn't return it like you planned?" asked Rigo.

"Yes, thanks to Carley we got the job done," replied Tony. "I'll tell you about it later but let's focus on this stuff first. So the same Jerrod Bellamy that owns a house in upscale D.C. is right here in Kingston. How do you explain that?" he asked rhetorically. "What else do we have here?"

"Well, I think you'll find this interesting," said Rob, sliding a sheet across to Tony. "According to the Federal Citizen Information Center, Bellamy works for a mid- level government agency called the Defense Contract Administration Agency."

"Wait, what? The Federal Citizen what?" asked Tony.

"I know," smiled Rob. "Who would believe that there's actually an online directory of Federal employees, right? But the bigger question is why is a member of the Defense Contract Management Agency in the Caribbean on a drug-running boat?"

"A very good question," replied Tony, "and I can't help wondering how he can afford to live in a million dollar house on a staffer's salary. Anything else?"

"Anne was able to answer some of those questions you sent her but we can talk about that later," said Rob, glancing at his watch. "Right now I think we should get back onto a regular schedule and begin preparing to shove off at daylight. Who has the 10:00 p.m. shift?"

"I do," answered Rigo Mejía. "Give me a couple of minutes and I'll get up on top."

"Actually, I think it might be a better idea to stay down on the main deck tonight, suggested Tony. "If there's a threat, it will come from the water or the pier and the lookout chair won't give you the best view. Maybe circling the boat on the main deck is a better plan. And just carry a side-arm so you don't look so conspicuous to anyone on the pier. Everybody else please lend a hand stowing away the supplies that were brought aboard this evening. Once that's done, get some sleep because tomorrow we return to the sea."

Everyone set about their assigned tasks and Rob, noticing that Carley was working nearby in the galley, motioned Tony out onto the salon's rear deck.

"I didn't want to mention this in front of the others, but one of the items you asked Anne to check into turned up some interesting information. You asked her to call St. John and see if she could track down Jill Harris."

"Yes, I did," acknowledged Tony with increased interest. "And…"

Rob consulted some hand-written notes he pulled from his pocket.

"She talked to someone named Jeri Addison who told her that Jill had returned to the US mainland about three years ago."

Rob paused to let the information sink in and then continued.

"But that's not the interesting part, my friend. This woman also told Anne that if she caught up with Jill she should tell her that your friend Erik Mueller was on St. John yesterday to meet you for lunch but that you never showed."

Tony shot Rob a look of surprise.

"But I don't know anyone named Erik Mueller."

"There's more," smiled Rob. "On a hunch, Anne checked the Defense Contract Administration Agency roster and guess whose name she found there?"

"Erik Mueller's?"

"Exactly! Now that's just way too much of a coincidence, don't you think?"

Tony swung back towards the glass doors that lead into the salon.

"Was there any word from the boat captain on Andros Island?"

"Only that he's still running the boat. Anne wasn't able to reach him personally, but she talked to someone at The Bay Club and your Captain Jimmy is still on the staff. She left a message for him to call her as soon as possible. Apparently he took a charter client out to explore several of the blue holes on the island. Who is this Jimmy guy, anyway?"

"He was the skipper of a boat that Frank, Jill I went diving on during our last mission. The boat was owned by Miles Adderly, the…"

"The guy Frank disappeared with," finished Rob. "Do you think Jimmy might know something?"

"I'm not sure, but during that dive Frank had a problem with the rebreather he was trying out and I remember him saying something about seeing some spheres. He dismissed it as just a panic attack hallucination but on the way back to the marina I saw him talking privately with Jimmy and now I'd like to know what they were discussing."

"Spheres? That seems like an odd thing to hallucinate about. Do you think he might have really seen something?"

"How soon can we be ready to get under way?"

"Fairly soon, I think. We can stow the supplies at sea just as well as we can here. When do you want to leave?"

"Immediately!" replied Tony.

Chapter 13

The next four days passed quickly aboard the Dolphin Diver as plans for the "mission" in the British Virgin Islands finally began to take shape. Thanks in large part to the initial leads provided by Anne, the mysterious Defense Contract Administration Agency became Tony's obsession. The fact that the merchant marine Jerrod Bellamy and someone named Erik Mueller both had ties to the same agency were, as Rob had pointed out, just too much of a coincidence. Tony wasn't surprised that someone was looking into his acquaintances on St. John and the fact that the man worked for an agency loosely tied to the Department of Defense probably meant that Buzz Edwards was behind the investigation. That too, was no surprise, since Tony had been held prisoner on Edwards' orders for more than five years before he had escaped less than two months ago. What *did* surprise Tony was that his plan to sail to the Caribbean and distract Edwards and his gang now seemed like the best possible course of action!

While Tony focused on the agents and the agency, used his computer experience and the ship-board radio to help Susan Fitzgerald create a super-secure network that would allow Tony, Linda and Jim to communicate without fear of interception or tracing once the Dolphin Diver reached its destination in the British Virgin Islands.

"It's much like the string of transactions I put together to disguise the transfer of your money," Rob had explained. "Even if Edwards and his buddies should locate one of you, they can't use your messages to locate any of the others and with our 128-bit encryption it would take years for them to figure out what you were actually saying to each other."

The second day out of Jamaica Anne reported that she had finally heard from Captain Jimmy and he had been very surprised and pleased to know that Tony was still "alive and kicking" to use the Bahamian's words. He told Anne that some reporter from Seattle was on Andros asking about Miles Adderly and Frank Morton. When pressed about the spheres

Frank had mentioned, Captain Jimmy gave Anne a strange message to pass along to Tony.

"Tell him they are very real and they may be connected to a place called the Guardian Blue Hole. I'll know more in a few days."

Another fact that came to light during the voyage to Road Town, BVI, was that Jim Barnes had apparently gone underground. At least all attempts to contact him at the U.S. Navy's AUTEC facility had failed. Calls were referred to a mid-level naval staffer who would only say that "Doctor Barnes is no longer associated with this facility."

Tony suspected that Jim had been moved, either for his own safety or due to some advancement in his research on the alien triangles, and that meant he was going to be very hard to find unless he decided to reveal his location voluntarily. It was one thing to have a super-secure communications network. It was quite another to get all the former NWIDI team members connected to it.

Through Anne, Tony had put out some anonymous feelers regarding Erik Mueller but, so far, nothing had turned up. However, he was confident he could track the man down once he could call some of his old contacts on St. Thomas and St. John by telephone.

"All hands prepare to make port," said Captain Braydon's voice over the ship's intercom system.

"Well, we must be getting close," commented Carley, who was sitting at one of the tables in the salon reading a book.

Tony grunted confirmation from across the table without looking up from his laptop.

"I'm going downstairs to set my hair on fire," smiled Carley, knowing Tony wasn't listening.

"Okay," he mumbled. "I'll be right down."

It wasn't until Carley had reached the stairway that Tony's brain registered what she had said.

"That's not funny, you know!" he shouted after her.

"What's not funny?" asked Rob, entering the salon from the hallway that led to his forward stateroom.

"Oh, nothing, she was just trying to be funny," replied Tony. "What's our ETA?"

"We're thirty minutes from the pier and it will take another thirty to secure the ship and clear customs before we can go ashore," replied Rob. "I negotiated a nice spot on the east side of the harbor near the commercial section of town."

"What about security?"

'I've contracted a local security service to post a guard at the foot of the gang plank twenty-four hours a day and the Captain and the three crew members are working out a schedule to make sure at least one of them is aboard and awake at all times. Those not on duty are free to come and go as they please but I assume they will all sleep aboard the Dolphin Diver unless they get a better offer. Everyone will check in at least once a day but that means it could take us twenty-four hours to make ready to sail if you decide to move the vessel. I hope that's okay."

"Yeah, that's fine," nodded Tony. "What about you?"

"Well, I'm at your disposal, of course, but I might fly up to Miami to meet Anne in a couple of days because I don't have any firm plans yet. Otherwise, I'd like to spend what free time I have exploring the islands. There's some fascinating history around here and it would be a shame not to check it out."

"Sounds good," replied Tony. "Before you take off for parts unknown, would you make sure everybody on board has a local cell phone and that all their numbers get programmed into mine? If I need somebody, I'll call. Otherwise I'd like them to enjoy as much time ashore as possible without leaving the ship unprotected."

"Sure, I'll get that done this afternoon," agreed Rob. "I paid everyone, as you requested, so they all have money in their pockets. I assume we're not providing meals aboard ship, right?"

"No, Carely has been dying to get off this boat since we left Kingston, so I'd rather pay everybody an extra daily allowance and let them find their own meals ashore. That way we don't have to worry about provisioning the ship until we're ready to leave."

"Any idea when that might be?" asked Rob. "We should probably give them a ballpark date, at least."

Tony looked up from his laptop for the first time and shrugged.

"I really don't have any idea, Rob. It could be a week or a month, I just don't know. I'll stay in touch with you, of course, but as far as the crew goes, let's take it a week at a time. If I don't sound the alarm by noon on Sunday, they can assume they have at least another week to enjoy the area."

"That'll work. I'll let everybody know before we tie up." Nodding at the now closed laptop, he asked, "What are you working so hard on?"

"Oh, I've been drafting my first message to Linda and Jim, assuming we can get them hooked in. I want to bring them up to speed with what's been going on in my life, but I don't want to write a book, either. I've been going back and forth with how much—or how little—to say."

"Well, good luck with that," smiled Rob. "You have quite a story and I can see why you're having a problem. I'll see you outside in a few minutes. Don't forget your passport."

As is the custom, the captain of the vessel hand-carried all the passports and the ship's manifest to the Customs House a short way down the pier while the rest of the crew waited on deck. The harbor seemed to be busy and the Dolphin Diver had already attracted the attention of several locals. As far as Tony could tell, she was the largest vessel in sight and her arrival had not gone unnoticed.

When the captain returned, he returned each crew member's passport along with a small, white card.

"That card is your thirty day Visitor's Card. Carry it with you at all times and do not lose it! However, it's not necessary to carry your passport so I suggest you lock it in the ship's safe, especially if you're going to be ashore. However, if you plan to travel over to St. Thomas or St. John, you'll need your passport to enter the United States."

Nicholas Banks had drawn the short straw and had the first watch so he set up a deck chair at the top of the gang plank to prevent anyone from attempting to board until the security guard arrived. With Tony in the lead, the remaining six crewmembers headed down the pier and stepped onto British Virgins Island soil.

***

A young black man opened the cell door and said, "Mr. Mueller, please follow me."

By observing the small window located high up on his cell's wall, Mueller knew he had spent the better part of three days in jail. His cell was equipped with a decent cot for sleeping and included a metal toilet and wash basin so he'd been comfortable enough, but other than being delivered regular meal trays, there had been no human contact since his arrest.

"Where are you taking me," he demanded as he followed the other man through a maze of narrow hallways.

The guard said nothing but finally stopped at an unmarked door, opened it and motioned Mueller through. In the center of what was apparently an interrogation room sat a large table surrounded by several straight back chairs. On the table was a small white box with his name hand-written on the side.

"Please have a seat. Someone will be right with you," said the man before closing the door from the other side.

Mueller heard a loud click from the door and guessed he was now locked in the room so he sat and waited. Several minutes later, the police officer who had transported him to the jail entered through another door, followed by the female customs agent. Anger started to rise in him but when he saw the scowl on her face, he quickly brightened.

"Mr. Mueller, you are free to go. Your belongings are in the box on the table and I've arranged for transportation back to your hotel."

"What?" exclaimed Mueller. "No apology? No explanation?"

The officer's eye locked on Mueller in an angry stare.

"Mr. Mueller, we have a legal right to hold you for seventy-two hours with probable cause. You were ordered to remain on the island by an agent of the U.S. Customs Service and we had credible information—in the form of a personal statement made by you—that you intended to violate that order. That's all the explanation you're going to get and no apology is necessary. Good day, Mr. Mueller."

With that, both the officer and the Customs agent turned and left the room, leaving the door to the station's lobby open.

Mueller waited until the two were out of sight and then reached for the box. He retrieved his wallet, his watch, his belt, his cell phone and some small change. He also found a three-by-five pink piece of paper from a telephone message pad. The "From" line contained the hand-written words "Mr. Edwards" and Mueller recognized the telephone number written below the name as his boss' private line. In the place where the message would normally be written were the large letters "ASAP" followed by several exclamation marks.

Mueller smiled broadly as he stuffed the paper into his shirt pocket. He had a feeling that his problems with the U.S. Customs Service would soon be over!

When he opened his hotel room door he half expected to see the place tossed from a police search but he was surprised to find everything pretty much as he had left it. The maid had been in, of course, but his clothes in the dresser appeared to be undisturbed and his brief case was still locked and standing beside the small writing desk. He thumbed in the combination and slowly opened the lid. Inside, next to his thick file on the NWIDI team, lay the Smith & Wesson .38 Special he had purchased along the St. Thomas waterfront the night he had arrived on the island.

Mueller ordered a bottle of Cutty Sark whisky from room service and when it arrived he poured himself a double and chugged it down. He was going to need it for his next task—a call to his boss, Buzz Edwards.

***

From the waterfront, Rob and Carley headed downtown to make the cell phone arrangements Tony had requested, Acosta and Mejía set out to explore the waterfront hotspots and the captain headed for the local branch of the International Maritime Association, of which he was a member.

Alone, Tony walked a few yards down the waterfront to the nearest pay phone and dialed the number Anne had provided during her last radio contact with the Dolphin Diver. The phone rang several times and Tony was about to give up when a man's voice answered.

"Hello?"

"Jack?" asked Tony. "Is this Jack King?"

"Yes, this is Jack King, who is this?"

"Jack, I know it's been a while, but this is Tony Nicoletti."

"Tony! My God, it's been years! How have you been? Are you in town?"

"I'm fine, Jack, and no, I'm not in town. I take it you never sold that run-down bar of yours."

"Same place, different day," replied the man on the other end of the line. "I've had a couple offers, but nothing that really spoke to me, so I still have the place. The last airport expansion almost gobbled me up and I figure I have another five years before they are forced to buy me out to lay more concrete. So what are you up to these days?"

"Well, I'm actually calling to ask a favor, Jack. I need some information."

"Well, I'd be happy to help if I can. You always used to tell me I was full of it, but I never thought you meant information! What can I do for you?"

"Someone over on St. John has apparently been asking around for me and I don't recognize the name so I'd like you to make a few calls and see what you can find out. I want to make sure it's not someone trying to use me to get to Jill."

"Is she with you? She stopped in here the night she left for the States and I got the feeling she hadn't heard from you in a while. She wasn't doing too well that night."

"She's fine," lied Tony, who hadn't seen or heard from Jill in more than five years. "But I need to check this guy out. Can you put an ear to the ground and see what you can learn about him?"

"Of course! What's the name?"

"Erik Mueller," replied Tony. "I'm sorry, but that's all I have."

"Wait a minute! Did you say Mueller? Hold on a second!"

Tony heard the telephone clank against the wood of Jack's bar. After a few seconds, Jack was back.

"Tony, this guy was in my place just a few nights ago! He was looking for you and he left me his card in case I saw you. He's a New York City cop—a detective, actually. Have you gotten yourself into some sort of trouble?"

"A cop, huh? Are you sure?"

"Well, I didn't actually see a badge, but that's what it says on his card. Do you want his phone number?"

Tony recorded the number in a small black notebook he had brought from the ship and then thanked his old friend.

"Jack, do you still have any friends on the local police force?"

"Of course," laughed Jack. "How do you think I keep this place open? I'll make a call and get back to you in an hour or two."

"Uh, I can't do that, I'm afraid. I'm traveling in the U.S. and I'm calling you from a phone booth. I'll have to call you back."

"Okay, whatever works for you," replied Jack. "I'm not sure my contact is even on duty, but why don't you call me back in a couple of hours—say before 5:00 p.m. my time."

"I'll do that, Jack, and thanks. I really appreciate this. Talk to you soon."

Tony walked slowly back to the Dolphin Diver processing the information he had just received. Was it just a coincidence that there was an Erik Mueller working for the Defense Contract Management Agency? And if so, then what was an NYPD detective doing on St. Thomas asking about him. Had something happened to one of his former NWIDI teammates? Or maybe something had happened to Jill and she had given his name since she had no living relatives that Tony had ever heard her mention. It was all he could do to keep himself from running back to the phone booth and dialing the New York number but he knew he had to wait. A careless mistake now would wipe out all his efforts to remain hidden from Edwards and his bunch.

As Tony approached the foot of the gang plank, the newly arrived guard stepped sideways to block his path.

"May I see some identification, sir?" asked the young man politely.

Tony reached for his wallet, and handed the guard his fake Belize driver's license.

"I'd prefer to see your Visitor's Card, sir. I have no idea what a driver's license from, er, Belize looks like," he said, glancing at the license again, "but I know what a BVI Visitor's Card looks like and I know how hard it is to get a duplicate or make a fake."

"I'm impressed!" commented Tony, removing his card and handing it to the guard who studied it briefly and then checked it against a list from his pocket.

"Thank you, Mr. Wykes," nodded the guard as he stepped aside. "You may board."

But instead of making his way up the gang plank, Tony glanced behind and around the other man. The only object in site was a small pack against the pier's rail.

"Are you planning to stand here for your entire shift?"

"Yes sir!" replied the guard proudly. "My supervisor wasn't able to provide any information about the location, but tomorrow I'll bring a portable chair. I've already called in to the office so my replacement will know what to expect."

"Well, my friend, I don't want you falling over from exhaustion, so follow me up the gang plank. For today, at least, your post is being moved onto the ship. What's your name, by the way?"

"Travis, sir" replied the guard holding his position. "But if my supervisor drives by and doesn't see me at my post, I'll be in big trouble. I think I'd better stay right here."

"Follow me!" demanded Tony. "I'll call you boss and square things away."

Two hours later Rob and Carley returned in a taxi and lugged two large shopping bags aboard the Dolphin Diver. Tony met them in the salon.

"How did it go?" he asked.

Carley plopped down on one of the benches at the nearest table and sighed.

"What a hassle!" she huffed. "You'd think we were trying to buy guns for the resistance!"

"Well, in their defense," smiled Rob, "we have only been in the country a few hours and we were paying in cash. And then we asked them to program all the numbers into each of the phones, so it probably did look like we were 'arming' a gang. Here's yours, Tony."

Rob handed Tony a Blackberry cell phone and answered his raised eyebrows without waiting for the question.

"Yours and mine were a little more expensive but this was the only model they had that included GPS capabilities and I figured we might both find that useful in our travels. The others are pretty basic models but they all have text messaging so you could, theoretically, send a single message to the entire crew all at once."

Tony looked at the large keyboard and snorted. "Yeah, like that will happen! Can it make telephone calls?"

"I'll help you," sighed Carley. "I just went through an hour-long training session and I feel like I could write the user's manual from memory. But first, I'm going to take a nap. I've been up since 5:00 a.m. and I'm exhausted."

"Is she okay?" asked Tony after the door down to the crew quarters had closed behind her.

"She's been acting a little tense, but it's probably just the extended ship-board life," replied Rob. "I suggested she find a bed and breakfast and stay ashore for a few days but I don't know if she'll take my advice. What have you been up to this afternoon?"

"Well, I called a buddy over on St. Thomas and learned that the Erik Mueller that's been looking for me is apparently an NYPD detective so our hit on the government agency list may have just been a coincidence."

"A detective, huh? What do you suppose that's all about?"

"I have no idea but I should have a better idea in a couple of hours. As far as I know, I've never been in any trouble in New York and even if I had it's been more than seven years since I was there, so the statute of limitations would have run out by now."

"Well, I see the guard service is in place so if you don't need anything more from me I'm going back ashore to check out a maritime museum I spotted on the way back from the cell phone store. I'll be back sometime after dinner. See you later?"

"Yes, I'll probably be here," nodded Tony. "Maybe I'll take Carley out to dinner and see if I can find out what's eating her but I'll be spending the night aboard. I want to make sure the hired guards and our own guys have things under control before I go too far away."

"I'll see you later, then," said Rob, standing to leave. "The phones all have their new owner's names on them. Would you pass them out if any of the others return before I do?"

Tony wandered the ship for the next hour making sure everything was secure and that all non-essential areas were locked up. He ran into Nicholas Banks on the bridge and chatted with him for a while before returning to the salon where he ran into Carley, almost literally.

"Hey, are you feeling any better?" he asked.

"Yes, I guess so. Are you ready to learn how to use your new phone?"

"Actually, I have a call to make but I'd like to make sure Caller ID is turned off, if that's possible."

Tony handed his new phone to Carley. She punched a few buttons and handed it back to him.

"There you go," she smiled. "I'll leave you to your call."

"No, wait, you don't need to leave," Tony replied. "This will just take a minute and then I thought maybe we could go ashore and get something to eat. What do you think?"

Carley smiled for the first time in hours.

"That would be nice."

Tony dialed the number of Jack King's bar and waited for his old friend to answer.

"Tony! I see you finally picked up a cell phone with Caller ID blocking! The last time you called you said you were at a pay phone—I thought you were more high-tech than that. "

"No, I'm actually a pretty low-tech guy," stammered Tony trying to cover his tracks. "As I told you, I'm traveling in the U.S. I did just get a new cell phone, but I didn't know my number was being blocked. I'll look into that. Did you find out anything about Erik Mueller?"

"I'll say! It seems that your Mr. Mueller has been in a fair amount of trouble during his short stay in the Islands. Customs has been all over his tail and he spent the last three days in jail because Customs felt he was a flight risk. He was just turned loose a couple of hours ago after some intervention directly from Washington, D.C. Apparently an agent over at Customs got quite a tongue-lashing for hassling him."

"Really! Any idea why Customs was interested in him in the first place?"

"Yes, and that's another weird thing. Apparently he went to Customs to claim a box that had arrived by private jet and when the agents opened it for inspection it had the appearance of a crude, homemade coffin. Customs suspected that Mueller was involved in some type of human trafficking so they ordered him to stay put while they conducted an investigation. Mueller apparently let it slip that he was planning to head back to New York so Customs ordered him held. Then some guy named Edwards from D.C. got involved and both the police and Customs backed off because..."

"Did you say Edwards?" Tony interrupted.

"Yup! That's what my contact said. Does that mean anything to you?"

"Maybe. Is there anything else?"

"Well, I guess Customs tried to check out Mueller's NYPD connection and came up cold but Edwards told them Mueller was deep undercover and that's why there was no record of him."

"And yet he gave you his business card," replied Tony. "That sounds like an odd move for someone who's deep undercover, don't you think?"

"It sure does, but the locals don't know about that card and I didn't see any reason to tell them. Only you and I know about that."

"Thanks, Jack! You watch your back, my friend. If our mystery man learns that you've been making inquiries, he may be back to find out why."

Chapter 14

Mueller put the glass down and considered pouring himself another double whiskey but he had second thoughts as he reached for the bottle. Instead, he lifted the receiver of his hotel room telephone and dialed a number in Washington D.C. The phone rang once and then beeped. Mueller keyed in his access code and waited while his call was routed to Edwards' cell phone.

"It's about time!" began Edwards without any greeting. "I sprung you out of that jail two hours ago!"

"Yes, sir," replied Mueller, "but there was the usual paperwork to wade through at the police department. I'm sorry you had to get involved again. They could only have held me a few more hours without pressing charges and I don't think they had anything substantial."

"Maybe, but I couldn't take that chance. They made some inquiries with NYPD and I needed to put a stop to that before somebody who didn't know any better blew your cover. As it stands now, your cop story has been substantiated and I don't think the local authorities will be asking any more questions. They think you're deep under cover so you have to stop telling people you're a cop."

"Ten-four," acknowledged Mueller. "Were you able to come up with any additional information on that box that was flown down here via Andros Island?"

"No, but that box really has the St. Thomas Customs office all bent out of shape! I convinced them that part of your undercover mission is to locate the intended recipient of the box, which is true. They shouldn't give you any more grief about the box, but they're also not going to hand it over to you. These Customs people are conducting their own investigation into the box's origin and its intended destination, so maybe they'll do some of your leg work for you. Just don't let them beat you to the answers!

"There's something else you should know. One of our Asian divisions apparently received some bad intel and dispatched a team to Seattle to eliminate Nicoletti before this box thing happened. They were unsuccessful but our man in Seattle has now confirmed that Nicoletti hasn't been there since he escaped from MX-2."

"Well, that's good to know because Nicoletti only had a few hangouts. St. John would have been my first guess, because of the woman, but Seattle would have been my second guess. I'm pretty sure he's not here yet and if he's not in Seattle, then where is he?"

"My first guess would have been Andros," replied Edwards. "And I still think he'll show up there, sooner or later. He and Frank Morton were old friends and Nicoletti will have to go investigate Morton's disappearance sooner or later. However, I have a person over at the State Department keeping close tabs on everyone who enters the Bahamas and so far no one matching Nicoletti's description has turned up. I still have his U.S. passport locked up at MX-2 and even if he has fake documents, he'll have a tough time getting back on U.S. soil without me knowing about it."

"Maybe," conceded Mueller, "but I'm still betting on the Virgin Islands. The arrival of that box is just too much of a coincidence and, after seeing the interior, I'd bet money it was used to ship a body—living or otherwise—from Andros to St. Thomas. If Morton really died on Andros, then maybe Nicoletti used the box to travel here without a passport or any other documentation."

"But how did he get to Andros in the first place and why wasn't he spotted by my people? On the other hand, if Morton is still alive, as I have always believed him to be, he may have used the box to finally make his escape from Andros Island. Either way, we know the final destination was St. Thomas, so keep your ears and eyes open—one of them is there, I'm sure of it!"

"What about the other team members?" asked Mueller. "Any chance they might lead us to Nicoletti—or even Morton?"

"Bad news there, I'm afraid," sighed Edwards. "We still haven't turned up any trace of the McBride woman or her husband and the professor we had under watch at the AUTEC facility has gone missing."

"Jim Barnes?" asked Mueller. "How could he go missing from one of the Navy's most secure facilities?"

"We suspect it was an inside job but if the Navy moved him, it was done at a very high level—even above our reach."

"Do you think they suspect anything?"

"It's being considered, but that's not your problem right now. You need to stay focused on Nicoletti and/or Morton. If you don't come up with something soon, I'm going to pull you back here and consider other options. In the mean time, I have a plan of my own that may get one of them to surface long enough for us to make a positive ID."

"If either one of them is here, I'll find him," assured Mueller.

"That would be a very good idea!" replied Edwards curtly before the line went dead.

***

Once they were seated and the waiter had served their wine, Tony told Carley about his earlier conversation with Jack King.

"So you don't know this Erik Mueller guy, huh?" asked Carley when Tony had finished his story.

"No, I don't know anyone by that name. I suppose it's possible he was at MX-2 using a different name, but I doubt it. Whatever organization Edwards really works for is much bigger than anything I ever imagined. I'm sure this agency we stumbled across is just the tip of the ice berg."

"Yeah, what about that agency?" asked Carley. "How does an entire agency stay in the shadows and provide cover for folks like Edwards, Mueller and what's his name—that sailor dude?"

"Bellamy," replied Tony. "And it's easy. There are many black ops outfits that don't even have names. At least this bunch operates out in the open with an office, a director and a budget. That's why I don't think we've found the top of the heap yet. Somewhere there's an unknown, undocumented group that's pulling the strings but we're going to have to work our way up the ladder one rung at a time. And my guess is that we'll find Edwards right near the top. He seemed to be in complete control at MX-2 and that kind of power isn't handed out to just anyone."

"So what are you going to do about Mueller?" asked Carley. "Are you going over to St. Thomas to confront him?"

"No, I can't risk blowing my cover and he has me at a big disadvantage. I have no idea what he looks like but he most certainly knows what I look like. No, I think I'm going to send Rob on a little reconnaissance mission. He's the only one of us traveling on a U.S. passport and that will attract the least amount of attention. He wants to do some exploring, anyway, and this will be the perfect opportunity. While he's on the U.S. side, I'm going to ask him to check out the house on St. John where Jill and I last lived, but I already know she's not there."

At the mention of Jill's name, Carley took a real interest in the conversation for the first time.

"How can you be sure?" she asked, silently relieved that she wouldn't be running into Tony's ex-girlfriend any time soon.

"I had Anne look into Jill's whereabouts several days ago," frowned Tony. "Apparently Jill moved back to the mainland about three years ago and she disappeared almost immediately. There's been no trace of her since the day she landed in Las Vegas. I'm afraid Edwards may have nabbed her and there are a million places where they could hold her in that maze of pseudo-military installations they have north of Vegas."

Carley's momentary euphoria quickly changed to concern for Tony. It was no wonder he'd been so depressed lately!

"Yeah, that would suck," she sympathized. "But you've always described her as a pretty independent woman. Maybe she just went underground for her own safety. After all, she left St. John on her own when she could have stayed here in the islands. Why would she do that if she didn't have a plan?"

Tony pondered that idea for a few seconds and then seemed to brighten a bit.

"You know, you're probably right! We developed some well placed contacts while we were working on the mystery of the Mayan spheres and she probably just called in a favor."

Tony leaned back in his chair, clasped his hands behind his head and smiled briefly.

"Hey!" he said, leaning across the table so fast it startled Carley. "How about we go dancing after we eat? I still owe you a night on the town from Jamaica."

At one point during the evening it occurred to Carley that she was having a good time because Tony, at least for the moment, was at peace over the fate of another woman. She quickly put that thought out of her mind, however, and vowed to enjoy the more relaxed Tony for as long as she could.

Several hours later, Tony and Carley stepped onto the deck of the Dolphin Diver arm-in-arm and laughing loudly. As Tony reached for the handle on the salon door, it opened briskly and he almost fell forward into the room. Howling with laughter, he stepped back to see a stern-faced Rob standing in the doorway.

"Gee, Dad, you didn't have to wait up for us," he managed to get out as he and Carley continued to laugh at almost everything.

"Tony, we have a problem," frowned Rob, "and I need you sober as quickly as possible. Let's get some coffee into you."

An hour later, Tony had finished an entire pot of coffee and Rob had covered about a hundred miles pacing back and forth in front of the table. Carley had long since made her way below to sleep off the alcohol.

"Now let me get this straight," said Tony, finally starting to sound coherent. "You're telling me that the NWIDI Learjet has gone missing?"

"Yes!" replied a frustrated Rob. "And one of your former pilots is also missing. Susan Fitzgerald was almost hysterical when she called Anne and she's terrified. Her husband went to the airport to do some routine maintenance this morning and when he didn't check in for supper, she started trying to track him down. According to the airport, the Learjet took off about 10:00 a.m. without filing a flight plan. Ten minutes later the local tower handed the aircraft off to Regional Air Control and that's the last anyone heard from your pilot."

Tony rubbed his forehead and tried to focus. He knew the Fitzgeralds pretty well and this was not typical behavior. They were normally inseparable and Fitz would never take off in the plane without checking in with Susan first. After all, she was the more skilled pilot of the two.

"Well, we have to start by assuming the worst," frowned Tony. "It's possible Fitz took the Learjet for a quick check-out flight and something went wrong. Have you contacted the Coast Guard?"

"No, I've been busy trying to sober you up, remember? But Susan has alerted the airport that the plane is missing and they will have done whatever protocol dictates. We'll hear from Anne as soon as they know anything. She's staying in contact with Susan."

"Another possibility," mumbled Tony, "is that the plane was stolen."

"Stolen?"

"Sure. Someone around the airport sees a guy working all alone on an expensive plane, he approaches and forces the pilot to fly the plane to some unknown location. Stranger things have happened."

"Not in my world," replied Rob, "but it's becoming more and more evident that we don't travel in the same circles. So, what do we do?"

"Nothing, for the moment. Let's give the authorities some time in case there's a logical explanation for all this. However, I'm concerned about Susan. If somebody did grab Fitz and the plane, then they might be looking for Susan, too."

"She called Anne from a phone booth somewhere, so I'm guessing she's already figured that out," nodded Rob. "But I doubt if she'll stray far from home until she hears from her husband."

"Can you still contact Anne by short-wave radio?" asked Tony as he chugged another cup of coffee."

Rob nodded.

"Okay, good. Call her and ask her to tell Susan to get to the airport as soon as possible. If she can reach Susan directly, she should do it from a pay phone, not her land-line or her cell. If Anne doesn't know how to reach Susan, then we'll just have to wait until Susan checks in again."

"The airport?" questioned Rob.

"Yes. It's one of the few places Susan will be willing to go to wait for word about Fitz. It's not a big airport, but the tower is manned twenty-four, seven and there's round-the-clock security, too. Tell her to find a place to hang out where she's in constant sight of other people—the tower itself would be perfect, if they'll let her in. It has very limited access and it would be easy for someone to keep an eye on her."

Rob disappeared forward towards his cabin to make the radio transmission, leaving Tony all alone in the salon. Although Tony had offered two possibilities for Fitz' disappearance, he had already decided which of the two was the most likely.

Tony poured himself another cup of coffee and turned to gaze out at the Road Town waterfront through the salon windows.

"Damn you, Edwards!" he shouted to the stillness.

***

Mueller stayed on the line until he heard a dial tone to make sure the transfer to Edwards had disconnected properly. When the phone was back in the cradle, he poured that whiskey and contemplated his next move. Of all the people on St. Thomas that Mueller had asked about Tony Nicoletti, only one person had acknowledged knowing him so that would be his first stop. But Mueller still believed that Nicoletti would show up at the house he had shared with the Harris woman and he planned to be there when that happened.

He paid the cabbie and entered the "Landing Strip" tavern. The run-down place was surprisingly busy for a Tuesday night but he elbowed his way to the bar and flagged down the bar tender.

"What can I get for you?" asked Jack King.

"I was in a few nights ago looking for a guy named Tony Nicoletti. I just wondered if you have heard from him since I was here."

"Er, no, of course not!" stammered the man behind the bar. "I told you the other night that I haven't seen or heard from him in more than five years."

Even without his special ops interrogation training, Mueller would have known the man was lying.

"Where is he?" demanded Mueller. "And I'm only going to ask you one more time."

"Hey, I'm telling you I haven't seen him, man! He called me earlier today from the States and asked about a woman he used to date here in the islands, but I haven't seen either one of them in a long time. Now get out of my place!"

"Is this guy bothering you, Mr. King?" asked a deep voice from behind Mueller. He turned to find himself staring into the chest of one of the biggest black men he'd ever seen.

"I was just leaving," he smiled, "and thank you for the information, Mr. King."

As Mueller side-stepped to maneuver around the big man, he looked back over his shoulder at the bar tender.

"Give Nicoletti my regards," he smiled.

When the taxi stopped in front of his hotel, he asked the driver to wait, with the meter running. Inside, he hurriedly packed a few of his belongings into a back pack and raced back out to the taxi. If he hurried he could just make the last ferry to St. John.

* * *

"Okay, I passed your message on to Anne," puffed Rob as he ran back into the salon. "Unfortunately she has no way to reach Susan, but she expects her to check in at 10:00 p.m."

Tony checked his watch and frowned. "Almost another hour! I hope we're not too late. Well, while we wait, let me tell you about a little mission I'd like you to do for me. You mentioned that you wanted to get over to the U.S. islands, right?"

Cautiously, Rob nodded.

"Okay, good! Apparently this guy named Mueller is over on St. Thomas looking for me and we're going to make him think he's hot on my trail. He tried to claim the box I had flown down on the Learjet and that got him into a little hot water with the local Customs office, but somebody sprung him and now he's back out on the street. I'm sure he's connected with Edwards and I want to keep him busy chasing ghosts until I can figure out how to deal with him permanently.

"While you're on St. Thomas you can do your exploring and I might even have you make a day trip over to St. John. How's that sound?"

"Well," smiled Rob, "I've known you just long enough to know that regardless of how good something sounds, there will be enough bumps in the road to make it, er, interesting. I'll be on the first boat in the morning but what about Susan?"

"I'll stay here and manage that problem," replied Tony. "But I'd like you to show me how to use that short-wave radio of yours and I'd like your permission to chat with Anne!"

"Permission granted," laughed Rob. "Anything special I should know about this Mueller guy?"

"I don't know anything myself," replied Tony. "I'll give you one contact on St. Thomas and another on St. John but please remember to use you phone in satellite mode anytime you make a call. We don't want Edwards or any of his henchmen tracking you down, now, do we?"

Tony and Rob continued to discuss Tony's plan until 9:45 p.m. and then made their way to Rob's stateroom to wait for Anne's scheduled call. At 10:10 p.m. the radio crackled and something remotely resembling Anne's voice blasted out of the unit's speaker. Rob adjusted several knobs on the set and reached for a microphone on the table.

"K9FJC, this is V3MJL. Go ahead, please"

"Rob, I just spoke to Ladybird and she's agreed to go to the location you suggested. However, as you can imagine, she's frantic. And there's been no word from the authorities yet. Over."

"Well no word is probably good news, in this case. Over."

"Ten-four. Please monitor this frequency until further notice and we'll let you know if we hear anything. Over."

"I'm going on a short mission for the boss, but he'll stay in touch with you using our established schedule. The last segment of the sequence is eight-zero-eight-one. Over."

"Eight-zero-eight-one. Roger that. And Roger the boss on this frequency, but what's this about a mission? Over."

"Nothing exciting. I'll tell you about it when we speak. V3MJL is clear for now. Over"

There was a pause before Anne responded with "K9FJC out."

Rob set the microphone down and shrugged.

"Well, that's about it for tonight, unless the Coast Guard comes up with something. At least Susan will be safe and now Anne has my sat-phone number in case an emergency comes up."

"Is that what those numbers were?" asked Tony, staring at the radio. "And I assume 'Ladybird' refers to Susan?"

"Hey, she's a female pilot, right?" laughed Rob. "It was the best I could do on short notice. As you probably noticed, we try to communicate as much in innuendo as possible and if you have to pass sensitive information, break it up and do it in pieces. Short wave radio communication has its strengths and weaknesses. On the good side, it's almost impossible to trace from a distance. On the other hand, it's wide open, unencrypted and simple to monitor."

"I did a lot of radio work in the military, so I'm familiar with the principles and with the digital frequency display—tuning should be pretty simple. But what's this other readout?"

"Ah, that's the transmit-receive offset. You'll need to remember to change both your main frequency and the offset every day just before your 4:00 p.m. transmission. Anne and I have worked out a scheme where we transmit on one frequency and receive on another to make it more difficult for anyone to monitor a conversation. There's a chart here in the desk drawer that shows the correct settings for each day of the week. If you can't make contact with Anne at the appointed time, that's the first thing to check."

"And how often do you check in?"

"Every six hours, at 10:00 a.m., 4:00 p.m., 10:00 p.m. and 4:00 a.m. but the 4:00 a.m. event only takes place if mutually agreed upon the evening before. There's no sense messing up a good night's sleep if there's nothing happening."

"Well, that all sounds simple enough," nodded Tony, "and tonight we'll monitor the current frequency in case Anne hears from Susan."

"That's right. If the Coast Guard locates the Learjet, they will contact Susan immediately, and she'll pass the info on to Anne. What do you think about the disappearance of a plane and its pilot?"

"Well," sighed Tony, "I don't think Fitz would have taken the plane for a test flight without checking in with Susan first. I know the Coast Guard is operating on the premise that the plane went down somewhere, but I don't believe that for a second. I think someone grabbed Fitz and the plane."

"But why?" questioned Rob. "Do you really think someone stole the plane?"

"That's a possibility, Rob, but I think the real target was Fitz, not the plane. The Learjet was just a convenient way to get him away from the airport."

"If the plane went down due to a malfunction, there's a good chance it went into water and the Coast Guard may never find it. However, if your theory is correct the plane has to be on land somewhere and it should turn up, sooner or later."

"Yes," frowned Tony, "but I think the longer Fitz is missing, the less likely we are to find him alive."

Chapter 15

After spending a restless first night in port, Tony was awake early Wednesday morning preparing information for Rob's "away trip" to St. Thomas. Tony was frustrated by the fact that he couldn't make the exploratory trip himself but it was just too risky so he would have to be content with doing his reconnaissance work second hand.

He found Carley in the galley preparing a light breakfast for those who had stayed onboard.

"Hey, I thought we were going to shut the kitchen down for a while," he commented.

"I am, but as long as I'm here I might as well make myself useful," Carley replied. "I might go ashore later, though, so don't count on lunch."

"Is everything okay?"

"Yes, I guess so. Maybe I'm just getting bored with boat life. This trip sounded a lot more exciting than it's turned out to be."

"Well, listen, Rob is going over to St. Thomas this morning to do some snooping around for me—why don't you go with him? There's a lot more activity on St. Thomas than there is here and maybe you can even help him with his cover. You know, a couple walking around together looks a lot less suspicious than a guy by himself, especially in a tourist spot like St. Thomas."

"I don't know," Carley frowned. "I don't feel much like a tourist."

"Would it help if I told you that the downtown area of Charlotte Amalie near the cruise ship terminal has some of the best shopping in all of the Caribbean?"

Carley brightened a bit and almost smiled.

"Well, it certainly wouldn't hurt your case," she finally replied. "Alright, if Rob doesn't mind me tagging along I guess it would be a good change of pace. How long is he going to be over there?"

"I'm not positive. I assume he'll come back tonight but I don't know what the transportation over and back is like. He's been talking about going to Miami to meet Anne sometime soon, so I don't think he wants to stay very long."

"Okay, as soon as I'm finished here I'll go throw together a backpack just in case we don't get back tonight. Don't let him leave without me!"

Tony poured himself a cup of coffee and left Carley to her work. As he stepped through the door onto the bridge he was greeted by Captain Braydon who was also sipping coffee in the elevated seat behind the wheel.

"Don't you ever get tired of this place, Captain?"

"Never!" replied the old salt. "Besides, I have the watch at the moment. What are you doing up so early?"

Tony leaned against the front of the bridge and sighed.

"I guess I'm trying to figure out what to do next. Rob is going over to St. Thomas to do some scouting for me but I'd really like to be going myself. I'm familiar with the geography and he's not. I also have a few friends over there that I might be able to talk into helping me."

"So why is Rob going instead of you?" asked the Captain.

"Well, it's complicated, but I think there's someone over there looking for me and I *really* don't want to be spotted. Plus there's this issue with my passport..."

"It's a fake, huh?" smiled Captain Braydon. "It was good enough to fool the authorities here, and they see a lot more British Commonwealth passports than the blokes over on St. Thomas. But if you're that concerned, let me ask around today when I go ashore. Maybe I can get you a ride over as a deckhand so you don't have to face anybody eyeball-to-eyeball. You would just be another name on a crew manifest."

"Hey, that would be great!" exclaimed Tony. "I'm still going to send Rob over today because now I've promised Carley a shopping trip if she accompanies him. However, based on what he turns up, I would love to get over there myself. Thanks, Captain! Let me know if you can work something out."

Tony headed back out to the salon and ran into Rob—literally—as he exited the bridge.

"Morning," mumbled Rob. "Is there anything to eat back there?"

"You're in luck, my friend, because Carley decided to fix breakfast this morning. But before you go, I need to talk to you about your trip to St. Thomas today. She seems pretty depressed, so I suggested that she accompany you. A couple together will look less conspicuous and she could use a shopping trip. I hope you don't mind."

"Ah, no, I guess that's okay. I hadn't really planned on spending much time in the market, but we should have time if we catch the last ferry back at 4:15 p.m. I guess we should get going as soon as possible. Do you have that info you were going to put together?"

"In my room," nodded Tony. "You get some breakfast and I'll meet you in the salon."

While Rob washed down the last of his scrambled eggs with some Gallon Jug coffee from Belize, Tony explained how to find the Landing Strip Tavern. He had drawn a rough map and jotted down Jack King's telephone number, along with several others he hoped Rob would have time to call. He also gave Rob a photograph Ann had dug up on the Internet of a man named Erik Mueller. There was no way to be sure it was the right Mueller, but it was all they had.

"Now remember, don't approach this Mueller guy directly. He's probably an ex-military type and he won't think twice about forcing you to talk if he thinks you are connected to me. Besides, the Captain is going to see if he can get me onto the island tomorrow or the next day. All I really need to know is whether or not Mueller is still there."

Just then Carley appeared through the door to the crew's quarters. She was carrying a worn backpack and smiling.

"Let me get my things and we'll be out of here," said Rob. "We're going to have to run if we want to make the 7:00 a.m. ferry."

When Rob dashed down the stairs, Tony reached into the pocket of his shorts and pulled out several bills.

"Here, take this and do me a favor, will you? There's this girl I'd like to buy a gift for and I'm not very good at that sort of thing."

Carley accepted the bills and fanned them out.

"There's five hundred dollars here," she frowned. "What do you want me to get her?"

"Well, I suspect that she's getting really tired of being a ship's cook, so get her something extravagant that will make her smile more!"

It took a second for the comment to sink in but when it did, Carley grinned from ear to ear.

"I just got paid, you know. I have spending money."

"Yes, but my guess is that you already have enough places to spend your wages. This is a little bonus—mad money to enjoy on St. Thomas—and no fair saving it for a rainy day!"

Once Rob and Carley were ashore, Tony refilled his cup and made his way down to his own cabin. He booted up the laptop Rob had helped him acquire in Belize City and, after a short struggle, managed to get it connected to the wireless Internet service provided by the port.

He spent the next hour using Google Earth to explore the islands off the coast of Miami for an airstrip that might be large enough to handle the NWIDI Learjet. He was positive Fitz wouldn't have taken the plane out alone without saying anything to Susan unless he had been forced to. The Coast Guard was searching the water for signs of a crash but Tony believed the plane might have been landed safely at some obscure airstrip. It bothered him, though, that the Learjet had not been logged in at any of the airports that report to the Federal Aviation Administration.

A knock on his door startled him just as he was coming to a conclusion he didn't want to accept.

"It's open," he called.

Captain Braydon opened the door and stuck his head in.

"Sorry to interrupt you but I just wanted to let you know that I'm going ashore for a while. Young Nickolas has the watch and, of course, the hired security guard is still dutifully guarding the foot of the gang plank. I'll see what I can find out about getting you to the U.S. side, but I may not have a definite answer for you until this evening."

"This evening is fine, Captain. I'll probably go ashore later, too, but I plan to return to the Dolphin Diver this evening because I'm very anxious to find out what Rob has to say when he returns.

"Hey, can I ask you a quick question before you go? Have you ever sailed a vessel into a Cuban port? More specifically, how hard would it be to get the Dolphin Diver in and out if that became necessary?"

The Captain scratched his head and thought for a moment before answering.

"Well, we'd probably have to leave Rob behind, since he's traveling on a U.S. passport, but otherwise it should be possible. I've never been in a Cuban port myself, but I know other captains who have and they don't count it as one of their most rewarding experiences. Why do you ask?"

"I have a friend who has gone missing and I'm afraid that he and his airplane—a very expensive private jet—have been kidnapped. The plane appears to have just disappeared off the planet and my guess is that he was forced to fly it to an airport in Cuba where his arrival would not have been reported to the authorities."

"You have some very interesting friends," smiled the Captain. "But if you decide to pay Fidel a visit, please give me as much advance notice as possible so I can acquire the necessary navigational charts. Good day, Mr. Wykes, and good luck."

***

By the time they stepped off the inter-island ferry and onto the dock at the Charlotte Amalie tourist marina it was 8:15 a.m. The ferry had been full to capacity, so it took another fifteen minutes to clear U.S. Immigration. As Carley scanned the area, she smiled.

"Wow! Look at the size of that cruise ship!"

"Yes, and I heard somebody on the ferry say there were four due in today. This is going to be a busy place once they offload five or six thousand tourists. Maybe we should hit some of the shops while there's still room to squeeze in. It's probably too early to pay a visit to this tavern Tony wants me to check out, anyway, so where would you like to start?"

For the next two hours Rob followed Carley from one shop to another until they all began to look alike. Carley had tried on clothes, she had tried on shoes and she had modeled jewelry but as far as Rob could tell she hadn't purchased a thing and he was wondering if she had brought any money. He was about to ask her about it when she spotted something in a window and dashed into the store, leaving Rob on the sidewalk alone. Taking advantage of the opportunity, he found a nearby bench and plopped down to rest his feet. Since their arrival, two more ships had docked and the passengers were beginning to come ashore by the dozens so Rob decided it was time to call a halt to the window shopping and take care of some of Tony's errands. He was mulling over how to break the news to Carley and almost didn't recognize her when she rejoined him.

"My God, lady, you look... stunning, is all I can think of!"

"You like?" she beamed as she handed him a shopping bag and twirled to give him the full effect. She had exchanged her blue jeans and plain blue blouse for a long, frilly sun dress, a floppy, brightly colored hat and elegant sandals with laces that wrapped part way up her calves. She was even clutching a small gold purse that matched the trim in her dress.

"Yes," nodded Rob. "I don't think I've ever seen you in a dress, Carley. Very nice!"

"Well, Tony told me to get something that would make me smile and when I saw this outfit on a mannequin it made me smile."

"I think it will make a lot of people smile, young lady!" He handed the shopping bag back to her and added, "Your old clothes?"

"Yes, and now I have to lug them around all day, but I couldn't help myself. I could probably have found these items for half the price away from the cruise terminal, but what the heck! You only live once, right?"

"That's what I've heard," smiled Rob. "So are you ready to see if we can track down this old friend of Tony's?"

"Yes, boss," laughed Carley as she hooked her arm through his.

On the street paralleling the cruise dock they found a vacant taxi and gave the driver the address of the Landing Strip Tavern. The four mile drive from the downtown marina and cruise ship docks to the tavern took them along the entire Charlotte Amalie waterfront district and both Rob and Carley gawked around like tourists, which is exactly how they wanted to appear.

When the cab slowed to a stop in the parking lot, Rob noticed that there were already cars parked nearby. The driver turned and asked if they wanted him to wait.

Rob looked at the meter and reached for his wallet.

"Ah, no thanks," replied Rob. "We're meeting a friend here and I don't know how long we'll be."

"Well, my name is Sammy and here's my card. Anytime you need a ride, anywhere on the island, you just call me and I'll pick you up. Enjoy your stay on St. Thomas, my friends."

The cabby accepted the U.S. twenty dollar bill from Rob and started to make change but Rob waved him off.

"Keep the change, Sammy. Depending on how our meeting goes, we may be talking again real soon."

Rob opened the door and followed Carley through into a dingy, dimly lit bar. To the right were two pool tables and beyond them a row of booths stretched down the far wall. Straight ahead at the bar the few early drinkers all had their eyes trained on Carley.

"Well, you're a hit so far," he whispered. "Let's check with the bartender"

"Can I help you folks?" asked the older man behind the bar. "I'm guessing you're lost, right?"

Rob smiled. "No, I don't think we're lost. This is the Landing Strip Tavern, isn't it?"

"Yes, for another year or so," replied the bartender laughing at his own private joke. "So how can I help you?"

"Are you Jack King?"

"It depends on who's asking."

Rob stepped closer to the bar and lowered his voice.

"We're friends of a man named Tony Nicoletti and he asked us to stop in and chat with you. Do you have a minute?"

The man was silent for a second as he processed Rob's comment.

"Yes, of course, come on back to my office where we can talk. Hey, Wanda, watch the bar, will you?"

In King's cramped, messy office Rob motioned for Carley to take the only guest chair and waited while King made his way around his desk and into his own chair.

"So you're friends of Tony, huh? How can I be sure of that?"

"Tony asked me to remind you that you still owe him twenty dollars from a bet you two had on the 2002 Superbowl game. He had the underdog Patriots and you had the Rams but he was called back to Seattle before the game and he's never collected."

King laughed and slammed his hand down on the desk.

"That's right! I'd forgotten all about the bet, but you could only have heard that story from Tony himself. How is he, anyway? I received a strange telephone call from him yesterday and I was sure he was back on St. Thomas but he insisted he was in the States somewhere."

Rob shook his head. "I don't think Tony has been on St. Thomas for a long time but we're actually here to follow up on that call you received yesterday. Do you happen to know if this Mueller guy is still on the island?"

"Not for sure, but he was definitely here yesterday because I had him thrown out of the bar. I don't like the looks of that guy and I told Tony so on the phone."

"Yes, he mentioned the conversation. He seemed to think you had a way to find out whether or not Mueller was still on the island. Is that true?"

"Well, I can make a couple of phone calls, I guess. Why don't you folks go back out to the bar and have Wanda mix you up something. I'll be along in a few minutes."

Rob was less than comfortable but Carley seemed to be secretly enjoying the stares and glances she was getting from the few seedy customers in the place. They had taken the booth closest to the front door, just in case, and Wanda had made them each a Long Island Iced Tea. About five minutes later, Jack King slid into the booth next to Carley and handed Rob a note.

"It would appear that he's still on the island because U.S. Customs is holding his passport. Apparently he got himself into a bit of trouble over some box or something. Anyway, that's the address of the hotel he was staying at and they say he hasn't checked out so I assume you can find him there. I'd be careful, though. He claims to be a New York City cop, but he looks like ex-military to me."

Rob studied the note and then slipped it into his shirt pocket. He pulled out the taxi driver's card and handed it to King.

"Can I get you to make one more call for me?"

King looked at the card and handed it back.

"Sure, but not to this guy. I'll hook you up with a friend of mine who knows every nook and cranny of this island. He also knows every person on the island and what their scam is. He owes me a favor, but I'm sure he'd appreciate a tip to cover his gas. I'll let you know when he's here."

King slid out of the booth and went back behind the bar, where he made a quick call on his cell phone. After flashing the "thumbs up" sign to Rob, he resumed whatever task he had been doing when Rob and Carley had walked in.

"Do you trust this guy?" asked an apprehensive Carley. "He seems like a real sleaze ball to me."

"I agree, but Tony has nothing but good things to say about him, so maybe he's okay. However, I'm not so sure about this driver he's hooked us up with. If anything feels wrong, follow my lead and we'll find our own transportation."

A few minutes later a horn honked outside and King nodded to Rob. In the parking lot, a clean, late model Jeep Wrangler with the top removed had pulled up close to the door. The engine was running and a young, stocky black man stood on the passenger's side, holding the door open.

As Rob and Carley approached, the man smiled and nodded

"G'day" he greeted. "My name is Henry. How may I be of service?"

Rob handed the man the note from Jack King.

"Henry, I would like to determine if a man named Erik Mueller is still on the island. According to Jack, he's registered at this hotel but we would like to be sure he hasn't slipped away during the night. What do you suggest?"

The other man scanned the note and handed it back, smiling.

"Today is your lucky day, my friend. My cousin James runs the travel desk at this place, so let's just give him a call and see what he says."

Rob nodded and Henry reached for his cell phone. A few minutes later he had the information Rob needed.

"Erik Mueller is still a guest at the hotel, but he's not currently in his room. My cousin called him a cab about an hour ago and this Mueller guy said something about catching the Red Hook Ferry over to St. John."

"How often does that ferry run?" asked Rob. "By the way, my name is Rob the lady's name is Carley."

"Well, Rob and Carley, the ferry runs about every hour and the dock is at the opposite end of the island. If you'd like to visit St. John I'd be happy to show you around, but the only way off that island is the ferry back to St. Thomas, so we could also just sit at the terminal on this side and wait."

"Unfortunately, we don't know what he looks like," frowned Rob, "but I might have an idea where he's going."

"It's up to you, but my cousin is sending a picture of him to my phone right now so we'll know what he looks like in just a minute."

"Let me make a call," said Rob, as he turned his back on Carley and the driver.

When he turned back around, he nodded to Henry,

"If you're available for the day, we'd like to hire you as our guide and our first stop will be St. John. Do you know the island well?"

"Like the back of my hand," smiled Henry broadly. "Hop in and we'll head over to the dock right now."

Once they were up to speed on the narrow two-lane highway, Carley leaned over and tried to talk to Rob above the sound of the wind rushing into the open Jeep.

"I take it you talked to Tony. Why is he sending us to St. John? I think Henry's idea of waiting at the dock makes more sense."

Rob turned his head to get as close to her ear as possible so the driver wouldn't overhear his response.

"He thinks he knows where Mueller is going. Did you know that Tony lived on St. John for a while?"

Carley frowned and nodded.

"Yes, with that Jill person, right? Is that where we're headed?"

"Yes, but only for a drive by. After that we'll stop someplace for lunch and then have our new best friend here take us back to the cruise ship terminal. There are some other people Tony wants me to call and then we can catch a boat back to the British side."

As Rob turned his head to reply he noticed the driver watching them in his mirror. When Rob made eye contact, the driver smiled and nodded before diverting his eyes away from the mirror.

"By the way, our friend thinks we're whispering sweet nothings in each other's ears, so smile a lot, okay?"

Rob's comment caught Carley completely off guard and made her laugh out loud rather than smile.

When they reached the dock, the departing ferry was already closed to vehicles, so Henry parked it and the three ran aboard just before the crew lifted the heavy ramp.

When they exited the ferry on the St. John side, Henry motioned them out of the flow of pedestrian traffic and pointed up the hill straight ahead.

"The place you told me about will be about five miles up that windy road. Give me a minute to find a taxi and I'll be right back. Please don't wander off."

The 'hill' Henry had pointed out provided a breathtaking view of the heavily wooded countryside and the surrounding bays of St. John. As the taxi negotiated a hairpin turn at the one thousand foot summit, Rob and Carley both gasped at the three hundred degree view of the many small islands visible off the "back" side of St. John.

"Beautiful, isn't it?" commented Henry from the passenger's seat. The house you're looking for is just down the road, so be on the lookout. It will be on your right as we pass by. I know you said you didn't want to stop, but just yell out if you see anything that changes your mind."

As the taxi slowed to a crawl, the occupants soon realized that nothing was visible except a high wooden fence.

When Rob saw a bright yellow piece of paper stapled to the gate, he called out.

"What's that? It looks like some sort of notice."

"This property has been sealed by the authorities," explained the driver as he brought the taxi to a stop. "There was a fire here a few days ago and there's an investigation in progress. That notice basically says, '*Keep out!*'"

Chapter 16

"A fire?" Rob asked the cabbie. "Was it serious?"

"Just some minor damage to the kitchen and the back porch but the place hasn't been occupied for a couple of years so the fire is suspicious. My brother-in-law is a volunteer fireman here on the island and he's conducting the investigation. That's why I was surprised when you asked to come up here. Do you know the owners?"

"No, not the owners, but we have a friend who lived here for a while and he asked us to swing by while we were in the Islands and check it out. I'm sure he won't be happy to hear about the fire but I guess those things happen. Do they have any idea what caused the fire?"

"Well," smiled the cabby, "you didn't get this from me but I hear they think it was started by a cigarette in the kitchen. That seems pretty strange for a house that's supposed to be vacant, huh?"

Rob nodded.

"Let me just peak through a crack in the fence and then we can be underway."

When he climbed back into the vehicle, he nodded to the driver and the taxi sped away. The highway looped around the back side of the island and eventually returned to Cruz Bay, where they had arrived on the ferry.

Rob paid the cab driver and suggested that they look for a place to have lunch before returning to St. Thomas.

Henry recommended a place not far away and led them to an upscale deli-style restaurant in a small shopping plaza called Mongoose Junction.

"Cute place," commented Carley as they were shown to a table. "And I really like the architecture of this plaza. It's very… Caribbean."

"Henry, did you ever get that photo from your cousin?" inquired Rob.

"I didn't hear anything come in, but let me check."

Henry stabbed at the keypad of his phone and nodded.

"Yes, here it is. Anybody you know?"

He handed his phone to Rob, who studied the image for a minute before passing it on to Carley. When she handed it back to Henry, she shook her head.

"He doesn't look familiar to me."

"Me neither," added Rob. "Does your cousin photograph all his clients?"

"No, of course not," replied Henry, slightly offended. "But this guy is developing a bit of a reputation on St. Thomas and the word is out to keep an eye on him. He's already had run-ins with the Customs officials and the local police so my cousin snapped this to pass around to all the 'foot soldiers' on the ground. By this afternoon every cab driver, bar tender and convenience store clerk on two islands will be watching for this guy."

"I see. Would you mind forwarding that to my phone? I'd like to pass it on to our friend who lived in that house up on the hill. In fact, I have a couple of other calls to make, so I'm going to step outside for a few minutes. Carley, would you order me a small chef salad and an iced tea?"

Rob found a bench a few yards from the front door and waited for Henry's photo to arrive. As soon as he had it, he forwarded it on to Tony and called him.

"Is this who I think it is?" asked Tony when he answered.

"Apparently Erik Mueller is making quite a name for himself over here. Does he look familiar to you?"

"No, I don't think I ever saw him around the MX-2 facility but I'm sure he's one of Edwards' men. Have you had a chance to make those other calls yet?"

"Not yet, but we did take a quick ride past the house a few minutes ago. There was a small fire a few days ago but no serious damage. Do you still think that's where Mueller is headed?"

"I do. Edwards would know by now that I spent some time there and if he thinks I'm in the area he would probably assume I'd go back to familiar ground to hide out. How's Carley doing?

"Pretty well, I think. She bought a new outfit that she's wearing right now and I must say, she's catching a lot of eyes today."

"Good. So what are your plans? Are you coming back tonight?"

"Yes, I think so, unless one of these calls I'm about to make changes my plans. How are things over there?"

"Cesar and I did some diving this morning. We took the Zodiac to a site just outside the bay and he got me started on this rebreather thing. It's pretty exotic and there's a lot to remember but I think I'll get the hang of it soon."

"Isn't that what Frank was using…"

"The day he disappeared," interrupted Tony. "Yes it is, but I may have to dive that same site someday to find out what really happened and I need to start preparing now. Besides, the ability to stay underwater for hours at a time fascinates me. Let me know if any of those other contacts I gave you pan out, okay?"

"Will do," replied Rob. "We're just sitting down for lunch, so I'll talk to you in an hour or two."

Rob dug a piece of paper out of his pocket and dialed the first number on the list Tony had given him. The phone rang a dozen times before Rob clicked End.

The second number yielded better results.

"Deep Six Scuba Shop," answered a deep male voice. "How may I help you?"

Rob introduced himself and explained that he was calling on behalf of Tony Nicoletti. Before he could finish, the man interrupted him with a series of questions about Tony. Rob responded with a story he and Tony had fabricated the night before and convinced the man that Tony was alive and well and living in Seattle and that Rob had arrived this morning on a cruise ship.

"So, Matt, what Tony wanted me to ask is whether or not anyone has been around your place asking about him."

"Actually, there was someone in here late last week— Friday or Saturday, maybe—asking about him. I was shocked because I hadn't heard Tony's name mentioned in several years, and that's what I told him. He pressed for information but I didn't really have anything to tell him and he finally left. Is my old dive buddy in some sort of trouble?"

"No, not trouble," replied Rob, "but somebody's been making a lot of inquiries and we're trying to figure out why. Thanks for your help, Matt."

Rob tried the last two numbers on the list but the first one had been disconnected and the second one went to voice mail.

Rob decided to wait until after lunch to call Tony back so he stuffed the phone into his pocket and returned to the restaurant. As he stepped inside, he immediately noticed that the table was empty and had been reset.

He flagged down a waiter.

"Did my friends move to another table?"

"Beats me! I took them menus and by the time I loaded up a tray with water glasses and returned to the table, they were gone. Are you staying for lunch, sir?"

"Ah, no. I need to locate my friends and get back to St. Thomas. Are you sure no one saw them leave?"

"No, I already asked. Maybe they didn't like the menu."

"Yeah, maybe," muttered Rob as he quickly made his way to the door.

Outside, he scanned the walkway that connected the shops in the complex but saw no one that resembled either Carley or Henry and he couldn't imagine why they would leave without letting him know. He had been sitting on a bench just a few yards away and they would surely have seen him when they exited the restaurant unless...

He dashed back inside and located the waiter he had just talked to.

"Is there another way out of here besides that door?"

"Yes, there's a door on the terrace. It's around the corner and at the end of the hall..."

Rob was gone before the young waiter could finish.

He hit the terrace door running, already imagining a dozen scenarios that all involved Carley and kidnapping.

He scanned the back side of the restaurant and the walkway that went left and right at the foot of the concrete steps. Opting for left, towards the ferry dock, he walked as fast as he could without looking too obvious. The sidewalk led down a gradual tree-covered slope and deposited him on the edge of the small plaza that greeted ferry passengers as they arrived on St. John.

Rob stopped short and stayed close to the trees while he searched for any sign of Carley or Henry. When he saw a young woman across the way talking on her cell phone it suddenly occurred to him that Carley had one of the new Dolphin Diver units in her purse and its number was programmed into his own cell.

On the verge of hyperventilating, he listened as the phone rang once and then switched to Carley's voicemail. Either her phone was off or she was using it to make a call herself!

Slowly, Rob made his way around the perimeter of the plaza looking for Carley. Her new outfit should be impossible to miss, he thought to himself. He was concentrating so hard on the small crowd awaiting the approaching ferry that the ring of his cell phone almost caused him to drop it.

"Don't move!" It was Carley's voice. "You're standing right next to him, so do not look to your left!"

"Next to who?"

"The man to your immediate left is Mueller! We saw him leaving the restaurant right after we were seated so we followed him. Sorry, but there wasn't time to alert you."

Rob turned slightly to his right, putting Mueller behind him and whispered into his phone.

"You almost gave me a heart attack, woman! Where are you?"

"Henry and I are across the plaza from you next to a big tree. We have eyes on him, so why don't you casually make your way over here?"

"On my way," replied Rob.

He slid his cell phone into his pocket and started to walk away when a voice behind him said, "Excuse me. I wonder if I could ask you a quick question."

Rob turned and found himself face to face with none other than Erik Mueller.

Mueller extended his hand to show Rob a small photo of Tony.

"Have you by any chance seen this man today? He's a friend of mine that I haven't seen in a long time and we were supposed to meet here today but we seem to have missed each other."

"No, I don't think so," stammered Rob, trying not to lose his composure.

"Okay, thanks. I'm just hanging out asking everybody I see because if he's on St. John, it seems like someone will have seen him. Dumb me, I lost the piece of paper I had his telephone number written on so I have no way to contact him."

Rob faked a smile.

"Well, good luck. I'm sure he'll turn up soon."

"What did he say to you?" demanded Carley as soon as Rob reached their position on the other side of the plaza.

"He showed me a picture of Tony and asked me if I'd seen him! I thought I was going to lose it for a second!"

"Now what?" frowned Carley. "I'm really hungry but I think we need to keep an eye on this guy and see what he's up to."

"I'll take care of that," offered Henry. "I have friends all over the island and we'll keep an eye on him. Why don't you two go back up the hill and have lunch—they probably wonder what the sudden disappearance was all about anyway. I'll stay here and if this guy takes off I'll make sure someone tails him and reports in. You can meet me here when you're finished eating and we'll figure out what to do next."

"Are you sure," queried Rob. "Aren't you hungry, too?"

"Oh, I'll grab something from my pal Jerome's food cart over there. We haven't chatted in several weeks and it will give me a chance to get caught up on the local gossip. I still have your phone number in my call list, so if anything exciting happens I'll let you know. Otherwise, enjoy your lunch and we'll meet up back here in about an hour."

"Well, okay, if you're sure that's alright with you."

Back at the restaurant, Rob and Carley made their apologies to the wait staff and were shown to a different table. Once the beverage part of their meal was ordered, Rob called Tony and brought him up to speed.

"So he's actually standing out on the sidewalk showing my picture, huh? He must really think I'm hiding out on St. John."

"He definitely does," agreed Rob. "Your trick with the shipment to the Customs Office has him convinced that you're in the area and he assumes that, sooner or later, you'll find your way to the ferry dock."

"It's the only way on or off the island, so he's playing his cards just the way I would. And if he's showing my picture all over the place, I may have to rethink my trip over there. Did it look like a recent photo?"

"It wasn't five years old, if that's what you're getting at. But it also wasn't too recent, because your hair was shorter than I've ever seen it."

"So it must have been taken while I was being held at MX-2! I think that confirms Mueller's connection to Edwards. Listen, the plan all along has been to keep Edwards and his bunch focused on the Virgin Islands rather than the Bahamas, so this is a very good development. Anything you can do to make him think he's hot on my trail would be a big help. What about those other numbers I gave you to call?"

"Disconnected, no answer and voicemail," replied Rob. "Except for the dive shop where a guy named Matt said Mueller had been in asking about you but got no useful information."

"Okay, we have what we need right there on St. John, so don't worry about the other numbers. Are you still coming back tonight?"

"That's the plan! Hey Carley wants to talk to you. Hold on."

"Tony, I have a plan I want to run by you. Your friend that owns the tavern hooked us up with a guy named Henry and he seems to know everybody on two islands, at least. In addition, he and his cronies are already watching Mueller because of the trouble he's been into. What if we got Henry to tell Mueller that he's seen you on St. John? That would certainly keep him busy for a while."

"Excellent idea!" replied Tony. "In fact, why don't you cook up a story that makes Mueller think I'm up at the house? That's what he already suspects so let's confirm his suspicions."

When they had said their good-byes, Carley handed the phone back to Rob and smiled broadly.

"We finally have a plan!" she announced, referring to Tony's struggle during the voyage from Belize to Tortola.

After ordering their food, Rob called Henry and explained the plan. Less than five minutes later, Henry walked through the front door of the restaurant laughing out loud.

"Did he take the bait?" asked Carley.

"Hook, line and sinker!" said Henry, still chuckling.

"That fool is on his way to break into a crime scene to find somebody who's not even there! Man, when the local police catch him they are going to lock him up for a long time."

"No!" shouted Carley too loudly.

Lowering her voice, she explained. "Henry, we want this guy occupied and believing that our friend is actually on St. John. You have to contact the authorities and ask them not to arrest him—at least not just yet."

"But if this guy's in jail, he won't bother your friend anymore."

"He's not bothering him now," interjected Rob. "You see, Mueller works for a large, international group and we want them to focus their collective attention here, on St. John, while our friend takes care of some business elsewhere. If Mueller goes to jail, the rest of them may start looking under rocks we'd really rather they not turn over. Do you get my drift?"

Henry nodded and grabbed for his cell phone. When he finished the call, he nodded again.

"Okay, if he enters the property up on the hill they will leave him alone until he exits, but they want to apprehend him in the act of committing a crime, so they have to grab him as he's leaving. Sorry, but that's the best I could do."

"Then that will have to do," replied Rob. "How will they know if he enters the property?"

"I arranged for him to get into the same cab we took and the driver is taking the long way around the back side of the island while one of the local policemen zips up the short way. The cabbie will let us know what happens up there."

"My friend, you just earned yourself a substantial bonus! Now order some lunch and relax for a few minutes."

About thirty minutes later Henry's phone rang and he checked the display.

"The cabbie," he said as he answered the call.

When he hung up, he was smiling.

"He didn't stop at the house but as they were passing it Mueller asked the driver if there were any restaurants nearby. The only thing up there is a small place at the viewpoint near the summit, so that's where he got out. He told the driver not to wait, but asked for his card, so I'm sure he'll unintentionally alert us when he decides to leave. That's when they will grab him."

"Wait, I don't get it," said Carley. "Is he going to the house or not?"

"Oh, I'm sure he is," smiled Rob. "He'll hang out at the viewpoint long enough for the cabbie to clear the area and then he'll walk back down the road to the house. It would have been too obvious to get dropped off in front of property posted with no trespassing signs. The cabbie would have reported that, for sure. This way, he just looks like a tourist who wants to spend the afternoon enjoying the view."

"So do we wait him out here?"

"Not me!" laughed Rob. "I think he'll stick it out in the house as long as he can waiting for a Tony who's never going to show up. He'll probably stay overnight, at least, and maybe several days, depending on his food supply. When he finally does leave, the local police are going to lock him up, so I think you and I have seen the last of him. I suggest we finish up here and then make our way back over to St. Thomas. We can do a little more shopping, if you want, and then catch the last ferry back to Tortola."

Henry's eyebrows raised at Rob's comment.

"I thought you arrived on a cruise ship."

"No, we're on a private vessel that's currently tied up over on Tortola," replied Rob, regretting the fact that he had given away unnecessary information.

"In that case, you don't need to return to St. Thomas at all, unless you want to. The same company that carried you to St. Thomas has a smaller passenger boat that crosses the channel from St. John over to Tortola's West End Marina at 3:00 p.m. From there you can take a taxi to Road Town. You'll be home in half the time and the drive along Tortola's south coast is spectacular."

Carley smiled.

"If the boat ride will be shorter, I'm all for it. We had a pretty rough trip this morning."

"It sounds good to me, too," agreed Rob, glancing at his watch. "We have about an hour and a half to kill, Henry. What do you suggest?"

"Well, I could take you to see a couple of the larger hotels nearby. The Westin has a beautiful property about a mile from here. Unfortunately, there isn't time for a trip to any of the popular beaches. However, we should probably start by purchasing your tickets because there's limited seating on the smaller inter-island boats."

The trio retraced Rob's earlier steps out the terrace door and down the hill to the plaza, where Henry led them to a small brightly painted stand at the edge of the dock. Rob paid for the tickets and then, as they regrouped beside the stand, he discretely handed Henry a fistful of bills.

"Will five hundred dollars cover your fees?"

The Islander smiled broadly and accepted the money.

"You are most generous, my friend. I will keep you up to date on the situation at the house and if you need anything, please don't hesitate to call me. It would be my pleasure to serve as your ears and eyes either here or on St. Thomas."

"Thank you, Henry, and either I or the friend we've mentioned might just take you up on that offer. I think we'll pass on the hotel tour and just hang out around here until it's time to leave. There's some interesting colonial architecture along the waterfront and I think I see some shops to explore, so if you have something to do, please feel free to call it a day."

"I'd be happy to stay until you depart, my friend, but I see that the Redhook ferry is just arriving, so if you're sure you will be okay here I might jump on and get back to St. Thomas before rush hour traffic gets started."

"By all means! You've been a great help today and I don't think we can get into too much trouble here. Thanks again, Henry"

Carley said her good-byes and Henry trotted across the plaza.

"Nice guy," commented Rob as Henry disappeared into the crowd waiting to board the ferry back to Redhook Bay.

"Very nice," agreed Carley, "and he knows *everyone*! I guess that's one of the benefits of living on an island—sooner or later you're related to almost everybody. That's probably one of the disadvantages, too."

Rob and Carley wandered two of the streets that emanated from the lower plaza until it was time to start looking for the boat that was to take them back to Tortola by way of West End Bay. When they didn't see anything that looked like a ferry at the dock, Rob returned to the stand where he had purchased the tickets but it was closed for the day. He asked several men standing nearby but no one seemed to know what he was talking about so he went back to the ferry dock and asked a taxi driver who pointed to the beach a dozen yards to the right of the main dock. There, a man was waving his arms and signaling for Rob to come to him. After collecting Carley, he waved back in acknowledgement.

"What's going on?" she asked as they hurried down to the beach.

"I think we should have asked more questions about this short cut home," he replied.

When they reached the man on the beach they could see that he was holding one end of a rope and that the other end was attached to a small, empty launch.

"We're going to West End Bay, explained Rob. "No fishing today."

"Yes, yes, this way, please. We will meet your vessel out in the bay. When you didn't arrive at the pier, they had to move to make room for another boat, so they called me to look for you. We usually find missing passengers up near the ticket stand."

"Wait a minute!" barked Rob suspiciously. "We just came from the dock and there wasn't any ferry there."

"That's probably true, sir, but that's not the dock the West End Ferry uses. If you check the back of your ticket you'll see that you were supposed to walk about one hundred yards north to the Municipal Pier. Now please hurry, because we have to meet the boat as it exits the inner harbor or they will continue on without you and you'll be stuck here until tomorrow!"

Rob started to reach for the tickets but the other man scolded him.

"Please, sir, get in the boat quickly so we can make our rendezvous."

Rob looked at Carley, who shrugged. Reluctantly, they climbed into the launch and sat on the seat in the middle of the small boat. With their backs to the beach, they didn't see the man in the trees signal a "thumbs up" to the launch operator.

Chapter 17

"Are you sure about this?" asked Carley as she and Rob settled onto the center seat of the small launch. The man who had waved to them pushed the boat off the beach and jumped into the bow. Nearly falling out in the process, he made his way to the back and fired up the outboard motor. They followed a zigzag course through the many anchored boats in the bay and headed for deeper water.

Rob glanced over his shoulder and saw that the other man was talking on his cell phone so he pulled the two tickets out of his shirt pocket and examined them carefully.

"Well, it does say that we were to proceed to the municipal pier and not the ferry dock," he shouted so Carley could hear him over the sound of the motor. "They even underlined 'not the ferry dock' so maybe we goofed."

"Maybe, but I sure hope we aren't going very far out into that rough bay in this little boat! This is worse than the trip this morning!"

Suddenly, the boat made a hard right turn and the pilot cut the speed to about half.

"There's your vessel!" he shouted, pointing to a fifty-foot day cruiser just off the port bow.

Ten minutes later, Rob and Carley were safely aboard a private power boat and seated on the covered aft deck with a half dozen other travelers.

"I'll bet you forgot to read the fine print on the back of your tickets," laughed a middle-aged man dressed in khaki shorts, a golf shirt and expensive looking leather sandals. "They get so few tourists on this run that they always forget to mention it at the ticket booth."

"Ah, that makes sense," nodded Rob. "Sorry if we held anyone up."

When no one responded, Rob turned to Carley to see how she was doing now that they were on a bigger vessel.

"Is everything okay?"

"Yes, fine, now that we're on a real boat. Do you suppose they have any water onboard?"

"Inside the main cabin in the small refrigerator," said a voice from behind a newspaper on the other side of the seating area. "They're a dollar each."

"Thanks," replied Carley to the newspaper.

When she returned, she had two plastic bottles of water and a Snickers candy bar. Rob raised his eyebrows and smiled as she handed him one of the bottles.

"What? I need a little chocolate to calm my nerves. I thought we were being kidnapped back there on the beach."

"The trip's not over," said the mysterious voice behind the newspaper.

The rest of the fifty minute ride was relatively smooth and uneventful. When the boat eased into a slip at the West End Marina, the other passengers, who probably rode this boat every day, automatically made their way to the starboard side. They waited for a young girl on the pier to open the railing and in seconds they were gone, headed home for the day. Rob tried to get a glimpse of the man who had been reading the newspaper but the angle was never right to see his face.

As the last of the regulars exited, Rob and Carley made their way to the side and stepped onto the pier.

"Where can we get a taxi to Road Town?" asked Rob, as the girl closed the railing.

"At the end of this pier, make a left and follow the boardwalk over to the parking lot. There should be one there," replied the girl without looking up from her work.

"Friendly girl," commented Carley sarcastically when they were a few yards away. "It seems like they come in two flavors here—too friendly and not friendly enough!"

As they walked along the small water-front commercial area they passed a number of businesses and restaurants. All the buildings were well maintained and painted in pastel pinks, blues and yellows. Bright white trim made them look crisp and inviting. To their left, yachts both large and small filled their view. Beyond the piers dozens more yachts rested at anchor in the narrow U-shaped bay known as Soper's Hole. To their right, a large tree-covered hill gazed down at the tiny, secluded harbor.

"This place is beautiful!" commented Carley. "Everything is so lush and green. It reminds me of home."

"Are you feeling a little homesick?"

"Yes, I guess I am. I think it's the uncertainty of this whole 'adventure' and not knowing how long we'll be gone. It's funny, because I thought this was going to be the trip of a lifetime and now I can't wait to get home. But that could be months away, couldn't it?"

"Yes, I'm afraid it could but you aren't committed to staying for the entire voyage, you know. The others signed on for the duration, but you're really here as a guest more than a member of the crew. We would miss you, for sure, but we can hire a local cook if you decide you've had enough of the high seas."

"Really? I feel better already, just knowing that there's a way out if I need it. Thanks, Rob. I guess I was feeling a little claustrophobic, in an open water kind of way."

"All I ask is that you explain your feelings to Tony one-on-one first. I know he doesn't express it, but he's very fond of you."

"Yeah, right! I'm about fourth in line, behind his 'mission' for Frank, his hatred of this guy named Edwards and his ex-girlfriend."

"I'm afraid you might be right about the first two, but I don't think he's still carrying much of a torch for Jill Harris. He's concerned about her safety, but he feels that way about all his old team members."

"It's more than concern, Rob. I can see it in his eyes when he mentions her name. Hey, there's a taxi."

Carley let lose a whistle that shocked Rob but it got the driver's attention and he whirled his vehicle around the circular parking lot and slid to a stop beside the pair.

Before getting in, Rob stuck his head in the passenger's side window and asked if the cabbie was willing to take them all the way to Road Town.

The cabbie flashed a big smile and replied, "Mister you just made my day! Hop in and I'll have you there in no time."

Rob guessed that fares to the far end of the island were few and far between for a reason so he asked the obvious next question.

"How much?"

"The fare is fifty dollars American, my friend, but I promise you it will be the most beautiful ten miles you've ever traveled. And I'm happy to stop at any of the lookouts along the way, too."

"That's a big promise, considering that we're from Belize, but we'll take you up on your offer. We're headed for the commercial marina on the far side of Road Town Harbor."

The driver was right. The trip along Tortola's southern coast was beautiful, but it wasn't the sea views that fascinated Rob and Carley. They had both seen more Caribbean coastline than they could remember. What really held their attention were the many private residences built on the steep hillside that was now on their left. The same pastel colors in a myriad of architectural miracles clung precariously to the mini-mountains as they passed through picturesque hamlets such as Boway, Havers and Nanny Cay. They were so caught up in viewing the homes that they didn't notice the cab slowing down until it had almost come to a stop.

Looking to the right, Rob realized that they were parked at one of the viewpoints the driver had mentioned.

"What's up?"

"Well, sir, I'm afraid I'm going to need a little more money than we first agreed on if you want to get back to the harbor unharmed."

Rob tensed, sensing what Carley had feared back on the beach. As discreetly as possible, he retrieved his cell phone and held it close to the back of the seat, where the driver couldn't see it.

"Are you kidding me?" shouted Rob, making eye contact with the driver in his rear view mirror. "Is this a robbery?"

"A what?" replied the driver, with a look of obvious surprise. "No, of course not! But it seems you forgot to mention that you were being followed. Now, I'm not opposed to a little car chase through the hills of Tortola, but it's going to cost you extra, my friend."

"What are you talking about?" demanded Carley. "There's no one following us!"

"I beg to disagree, young lady. A car has been following us since we pulled out of the parking lot back at Soper's Hole. No matter how slow or fast I go, it matches our speed and when I pulled into this turnout, it pulled over into the one just back down the road—I can see the car in my mirror right now.

"I don't know if you two have gotten yourselves into trouble here on Tortola or if it's just somebody looking to relieve rich tourists of their valuables, but I didn't bargain for a fight and that's going to cost you extra."

Resisting the urge to turn and look out the back window, Rob raised his cell phone and dialed Tony. While the phone was ringing, he turned to Carley.

"Okay, let's don't tip our new friend off any sooner than necessary. Carley, open your door, step out and pretend to be enjoying the view. As soon as I'm off the phone with Tony jump back in here and slam the door. Driver, the second she's back in, do your magic. We'll negotiate your fee when we reach our destination."

Tony came on the line in the middle of Rob's explanation.

"What's going on? Is everything alright?"

"We're coming in hot, boss!" replied Rob. "It looks like we've picked up a tail and our cab driver is going to try to lose it but you might want to be ready on your end in case we can't shake it out here."

"Where are you? Is Carley okay?"

"Yes, she's okay and we're currently just north of Sea Cow Bay on the south coast highway. I'm looking at a map the driver just handed me and it looks like we have some pretty wild road between us and home."

"We'll be waiting for you at the ship, but be careful out there. Shall I call the local police?"

Rob passed Tony's question on to the driver, who shook his head.

"No police, but you could send a prayer or two our way. Stay tuned and I'll let you know when we get close."

Rob ended his call to Tony and patted the driver on the right shoulder.

"We're in your hands, my friend, but we'll have help waiting if and when we reach the ship. By the way, I'm Rob and this is Carley."

"My name is Samuel, and we will reach your ship, I assure you. I'm just waiting for the right opportunity and I think I see it now. Hang on!"

Samuel launched the cab out onto the highway in front of a large cargo truck. With the gas pedal on the floor, he put as much distance between his taxi and the truck as he could before breaking hard for what would be the first of many sharp, blind curves as the road climbed up away from the sea and onto the steep hillside. By lurching out in front of the truck, the cabbie had put a significant road block between himself and the other car but he could see the chase car darting in and out of the other lane, looking for a chance to pass the truck.

Carley gasped as the taxi's tires squealed negotiating the sharp right turn but she kept her attention riveted to the road ahead, providing an extra set of eyes for the driver. At this speed, an oncoming car in their lane wouldn't stand a chance of getting out of the way.

After about five minutes of slamming back and forth from left turn to right turn, the road straightened out for a short stretch.

"Everyone doing okay?" asked Rob, rhetorically.

"So far, so good," replied Samuel, "but that was just a warm-up. The really interesting part of the road is just ahead so hang on and keep your eyes out for anything—including cars—in the road."

After negotiating several miles of hairpin turns and steep hills, both up and down, the road suddenly dropped back down to the beach as it passed through Slaney and Fisher Estates. Samuel was forced to slow down due to congestion in both villages and by the time the road opened up again, Rob could see the chase car in the distance. He started to mention it, but the driver interrupted him.

"I see it. I'm going to drop off the main highway and try to lose him, but this might be a good time to call you friend back. Tell him we're across the harbor, about a mile away."

As the taxi shot through a gradual left bend, a car in the oncoming lane forced Samuel onto the soft shoulder and the rear end started to slide. He quickly regained control and then cranked the car around a hard right turn onto a side street. Two blocks later, at the water front, he made a left and eased the taxi into a parking lot that was shielded from the street by a row of bushy, flowering trees.

"Keep your eyes open for him!" shouted Samuel, as he put his cell phone to his ear.

Rob heard him give someone a description of the vehicle that had been following them and then there was a long pause before the driver cursed, flipped his phone shut and moved the taxi down the parking lot to a place where the trees provided the maximum protection.

"He didn't see us pull off the highway, but he quickly realized he had lost us and he's turning around right now. He should be coming down this street right at us in a couple of minutes."

As Samuel was explaining the situation, another taxi crawled down the street he had just indicated and before it had passed yet another taxi passed going the opposite direction. Soon the street on the other side of the trees was clogged with taxis.

"What's going on?" asked Carley.

"I believe you call it a flash mob," smiled Samuel from the front seat. "And look! Here comes our friend. Duck down in case he spots the car!"

And with that, he leaned over in the seat, as did Rob and Carley, making the cab look empty.

When Samuel's cell phone rang, he popped up, put the car in gear and sped out the opposite end of the lot opposite from where they had entered. He pulled out between two other cabs that had stopped to allow him to merge into the bumper-to-bumper stream of yellow and called to his passengers in the back seat.

"You can sit up now!"

Five minutes later, Samuel's taxi screeched to a stop at the end of Pier 1 and he turned to face Rob and Carley.

"You two should make your break while my buddies still have your new friend bottled up in traffic on the other side of the harbor. The farther away from here I get, the less chance there is that he will track you down."

Carley and Rob quickly gathered their belongings and exited the cab. Rob went around to the driver's window and handed Samuel three bills.

"There's fifty for the regular fare and another two hundred for the roller coaster ride. Will that cover it?"

Samuel smiled, accepted the bills and handed Rob a business card.

"Yes, it will, and there's enough there to buy a round of beers for my friends in the flash mob. Call me if you need anything. I usually hang out at the other end of the island, but I can get here pretty fast, as you just saw. Or I can put you in touch with one of my buddies down here."

The two men shook hands and the cab was out of sight seconds later. When Rob reached the end of the pier, Tony and Carley were waiting at the top of the gang plank.

"Any idea who was following you?" asked Tony as Rob stepped onto the Dolphin Diver.

"None whatsoever. I didn't notice anyone following us today, did you Carley?"

"Nope. And the only person who knew we were going to be arriving on that boat was Henry."

"Henry?" asked Tony.

"Henry is a guy your friend Jack King set us up with when we left his tavern this morning. Unfortunately he knows more about us than I would like, but he seems like a pretty good guy."

"Does he know where the Dolphin Diver is tied up?"

"Not exactly, but he knows Carley and I were headed for Tortola. I don't think I ever mentioned the type of vessel or an exact location, but it wouldn't take too much to find us."

"In that case, we need to be prepared for a visit. And I think I'll give Jack a call and see what's up. Maybe he's working for the other side these days."

***

Erik Mueller had a hearty lunch and killed a couple of hours at the Coral Bay Viewpoint before walking back down the hill towards the house he had visited a week earlier with the real estate agent named Jeri Addison. Partway down the hill he veered off into the woods and hiked up the steep slope that would position him high above the house. He knew from his previous visit that the back of the property was secured by a high cliff but his military training had prepared him for just such a challenge. From his backpack he retrieved a large coil of black, nylon cord and a pair of leather gloves. He secured the cord to the base of a small tree, tossed the other end over the edge, slipped his arms through the straps of his backpack and silently repelled down the rocky face and onto the property in less than a minute.

Mueller surveyed the fire damage near the back door and discovered that the kitchen window he had left unlatched was now secure—probably the work of whoever had made the temporary repairs to the rear of the house. He made his way around the right corner of the building and tested the master bedroom window. Seconds later he hoisted his backpack through the now-open window and then crawled in after it. He had selected this room on his earlier walk-through and short-circuited the window sensor in anticipation of his return. After removing his shoes, he laid his pack on the large king-sized bed and exchanged the gloves for a small tool kit. Stopping every few steps to listen, he made his way to the alarm system's digital keypad located near the front door. With the skill of a surgeon, he removed the faceplate and snipped one of the wires that led to the horn mounted on the outside of the house. Next, he carefully disconnected the telephone cable that allowed the built-in auto-dialer to contact the outside world. He reinstalled the faceplate to hide his modifications and stepped back to admire his work. The alarm system was still enabled and it would still respond correctly to the keypad, but it could no longer notify anyone of an intrusion.

Mueller returned to the bedroom and changed from his street clothes into a more comfortable set of lightweight sweats. He unpacked three U.S. Army issue MREs (Meals Ready to Eat) and set them on top of the dresser. Back during his days in Iraq, he could survive for five days on three MREs, but he hoped he wouldn't be in the house that long. He hoped Tony Nicoletti would put in an appearance soon and fall into his waiting trap.

Mueller's final act, before laying down for a nap, was to unpack his .38 Special and place it in the nightstand drawer beside the bed.

***

"Wow! It sure doesn't seem like this is just our second day in the Virgin Islands," commented Carley, as she sipped her wine.

Tony, Rob and Carley were enjoying the evening breezes from the rear deck of the Dolphin Diver and discussing the current situation.

"I know," agreed Rob. "Today was like a week's worth of excitement compressed into ten hours but I feel good about it. We got a lot accomplished."

Tony nodded and raised his beer bottle to toast the other two.

"Here's to you! In one short day you not only found Erik Mueller but you also got him pinned down and focused on St. John instead of on the Bahamas. A major accomplishment, for which you will be richly rewarded, I'm sure!"

"Well, I don't know about Carley, but my reward is waiting for me in Miami. I talked to Ann by short wave a while ago and I think I'm going to see if I can make arrangements to meet her in the next day or two if things are under control here. Is that okay with you, Tony?"

"Sure, sure! I made that trip a bunch of times and there are several flights a day from St. Thomas to Miami. Look for non-stop flights, though, or you will end up changing planes in Puerto Rico. American Airlines used to have three direct flights a day to Miami."

"Good to know. So what are your plans? Should I plan on bringing Ann back here?"

"That would be great, unless she wants to go back to Belize right away. I think we have Mueller handled for a few days but eventually he's going to give up waiting for me and leave the house. At that point we lose him to the local authorities and then I'll have to find another way to keep Edwards and his team from thinking about South Bimini. When that time comes, I'd really like to have you back on board in case we decide to move the boat. However, your family duties need to come first, so whatever works out for you."

Rob glanced at Carley and made eye contact for just an instant.

"Yes, you're right about that. I'll see how Ann feels about it, but maybe she'd like to spend a few days on the Dolphin Diver and then fly back to Belize on her own. I know she wants to see the ship, but I doubt if she'll want to make a long stay out of it."

Just then, Rob's cell phone rang.

After several minutes of discussion, he hung up and wrinkled his brow.

"That was Henry," he explained. "He promised to call when he heard something from the house but he just told me Mueller never showed up. The local police have two people watching the house from the woods across the street and they haven't seen anyone around it all day."

"Are they watching the back, too?" asked Tony.

"He didn't say, but I would assume that trained police would be smart enough to figure that out, wouldn't you?"

"Not necessarily. If they know the property, they know that the back is protected by a fairly high rock cliff face. It always made Jill feel secure but I used to practice repelling down it when she was away from the house. If our guy is the paramilitary type he's already inside the house!"

"So much for a good plan! I'll call him back and let him know."

"No, don't do that. The police would probably storm the place and alert Mueller. This way, at least we know where he is. Besides, if he leaves the way he came in—or if the police think he's not there and call off the stake-out—he might stay out of jail and we can continue to use him. This news actually improves an already good day!"

"Well, in that case, I think I'll go down below and start working on travel arrangements while I wait for Ann's call on the radio. Good night, all."

When Rob was gone, Carley refilled her wine glass and pulled another beer out of the refrigerator for Tony.

"I know I should have mentioned this earlier but you look amazing in that new outfit," he said with a smile.

"Thank you. Tony, but we need to talk."

Chapter 18

"I don't like the sound of that," frowned Tony as he accepted the bottle of beer from Carley. "Is this about the car chase this afternoon? Because if it is…"

"No, Tony, it's not that. In fact, that was the first interesting thing that's happened in days. No, the problem is that I'm really not enjoying this trip as much as I thought I would. When I'm on board the Dolphin Diver I feel really confined and on top of that I'm really, really home sick. This is the first time I've been away from home since my days in Guatemala. I thought it would be fun, but I really don't enjoy ship life and I think I want to go back to Belize."

Tony was silent for a moment.

"Really? When Rob invited you to join us on this trip you sounded so excited to get out of that dingy bar and see the world and now—less than three weeks later—you're ready to go home? What happened?"

"Honestly, I don't know. I'm not sure what I expected, but it wasn't this. I'm sorry to let you and the rest of the crew down, but I just can't do this anymore. This is your quest and if you weren't chasing Erik Mueller, you'd be chasing after someone else. And that's fine, for you. But not for me."

Tony put his arm around Carley's shoulders and she rolled into his hug.

Long minutes later, he asked, "Are you sure there isn't something else?"

Carley didn't reply, but instead shook her head slightly and sobbed.

***

Mueller had sat in the dark house all night but he couldn't risk turning on any lights in case Nicoletti arrived during the night. It was now 6:30 a.m. and fully daylight so he unpacked the three muffins he had bought at the viewpoint and made his way to the kitchen. He silently searched the cupboards, knowing in advance that any food he found wouldn't be edible. When he came to a stack of small plates, he pulled one down and set it on the counter. Continuing his search, he located glasses and retrieved one of those as well. In a drawer next to the stove he found a small supply of towels and as he reached for one his fingers touched something odd. He pushed the remaining towels aside and saw a framed photograph of a man and a woman on a beach. He immediately recognized the man as Tony Nicoletti and he assumed the woman must be Jill Harris, although he had never seen a picture of her.

Mueller removed the photo and carefully replaced the towels, minus the one he planned to use. At the sink, he rinsed off the plate and glass and then dried them with the towel. He let the cold water run for several minutes to flush the pipes and then filled the glass.

Back in the bedroom, he nibbled on a muffin and drank the water as he studied the photograph. When he got back to St. Thomas he would fax the picture to Edwards but for now it would serve as a constant reminder of the task at hand. Mueller leaned the photo against the lamp on the end table next to the bed so that it would be the first thing he saw each morning.

***

Tony had been awake for a long time, but he remained very still so as not to wake Carley. He had silently considered several courses of action and then spent the last hour working out the details of the one he had decided to pursue.

Carley stirred and mumbled something in her sleep. When she rolled over, her arm brushed Tony and her eyes suddenly snapped open.

"Good morning, sleepy head," smiled Tony as he rolled to face her.

Carley's look of shock slowly morphed into a smile.

"Good morning yourself, sailor."

Thirty minutes later, Tony rolled out of bed and pulled on some shorts and a t-shirt.

"How about if I go figure out how to make a pot of coffee?

"That's a sweet thought, but in the interest of everyone's health, maybe I should do that," replied Carley from the bed. "How many crew members are aboard?"

"Just you and I, Rob and whoever's on the bridge, I think. But the others come and go all the time, so it wouldn't hurt to make a full urn. You relax, I'm sure I can handle this."

And with that, Tony was out the door. When he reached the ship's salon, he was surprised to see Rob sitting at one of the tables with a mug of coffee.

"I was just coming to do that!" greeted Tony.

He took two mugs from the galley and filled them from the large stainless steel urn. When he turned, Rob was smiling.

"You must be really thirsty."

"Ah, no, one is for a friend. Listen, what do you have planned for today?"

"Nothing special, but I'm going to fly up to Miami tomorrow and return the next day with Ann. Why?'

"I'd like to talk to you about a plan I've been working on. Do we know the whereabouts of the ship's divemaster?"

"Yes, as a matter of fact Cesar was just here a few minutes ago. I think he might be up on the bridge talking to the Captain."

"Good! I'd like to talk to him, too. Can we plan to meet here in about an hour?"

"Sure," replied Rob. "You go deliver your coffee and tell Carley I'll cook breakfast this morning since it was my idea to take that no-name ferry back from St. John yesterday."

An hour later, Tony, Carley, Rob, Cesar and Captain Braydon were seated at the largest of the salon tables and Tony had a large nautical map of the British Virgin Islands spread out in front of them.

"So right here is Leinster Bay. It's the closet water approach to the house and I used to snorkel there all the time so I know the area pretty well. The Dolphin Diver would have to stay some distance off shore, but I could scuba in to the beach, hike up the hill, do my thing and be back to the boat in about an hour. What do you think?"

"It seems like a lot of work just to rattle Mueller's cage," replied Carley with a frown.

"Not to mention risky," added Rob. "You realize that if you were to be stopped on the island you'd have an immigration issue, right? You've traveling as a citizen of Belize—you can't just walk out of the water and onto U.S. soil."

"Noted," replied Tony, "but other than that, what do you think? On the way back we can stop at Norman Island and do a little underwater treasure hunting. There's supposed to be pirate booty buried somewhere around there."

"What about the rest of the crew?" asked the Captain. "If they return to the pier and find the vessel gone, they will think we've abandoned them!"

"I thought of that," smiled Tony. "They all have ship-issued cell phones and, with any luck, they have them powered on. We can send them all a text explaining that the ship is only out for the day and will return by nightfall. We can also leave that message with the guard, who we can leave on the pier where the gang plank would normally rest."

"Well, I suppose if we're not going too far we can survive without an engineer and a first mate," conceded the Captain. "But before I agree, I must check my charts and see if there's enough depth in this bay to handle the Dolphin Diver."

The captain spun and headed for the bridge.

"Well, while he's checking on that, I have some big news to share," announced Rob.

"Last night Ann told me that she received a call earlier in the day from the dolphin research center back in Belize and they've finally had a break-through in their research efforts! A couple of days ago one of the technicians installed an incorrect component in a new version of the translator module and it suddenly began translating the dolphins' simple messages. Ann says the dolphins were almost as excited as the humans!"

Cesar Acosta gasped out loud.

"Is *that* the research you were telling us about? Someone has actually built a device that can translate dolphin communications?"

"Yes, although I must stress that it's still in the early stages of development. However, it seems that the unintended component change solved two problems because the device now translates in *both directions*. We can essentially communicate with dolphins in their own language, although we are only at the grade school level so far. Much work still needs to be done, but this was the crucial first step. Needless to say, the Dolphin Diver will be playing a long and very important part in this incredible research a few months from now."

"You can count me in for the duration," stated Cesar emphatically. "I want to be in the water, nose to nose with one of those beautiful creatures and see the expression on its face when I say, '*Hola!*' in its own language!"

The Captain had returned midway through Rob's explanation but he had heard enough to make a decision.

"I'd be honored to remain on for the rest of my days, if you'll have me."

"Me, too," added Tony. "I can't think of another place I'd rather be as soon as I finish this little task I've already undertaken."

All four men turned to Carley and stared.

"Sorry, but I've had enough sea life," she apologized. "Maybe Rob can find a place for me in the office."

"I promise you I will make that happen, Carley! Now what about this harebrained idea of Tony's, Captain? Is there enough depth for the ship?"

"More than enough and we can be ready to shove off in thirty minutes."

It actually took almost an hour to get everything re-stowed and the trip through the Sir Francis Drake Channel took another ninety minutes but talk about the dolphin research breakthrough made the time pass quickly.

When the Captain had dropped the bow anchor, he came into the salon.

"The Dolphin Diver is secure, Tony. If you're still planning to go for a swim, now would be a good time. The water is calm and there aren't many boats in the bay."

"I still don't understand why you don't take the Zodiac in to the beach instead of swimming all that way," commented Cesar.

"For one thing, I need the practice with the rebreather. And secondly, as Rob pointed out earlier, St. John is U.S. soil. Pulling the Zodiac up on shore would be much more likely to attract attention than me slipping out of the water and into the bushes. So enough talking—let's get wet!"

The Dolphin Diver had anchored nearly a half mile from shore but Tony put his high-thrust swim fins to work and reached the inner bay in no time. He surfaced, got his bearings and then descended again. The east end of the beach was nearly deserted and he aimed for a spot near a small cluster of mangrove. When the water became too shallow to swim, he stood and quickly made his way into the bushes just behind the narrow beach. He pulled a net bag out of a pouch on his utility belt and packed his dive gear into it. Unzipping the lightweight, black dive skin, he tossed the bag over his shoulder and started up the hill towards the house he and Jill had shared for several months. It had been more than five years since his last trek, but he soon found the path he had followed many times in the past.

As he reached the top of the hill, he veered off to the right and climbed through the trees to the cliff that overlooked the house. Just as he had suspected, Mueller had used a length of black military paracord to repel down the face of the wall.

Using his own piece of cord that he had specifically cut to be a little longer than twice the height of the cliff, Tony slipped one end of the cord through the strap of a U.S. Army canteen he had taken from his private supply room onboard the Dolphin Diver. Holding both ends of the cord firmly in his left hand, he played out the cord and let the growing loop lower the canteen to the ground right beside Mueller's rope. When the canteen came to rest, Tony released one end of the rope and gently pulled it through the strap and back up the hill.

He coiled the rope, re-shouldered his dive gear and vanished back down the hill confident that Mueller would find the canteen on his next perimeter check.

"How did it go?" asked Rob as Tony splashed up onto the dive platform of the Dolphin Diver and removed his mask.

"Mission accomplished," he smiled. "Mueller will believe I was inside the fenced property with him and he will spend hours searching every nook and cranny for me. But more importantly, he will be absolutely positive that I'm on St. John. My guess is that he will withdraw to a sniper position at the top of the cliff and patiently wait for my return. At least that's what I would do."

Tony dried off, chugged a bottle of water to help the dry-mouth caused by the rebreather and then made his way to the bridge where he pointed out their next destination near Norman Island. Once the ship was underway, he returned to the salon.

"Okay, folks, now we're going to have some fun. The Captain is taking us to a place called 'The Caves' on the coast of Norman Island. This is the same place that Robert Louis Stevenson described in his book *Treasure Island* and Norman Island is often called Treasure Island. However, this part of the Virgin Islands was once home to many pirates and legend has it that more than one of them stashed their loot in one of the three caves here. I've snorkeled here several times, so this time I'm going to dive. Whether you dive or snorkel, be sure to carry an underwater light because one of the caves goes back more than seventy feet and it gets very dark."

Rob and Carley chose to snorkel, but Cesar donned a rebreather and paired up with Tony. The Captain elected to stay aboard the ship.

As Tony and Cesar slid beneath the surface, they gave each other the "OK" sign, the universal sign that everything was normal. They leveled off at about thirty feet and headed directly towards the largest of the three caves. The surge was a little rough outside the entrance, but once inside it became very calm and clear. Cesar already had his light on and was exploring the wall to the left while Tony focused his attention on the rock formations below them. Huge boulders that had once been part of the island were tossed like pebbles on the bottom, completely obscuring the cave floor. They explored the large outer chamber for more than fifteen minutes before moving further in.

The cave grew darker with each kick and soon Tony was forced to use his light, too. It's broad, intense beam created a wide cone of light in front of him and he moved cautiously through the cave in awe of the power of nature. He could see Cesar's light to his left and as the cave narrowed, they were suddenly side by side. Ahead, the sand was rising up to meet them and soon they were standing in waist deep water with their mouth pieces out.

Tony pointed his light towards the back of the cave.

"Shall we check it out? There's supposed to be another small cave back there."

"Sure!" replied Cesar. "Is that where the treasure is?"

Tony laughed as the two men splashed up onto a dry strip of sand along the back wall.

"Well, I've never been back here but I'm sure a lot of other people have and if there ever was any treasure in this cave it would be long gone. Besides, the big stash is supposed to be up on the hill overlooking the bay."

"Now you tell me!" joked Cesar. "Hey, check this out!"

His light had caught the top half of a small opening that was partially filled with sand. He carefully got down on his hands and knees and peered through the hole with his light.

"What do you see?"

"There's definitely a second chamber back there but we would need shovels to get in. This opening is just too small. It looks like there are a lot of small bones in there, so I'm guessing what goes in doesn't necessarily come out."

Cesar set his light on the sand, partially sticking into the hole so he could use his arms to help push the added weight of his gear erect. Just as he reached down to retrieve the light, something hit it and it disappeared into the small chamber.

"What was that?" he yelled.

"I don't know, but let's get out of here before whatever lives in there decides to add our bones to that pile!"

Tony began backing into the water but Cesar turned and ran as fast as he could until he was waist deep. Using Tony's light the two kicked along the surface shoulder to shoulder until they were back at the entrance. While they floated there resting, they both kept a close eye on the interior of the cave.

"There's another cave off to the right, if you want some more excitement," laughed Tony.

"No thanks, I'm good. Where do you suppose Rob and Carley are?"

Tony used his arms to rotate towards the Dolphin Diver a hundred yards away.

"I'd say they're home having a beer," he laughed as he waved back at the boat. "Shall we head back, too?"

The midday sun was intense, so both men descended to about fifteen feet and slowly kicked their way back to the Dolphin Diver. About fifty feet from the boat, Tony spotted something headed directly towards them. He grabbed Cesar's arm and pointed. Cesar gave the thumbs up sign and both men raced for the surface. When their heads broke the surface, they were both wielding nasty looking dive knives and scanning the surface for any sign of the critter. Cesar put his face in the water and looked below them, but when he reappeared he just shrugged. Cautiously, the men started for the boat on the surface but before they had traveled two body-lengths they were confronted by a dolphin that looked like it was going to attack them. Instead, it stopped just a couple of feet in front of them and assumed an almost vertical position. By the time Tony could get his head out of the water, the dolphin was whistling, clicking, moaning, grunting and squeaking at the two men. It dove deep below the surface for a second but soon returned to repeat the performance.

"I've never heard of one of these things harming humans, but I think we may have stumbled across Crazy Charlie here," shouted Cesar. "Let's slowly make our way to the boat but keep your head out of water and keep an eye on this one."

Tony did as instructed but every few seconds the dolphin would pop up right in front of the two divers and read them the riot act.

"Maybe it's trying to warn us about that cave," called Tony.

When he looked to see if Cesar had heard him, he noticed that the other man had a small underwater camera trained on the dolphin. By the time they reached the dive platform, Rob, Carley and the Captain were there to help them out of the water. The dolphin continued to scold them until they were completely out of the water and then it disappeared as quickly as it had appeared.

"Wow, that was strange!" said Tony as he removed his mask and brushed his wet hair back. "What the heck was going on out there?"

Carley accepted Tony's gear and placed it in the rinse tank.

"It sounded like you were getting yelled at pretty good. What did you guys do to that poor thing?"

"Nothing. We had a little excitement of our own in the back of the big cave, but this guy just charged at us as we were approaching the boat."

Rob was helping Cesar with his gear.

"Excitement? Was it buried treasure kind of excitement?"

Tony laughed and put his arm around Cesar's shoulder.

"No, our divemaster, here, put his light where it didn't belong and something grabbed it away from him. Maybe our dolphin friend was trying to warn us to stay away."

Cesar sat down on one of the plastic benches molded into the dive platform and handed Rob his camera.

"It wasn't just one dolphin, Tony, and I don't think it had anything to do with the cave. They were trying to tell us something, but I don't think it had to do with the cave."

"How do you know it was more than one?" challenged Tony.

"Check out the pictures. There were at least three unique animals, maybe more. And if they were warning us about the cave, I think they would have placed themselves between us and the cave. Instead, they stayed between us and the boat as if they were trying to prevent us from leaving the water until we received their message. They all delivered the exact same message, by the way. You can verify that by downloading the MP3 file I recorded on the camera."

"What?" shouted Rob. "You actually have an audio recording of that performance? Cesar, you're a genius!"

Rob disappeared with Cesar's camera and left him standing on the dive platform holding his gear.

Carley took over and got Cesar's gear taken care of while the two divers climbed the ladder to the main deck and wrapped up in towels. The Captain raised the anchor and soon they were headed back to Road Town Harbor. Rob finally reappeared from his cabin and joined Tony, Carley and Cesar in the salon.

"We'll know in a few hours," he announced as he sat down.

"We'll know *what*?" asked Tony. "Where the heck have you been for the last half hour?"

"I transmitted Cesar's audio file off to Anne and she's emailing it to Belize. In a few hours we'll know what those dolphins were trying to tell you. There were several different ones, by the way. Cesar probably recognized different markings on them, but you can also hear the difference in their voices."

"The research project!" shouted Tony, finally realizing why Rob had been so excited to get his hands on Cesar's camera. "They will be able to tell us what the dolphins were saying!"

***

Mueller examined the canteen, but he already knew who it belonged to. As he turned it over, his face reddened. Scrawled on the back in black marker was the name *"T. Nicoletti"*

Mueller got down on the ground and looked for any indication that the canteen had been dropped from the top of the cliff but he didn't find any indentations in the ground. That meant that Nicoletti had probably used Mueller's own rope to enter the fenced yard. He had then gone back up the rope or...

Mueller dropped to one knee and carefully scanned the back yard.

"Are you still here?" he whispered to himself.

Chapter 19

When engineer Rigo Mejía and first mate Nickolas Banks reached the top of the gang plank they were surprised to see the rest of the crew sitting in the ship's salon.

Concerned that they had missed a crew meeting, they both asked, simultaneously, "What's up?"

"Oh, Tony got lectured by a dolphin this morning and we're just waiting to find out what the scolding was all about," replied Rob.

Rigo nodded and then did a double take.

"I see… wait, what? Did you say you are waiting to find out what a dolphin told Tony? What did we miss?"

"That's right!" exclaimed Rob. You weren't here when I made the big announcement. Our dolphin research team back in Belize has been working for several years on a device that would translate the language of the dolphins into English, and vice-versa. I couldn't tell you that earlier in the trip when I talked about the future of the Dolphin Diver but they are going public with the news tomorrow. Anyway, Cesar managed to record a repeating message several dolphins were delivering to Tony and we're waiting to hear back from the lab right now. Well, actually we're waiting to hear from my wife, who is waiting to hear from the lab…"

"Are you serious?" exclaimed Rigo. "Is that what the Dolphin Diver will be doing? Man, where do I sign up?"

Rob laughed and addressed the entire crew.

"Okay, here's the deal. The researchers have been working with a very select group of dolphins out on Turnefee Atoll, where I live. They still have some work to do before they will be ready to send their devices out into the open sea— probably a couple of month's worth of work, maybe more. Hopefully, that will give us time to complete Tony's mission and get the boat back to Belize City. At that point, any of you who wish to remain onboard will be given the opportunity to sign on as permanent employees of Turneffe Wild Dolphin Institute. The salary probably won't be as good as what Tony pays, but you will have an opportunity to be a part of history. Using the Dolphin Diver, we hope to visit dolphin pods all over the globe and fine tune the new device, as necessary, for any regional and species language differences. We will also be listening very carefully to what the dolphins have to say and, when necessary, taking action to protect them. I hope to be on a number of voyages and the Captain has already opted in. Tony has also expressed an interest in staying on, depending on how his current project turns out. You don't have to make a decision right now, but you have all proven that you can work together as a team, so I'm officially extending you an offer to work with us."

Suddenly the room was buzzing with chatter about the implications of the research and the possibility of working on the ship. Tony glanced at Carley, who was sullen and silent. He motioned with his head for her to join him on the aft deck, behind the salon.

"Are you still sure you want to abandon ship?" he asked.

Carley didn't answer immediately but instead leaned gently against Tony as they stared off the stern towards the entrance to Road Town Bay.

"Yes, I think I'm going to take Rob up on his offer of an office job. I'm not excited about going back to long days behind the bar babysitting a bunch of drunks but I'm not interested in spending my life on a boat, either, especially not as a cook! And what do you see yourself doing, Tony? They already have a much younger diver and space will be at a premium so you'll probably have to convert your private room back into a bunk bed setup. How comfortable is *that* going to be?"

Now it was Tony's turn to be silent for a while.

"Well, I guess I didn't think it through too well, but you're right—I won't be running the show anymore and I'll have to pull my own weight. Maybe I can be the security officer, if they need such a thing. And I could be Cesar's backup diver, I suppose."

"Or you could work in the office with me," smiled Carley. "I'd be happy to put in a good word for you."

***

Mueller held his position on one knee for several long minutes, afraid that he may have already alerted his prey. When he finally stood upright again, he slowly backed away from the canteen and into the corner of the lot. His trained eyes watched the back and side yards for any sign of motion but the area seemed to be secure. From this vantage point he couldn't see the front or other side of the house so he quietly made his way along the high chain link fence that ran down the east side of the property. When he reached the front corner of the house, he paused and listened for more than a minute but all he heard was a slight rustling of the leaves from the afternoon breeze.

The large front yard contained a number of trees and ornamental shrubs that would provide good cover for anyone trained in covert ops and Mueller had read Nicoletti's file enough times to know that he had served behind enemy lines in Southeast Asia back in the early 1970s. But Mueller had also been in the Special Forces some fifteen year later and he had rigged some surprises for just this occasion. He pulled the black-market handgun out of his waist band and crouched behind a bougainvillea bush. His task now was to coax Nicoletti out of hiding and towards one of his traps.

***

Through the open door of the salon, Tony heard a phone ring and turned to see Rob reach for his cell. Ushering Carley ahead of him, he moved them quickly back inside to hear the news from the research team back on Belize.

While Rob listened to whoever was on the other end of the call, he smiled, frowned, and showed signs of concern. The room was absolutely silent until he took the phone from his ear and pressed the end button.

"Well?" demanded an impatient Tony. "Why was I getting yelled at?"

Rob paused to collect his thoughts before speaking.

"You weren't getting yelled at, Tony, you were being summoned. The dolphins were saying, and I quote, *'Your assistance is urgently requested at 24 30 dot 74 north 77 43 dot 23 west. One of us will serve as your guide when you arrive. Bring your ship and crew.'* And then comes a part that doesn't make any sense and may actually be a bad translation. The message seems to end with a word we can't translate followed by the string of letters and numbers *'AF18674201'* and then it repeats."

Tony dropped onto a bench with a shocked look on his face.

"That's Frank Morton's Air Force serial number! But only a few people on Earth would know that today. He must have included it as his way of letting me know the message was really from him. And the other numbers..."

"They're coordinates of a very bizarre place called the Guardian Blue Hole on Andros Island, in the Bahamas. Are you familiar with it?"

"No, it's not a place we visited when the NWIDI team was on Andros. What do you mean bizarre?"

"It's the biggest blue hole ever discovered and large portions of it are still unexplored. Those portions that have been explored extend more than a half-mile horizontally and some of the caves are more than four hundred feet below the surface of the island. The entire system is filled with water, of course, so it seems like an unusual place for a meeting."

"Captain, how soon can we be ready to be under way?" asked Tony.

"We'll need to arrange for provisions and a considerable amount of fuel, and today is already more than half over. If we're lucky, I think we could have the vessel ready by late Saturday evening and depart at first light Sunday morning."

"Make it happen," stated Tony decisively. "The rest of you should wrap up whatever activities you have going on ashore and be back onboard by 2100 hours Saturday night. I want everyone to spend Saturday night aboard the Dolphin

Diver so we can leave as early as possible Sunday morning. Rob, will you and Ann be back by then?"

Rob nodded.

"I've already purchased non-refundable tickets so I guess Ann will be making the trip with us whether she wants to or not. Captain, how long will we be at sea?"

"Five days, more or less, assuming no problems and no stops."

"There will be *no* problems and *no* stops!" insisted Tony. "And Cesar, I have a feeling you and I are going to be using those rebreathers so I need to get in as many dives as possible between now and Sunday. And they need to be deep dives."

"I'm at your disposal," acknowledged Cesar. "How deep will you need to go?"

"If we're headed to the place I think we are, we will be visiting a site that's about three hundred fifty feet down. Can you get me up to speed for something like that in two and a half days?"

Before Cesar could answer, Rob interrupted.

"Tony could I talk to you outside for a second?"

On the rear deck, Rob spoke softly so the others, inside, couldn't hear.

"Tony, it's none of my business, of course, but don't you think it might be time to let them in on your NWIDI adventures and, in particular, the events that led up to Frank's disappearance? In a few days you're going to ask them to risk their necks and I think it would help if they knew why this means so much to you."

Tony thought for a minute and then nodded.

"Yes, you're probably right, but it has to be an abbreviated version that omits some of the details you are aware of. We're going to lose Carley, you know."

"Yes, I know. She told me about her feelings, but I made her promise to talk to you about it and after last night I thought maybe…"

"Yes, me, too, but her mind seems to be made up. I don't know if she'll make the trip to the Bahamas with us or not, but I think we should hire a cook here because the talent pool up there will be very slim compared to what we have available here in the Virgin Islands."

"I'll take care of it this afternoon because I have reservations on a 9:10 a.m. flight tomorrow morning. And Carley asked me to book her on the same flight, so I think that answers your question about the trip north."

"Well, so be it! I tried to change her mind, but she really doesn't like ship life so she needs to go home. Things may get a bit exciting when we get to the Bahamas and we'll need the full attention and commitment of everybody onboard. Let's go back inside and I'll brief the rest."

Nearly an hour later Tony gazed into several stunned faces after telling them about the old NWIDI team and their adventures, including the disappearance of Frank Morton and Miles Adderly at an unusual underwater site that was intentionally left off U.S. Naval charts. Rob knew a lot more of the story than Tony had divulged and Carley knew a few facts that Tony had not shared during his briefing but they both kept silent.

"So, we're off to see what's so important that a group of dolphins would bring me a message from my old friend, who apparently isn't dead after all. Is everybody up for this?"

"Maybe this would be a good time for me to let you all know that I won't be joining you," said Carley softly, as she rose. "I've discussed my plans with Tony and Rob, but I would like the rest of you to hear it directly from me because I want you to know that my decision to return to Belize tomorrow doesn't have anything to do with any of you. I just can't handle the claustrophobia I feel when I'm onboard and it doesn't sound like there's going to be much opportunity to be ashore in the foreseeable future. I hope to be working for the dolphin research group when I get home, and I look forward to seeing you all often, just not out here—not at sea."

There was a long, awkward silence after she sat back down before Rob finally spoke.

"With the research developments I mentioned earlier, there will be a very real need for someone who understands the Dolphin Diver and life aboard her. Carley will probably be our vessel coordinator and responsible for making sure the rest of you have what you need for long voyages at sea, so I suggest you be very nice to her until she leaves!"

Rob's comment broke the dark mood and soon everyone was laughing, including Carley.

"Okay, team, there's a lot of work to do, so let's get started," announced Tony. "If you have business ashore, please coordinate with Rob so he knows when you'll be away. I'm sorry to cut this port stay short, but I had no idea we would be pulling out this soon. Cesar, if you'll stay behind, the rest of you are free to go. And don't forget, everybody back onboard no later than 2100 hours Saturday."

The salon was empty in a minute as everyone began preparing for sea duty again. Tony retrieved a chart from the bridge and spread it out between himself and Cesar Acosta.

"So here's where I think we're going to end up," began Tony. "This chart, and other, newer ones, indicates a slowly sloping bottom along this coast of South Bimini Island. The truth is that there's a three hundred fifty foot vertical wall very close to the low water level on the beach. What I didn't mention to the rest of the crew is that this wall appears to be artificial. That is to say, it's man-made. Exactly why the Navy is hiding this fact from the world is unknown, but you can probably imagine a number of scenarios that would warrant such action—a secret military base, for example."

"You don't sound very convinced that it's a military installation," laughed Cesar.

"Not one built by *our* military, that's for sure!" replied Tony. "There's no reason for the others to know this, but I have a hunch you're going to see it first-hand pretty soon, so I'm going to share something with you that only a handful of other people know. I've seen a video of the bottom, taken by another young divemaster, that clearly shows a triangular structure protruding from the sand more than three hundred fifty feet below the surface. Around the perimeter of this structure are strange symbols that are unknown to archaeologists and anthropologists."

"The ruins of an unknown ancient civilization?" shouted Cesar.

"Not ruins and not ancient, but definitely something built by an unknown civilization," replied Tony. "I think we'll have a chance to answer that question in a few days."

***

Mueller had been holding his position behind the large, flowering bush for many minutes and he would have remained there for many more had he not heard a sound from the back yard. Assuming that Nicoletti had somehow circled around behind him, he streaked across the front yard and took cover behind a large tree on the far side of the lot. In a flash he was up the tree and perched on a large limb that provided a view of the entire front yard and most of the west side he had been unable to see until now.

Absolutely motionless and barely breathing, he scanned the property for any sign of his target but he saw no one below. The island of St. John was in full bloom this time of year and a multitude of aromas flooded his senses, but a hint of one smell didn't fit. Mueller sniffed several times to be sure, but there was no doubt. Somewhere nearby, someone was smoking a cigarette!

***

By mid-afternoon, Tony and Cesar were just off Boughers Point, less than a mile from the harbor, but far enough out into open water to avoid the pollution that's unavoidable in a busy port. Their first dive had been a quick check out trip down to ninety feet. The visibility in this area wasn't the greatest, but as long as they stayed within twenty feet of each other they could communicate with hand signals and Cesar could observe Tony's management of the rebreather.

"Okay, you're doing fine," commented Cesar, as they clung to the rope around the perimeter of the Zodiac. "This time, let's try two hundred feet. That will probably be a new milestone for you, right?"

"You bet it will! I may have accidently made it down to one-fifty a time or two, but that's really pushing it with regular scuba gear."

"It is, but you have to forget all those warnings that were drilled into you during your open-circuit scuba training. These closed-circuit rebreathers will make three hundred seem like one hundred. Just don't let your depth gauge panic you into doing something stupid. The rebreather's computer display will tell you everything you need to know and it will let you know if something's wrong. Respect it and your dive will be fine.

"Also, remember your decompression stops. At depths above one-fifty you can get away with a five-minute stop at fifteen feet, but below that you're playing by a whole different set of rules. On our way back up we're going to stop at one-sixty-five and then again every fifteen feet until we reach the surface. We'll do two minutes each at the first four stops, five minutes each at the next three and ten minutes each at the next three and, finally we'll do a fifteen minute stop at the fifteen-foot level. That means that it's going to take us almost seventy minutes just to get back to the surface—longer than most single-tank dives last using conventional scuba."

"Wait a minute, Cesar! I need to write this down because I'll never remember all those numbers," interrupted Tony.

"Your rebreather's computer will keep track of all that for you, and I will also provide the information on an underwater slate in case of a computer failure. But you don't need to memorize it because it all changes as we go deeper. There's another set of numbers for a three-hundred-foot dive and if we really end up below three-fifty, we'll use yet another set of numbers. The stops are always at every fifteen feet, but the time at each stop increases as your maximum depth increases. Got it?"

"Oh yeah, I've got it alright!" replied Tony. "I don't remember Frank mentioning anything about this when he was getting checked out."

"Yes, but his first deep dive was also his last, wasn't it?" replied a frustrated Cesar.

***

Mueller very carefully climbed up into the big white cedar tree so he could see over the high wooden fence that secured the front of the property. It only took a minute for his trained eyes to spot the two individuals on the other side of the road. They were partially blocked by some brush so he couldn't see their faces but he could tell that they were wearing uniforms of some kind and it was obvious they were watching the property. He knew the place was posted while the fire was being investigated, but why would the police hide in the bushes? Why not relax in the relative comfort of a squad car or jeep or whatever they used on this chunk of rock called St. John?

His momentary focus on the stake-out team had distracted him from his primary mission and he suddenly realized that he had his back to the house and Tony Nicoletti. Mueller shifted to a position that would allow him to keep his eyes on both sides of the fence and waited. Periodically a car would pass by on the road below and that always got the attention of his new neighbors in the woods, but they never showed themselves and there was no sign of life at all near the house. He hadn't been prepared for an extended stay in a tree and he was getting very thirsty. Soon he would have to give up his vantage point and return to the house. If Nicoletti wouldn't bring the fight to him, he would just have to take it to Nicoletti.

***

"I'm as wrinkled as a prune!" laughed Tony as he brushed his hair back and shook the water out of his face.

"Well, we've spent more than three hours in the water today," replied Cesar. "Are you chilled?"

Tony shook his head and laughed.

"Not too bad, but I could sure use some food! On a *real* dive boat you at least get a piece of fruit between dives!"

"It's kind of hard to eat underwater, my friend, and if we dive to three-hundred-fifty feet we could be down there for three hours or more. This was a stamina check to see how you would do."

Cesar opened his dry bag and pulled out two thick roast beef sandwiches.

"Fortunately, your thoughtful divemaster came prepared for today's adventure. Would you like a beer to wash this down with?"

The noise of the Zodiac's engine made talking difficult, so Tony ate and pondered his next move as Cesar piloted the craft back to the Dolphin Diver. Tony kept expecting to wake up from some strange dream and find that he was still being held captive under the Cancun airport. His no-nonsense mind couldn't accept that Frank was still alive and that he had found a way to send him a message by dolphin. Too many of today's events seemed contrived and unbelievable. It was all unreal—and unacceptable. And yet, here he was, wolfing down a sandwich after surviving a dive to two-hundred thirty-seven feet. He had no idea what awaited him in the Bahamas, but he was beginning to feel like the Tony Nicoletti that—thirty years earlier—had parachuted into the jungles of Thailand, Laos and Cambodia not knowing what awaited him on the ground. And he liked the feeling—he liked it very much!

Chapter 20

Rob was waiting at the rear dive platform when Cesar touched the nose of the Zodiac against the Dolphin Diver. He caught the line Tony had thrown and held the small inflatable craft steady as the two divers stepped onto the larger boat.

"So, how did he do?" Rob asked Cesar.

"He survived a dive to two-hundred thirty-seven feet, that's how he did," shouted Tony before Cesar could reply. "These things are amazing, to say the least. Tomorrow we do the big three-hundred, right Cesar?"

"If you say so, boss, but we'll need the Dolphin Diver for support on that one. And in the afternoon we'll practice bail-outs so you'll know what to do if you run into equipment problems down there."

"We'll need to coordinate with the captain on that because they will want to start loading supplies for the trip pretty soon. Why can't we take the Zodiac?"

"We need to hang a number of safety tanks over the side—some at a hundred feet, and some at two hundred feet—and that much weight would pull this little guy to the bottom!"

"Okay, then let me find out what tomorrow's schedule is like before we plan anything. The big dive may have to wait until we get to the Bahamas. Rob, you'll be taking off early, right?"

"Yes, our plane leaves at 9:10 a.m. so we need to be on that first ferry at 7:00 a.m. Are you going over to the airport to see us off?"

"No, I don't think should risk it. But I'll ride over to the ferry dock with you and say my good-byes there."

"Aren't you only going to be gone one night?" asked a confused Cesar.

"Yes, but Carley is going with me as far as Miami and she won't be returning," frowned Rob. "Tonight will be her last night aboard ship."

"Wow, I forgot about that! We need to have a party for her!" shouted Cesar. "What do you say, guys? Let me get my gear stowed and then I'll run into town and pick up some party fixings. I know you two both have plenty to do, so let me handle this, okay?"

Tony and Rob looked at each other and smiled.

"Go for it!" they replied in unison.

Tony helped Cesar rinse and store the rebreathers and their personal dive gear before showering and changing into shorts and a t-shirt. After resting for a few minutes, he made his way up and forward to Rob's stateroom. When he knocked on the door, he heard Rob yell, "It's open!"

As he pushed the door open he realized that Rob was on the radio with Anne so he just waved and quietly took a seat.

"Anne, Tony just arrived—could you please repeat what you just said, over."

"Hello, Tony, I hear you had an exciting day. I was just telling Rob that our team on Turneffe is really scratching their heads over this break-through they made. After they recovered from their initial excitement, they retraced their steps to better understand how it happened but they are still stumped. The component that was incorrectly substituted had been placed in a small parts bin that has always been used for the correct item. The container was even labeled as the one containing the correct item, but instead it was full of the substitute. What's even stranger is that the substitute component isn't even an item they normally stock! Over."

Tony scooted up to Rob's desk and accepted the microphone from him.

"Are you suggesting that someone made an intentional substitution, knowing that doing so would advance your research by months? Over."

"I know it sounds crazy, guys, but that's the current theory. The project director has questioned everyone who has access to the supply room and they all swear that they don't know anything about it. Work is pressing on at an increased pace, now that they're finally getting results, but this is still a big mystery. Over."

"Anne, has anybody checked to see when the bin was last refilled?" asked Rob. "Sorry, over."

"As you know, dear, many of the items in that storeroom are very expensive, so detailed usage records are kept to satisfy the board of directors. The item that should have been used was last issued about a week ago and the records show that the quantity on hand went to zero. Other records show that a replenishment order was already in the pipeline and that it arrived three days ago—the same morning that the lucky technician who made the discovery needed one of the components to complete a new translation device. Over."

Tony looked at Rob and raised his eyebrows.

"Is this for real?" he asked with a puzzled look on his face.

When neither man responded by radio, Anne continued.

"Tony, I have a special message for you from Belize. Emma has specifically asked about you and she wants you to know that she didn't mean to scare you. Over."

Tony looked at Rob and shrugged.

"Emma?" he asked, without keying the microphone.

"The dolphin that scared you the night I showed you the lab," laughed Rob. "You certainly do have a way with the ladies, my friend!"

This time Tony did key the mic.

"Anne, please tell Emma that I don't get mad, I get even! Over."

"10-4, Tony! I'll pass the word along. Listen guys, the only other thing I have is that there's still no news on the missing pilot, Fitz. His wife is a wreck, of course, but she's keeping pressure on the military to continue their search. Unfortunately, I think they've pretty much decided that the plane went down. The FAA has turned up an unidentified radar trace that fits the time of departure window and the object was flying at an unusually low altitude just west of

Homestead, Florida. It was headed due south, right out over the southern glades area. If it went down out in the swamps, it would have sunk and it might never be spotted again. I'm sorry. Over"

Tony hung his head and sighed before responding.

"Thanks, Anne. Listen, I know we've been fanatics about keeping our location secret, but once you and Rob leave Miami this radio will be useless so I'd like you to give Susan Fitzgerald Rob's new satellite phone number and ask her to call him if anything changes. Just don't mention where we are, or that I'm here at all, in case your calls are being monitored. Over."

"I'll get in touch with her tonight, Tony. Again, I'm terribly sorry about your friend. Good bye, guys. Over."

Tony stood and left the room so Rob and his wife could say their good-byes privately. When he entered the salon, he was surprised to see Carley in the galley.

"See you just can't get enough of this place! Less than twenty four hours to go and you're in here cooking."

"I'm just making myself a snack," she replied softly. "Would you like anything?"

"Yes, I'd like you to change your mind about leaving the ship. Is there any chance of that?"

"No, I'm afraid not. What were you and Rob up to?"

"He's on the radio with Anne and she was giving me an update on Fitz, the NWIDI pilot that went missing a couple of days ago. He still hasn't been found, by the way."

"Sorry. Are you sure you don't want a sandwich or something while I have all the fixings out?"

"Tell you what. I'll make my own sandwich if you'll have a beer with me while I eat it. Is that a deal?"

"Deal," replied Carley with a hint of a smile. "Where did Cesar go racing off to? I don't think I've ever seen him move that fast."

"I don't know," lied Tony. "Are you all packed?"

"Yes, except for a few last minute things. "

"How about an afternoon stroll around downtown and a glass of wine somewhere? We'll come back early because you have to be on a 7:00 a.m. ferry in the morning."

Carley thought about it for a minute, considered declining and finally accepted.

"Great!" smiled Tony. "Let me just tell Rob something I forgot about earlier and I'll be right back."

* * *

Mueller carefully made his way down the tree and landed softly in the grass below it. Whatever the two local cops were up to across the street would have to wait until later—his primary concern was eliminating Tony Nicoletti so he could get off this island and return to Washington, D.C.

Like the front yard, the west side of the house was heavily wooded, with many large, flowering bushes but from his earlier vantage point in the tree he had seen no signs of activity. If Nicoletti were still here, he must have slipped back into the house. Mueller made his way along the side of the house and crouched below the bedroom window he had originally used to gain entry. He listened for several minutes but heard nothing so he made his way around to the back door. It was still standing wide open, just the way he had left it when he had entered the back yard to examine the mysterious canteen. He removed the pistol from his waistband and entered the house ready for anything.

After a thorough search of the interior, Mueller was beginning to doubt his own instincts. Except for the canteen, he had seen no evidence of Nicoletti inside or outside the house. It was like the man had never been there and yet the canteen was proof positive that he had been on the property earlier in the day!

Mueller retreated to the bedroom and flopped onto the bed to ponder the situation. If Nicoletti weren't still on the property, what had made him leave before Mueller could grab him? Would he be back or had he been frightened off for good? The fact that he had dropped a canteen seemed to suggest that he left in a hurry, unless…

"Bait!" shouted Mueller out loud. "He wants me to stay here!"

Angry at himself for being duped, he quickly reassembled his backpack, gave the house a quick once-over and climbed the rope to the cliff overlooking the house. After untying his rope he cut a small branch off an evergreen and used it to erase any evidence that he had been there. He made his way down the hill to the beach and began the long hike back to Cruz Bay and the main business district of St. John, where he was now positive he would find—and dispose of— Tony Nicoletti.

***

Road Town was spread out along the edge of a half-mile wide bay and Tony and Carley had taken a cab from the commercial docks, on the east side, around to the shopping area on the west side.

As they exited the cab, Carley stopped and looked around.

"Maybe this wasn't such a good idea. I think this is the spot where Rob and I hid from the car that chased us yesterday."

Tony turned to question the driver but the cab sped off before he could say anything. He looked back at Carley and shrugged.

"Well, I guess we'll just have to make the best of it. Which, way, kid?"

They walked the length of several streets lined with small shops of all kinds but Carley didn't seem to be interested in any of them.

"No souvenirs to take back to Belize?" Tony finally asked.

Carley shook her head and looked away.

"Okay, maybe it's time for that glass of wine. We're stopping at the next restaurant we come to."

When they were seated and had placed their order, Tony reached across the table and took Carley's hands.

"Are you sure I can't change your mind about staying?"

Carley bit her lip and shook her head.

"No, Tony, my mind is made up. I feel like I'm lost in the jungle, going around and around in circles with no purpose. I just want to get home and back to familiar surroundings."

"But isn't that how you felt when I first met you? When you were back in Belize? Didn't you once tell me that you were just treading water and going nowhere in your life?"

Carley looked up at Tony and stared deep into his eyes for a moment.

"Yes, I did say that. And maybe that's my problem out here, too. I thought the 'excitement' of the voyage would change things, but perhaps the problem is inside, not outside. I really envy you, you know it? You have such a strong sense of purpose. Even when we were in route and you were struggling with a plan of action, you at least knew you were going to do *something*. You were driven, and I've just been along for the ride."

"So you need to find your own purpose, Carley, and I'm not sure going to work for the dolphin research group is the right move. What energizes you? What gets your motor running?"

"To tell you the truth, I haven't felt deeply about anything since I walked out of the jungles of Guatemala years ago. The things I saw—the horror and injustices—left me dead inside."

Tony squeezed her hands.

"I'm sorry, and I know how you feel. These days the military calls it post-traumatic stress disorder, or PTSD, and it's a recognized disability but back in my day you were just supposed to 'man up' and deal with it. Maybe you should see someone when you get home and try to work through it."

"I doubt if there's a doctor anywhere in Belize capable of treating it, if that's even what's wrong with me. And even if there were, there's no real cure. You can't un-see the horrors."

R.J. Archer

"True, Carley, but there are medications that can help control it and make your life more normal. Promise me you'll get some help, even if it means leaving Belize to do it. I had a good friend in the Army that suffered with PTSD for years after we came back from Southeast Asia before he finally blew his brains out with a shotgun."

Carley was staring off into the distance and didn't hear Tony's last comment.

"Carley! Are you alright?"

She nodded her head slightly but did not make eye contact.

"Don't look around," she finally said softly, "but I think the guy in the corner booth is following us. And I think it might be the same guy that chased the taxi yesterday."

"Are you sure?" asked Tony. "I haven't noticed anybody tailing us, and I'm trained in this kind of thing."

"Maybe, but I have a feeling he's watching us. Snapping her head around to face Tony, she whispered, "He's looking right at me!"

"It's not unusual for a guy to look at a pretty girl," laughed Tony. "I doubt if we can have him arrested for that."

"Okay, listen to me. I'm going to describe him in detail so you know who I'm talking about and then let's move down the street to another place. If he doesn't follow us, then you can laugh at me."

Carley rattled off a description and chugged the last of her wine. Tony drained his beer and the two slid out of the booth, making a conscious effort not to look in the man's direction. They casually wandered down the street in the direction they had been traveling and soon came to another tavern decorated like a traditional English pub.

"All the way to the back," insisted Tony and they entered the dark interior and stopped while their eyes adjusted.

They took the booth in the far corner and Tony sat facing the door. A barmaid had followed them to the booth and before she had finished taking their order, the man Carley had spotted appeared in the doorway. After a minute to adjust to the darkness and scan the room, he took a seat at a small table in the shadows in the opposite corner from their table.

"You're absolutely right," said Tony. He had his head facing Carley, but his eyes were cranked all the way to the right as he watched the other man. "I don't know how I missed it, but that guy is definitely following us and he's good. I guess the next question is who is he following—you or me?"

"Why would anybody be following me?"

"Well, he wasn't following *me* yesterday on St. John, and I doubt if Rob has any enemies in the Virgin Islands so the logical choice seems to be you, my dear. What heinous crimes are you wanted for that you forgot to tell us about?"

"Tony, that's not funny! I'm not wanted for…"

"I know, but I couldn't help yanking your chain. However, there is some truth to the fact that you might be the face he recognizes because I'm pretty sure I've never seen him before. Did you notice anything strange yesterday?"

"Actually, there were several strange things about yesterday. First there was Henry, who we picked up courtesy of your buddy Jack King. He was with us all day, and very helpful, I might add, until the very end of the day when he neglected to tell us where the inter-island shuttle boarded. We almost missed it because of that. Then there was our chance encounter with Erik Mueller. He actually talked to Rob in the central plaza, but I was out of sight at the time. And, of course, there was the exciting taxi ride that you already know about. Oh! And there was this creepy guy on the boat coming home that made several remarks from behind his newspaper but never revealed his face."

"Whoa, back up the bus! Tell me more about this guy Jack set you up with."

"Well, like I said, he was with us every minute of the day and by afternoon he knew a lot about Mueller. We never mentioned you by name but Rob mentioned that we had a 'friend' that had lived in the house up on the hill and that Mueller was after him."

Tony pulled his cell phone out of his pocket and held up his index finger to interrupt Carley as he dialed.

"Jack! Hey, it's Tony Nicoletti here. Yes, I know, she's a great looking gal. Jack what exactly are you involved in?"

For the next ten minutes Tony grilled Jack King about his recent activities, about his hired hand, Henry, and about who might have an interest in Tony and his friends other than Erick Mueller. When he finally ended the call, he shook his head.

"He's lying! He claims to know nothing but he's lying. However, I don't think he's in cahoots with Edwards and his bunch, either."

"What did he say about Henry?" asked Carley.

"Nothing! He claims Henry is just a trusted friend, but there's more to it than that. I could sense it in his voice. Did this Henry ever say how he knows Jack? Was he a bartender, maybe?"

Carley thought for a minute before replying.

"No, I don't think he ever said. King told us Henry owed him a favor, but that's all. And Henry was driving a fairly new Jeep, which must be hard to come by on St. Thomas, but he never said what he did for a living."

"What about a last name that we could trace?"

Carley shook her head.

"No, he never offered and I guess we never asked. We didn't suspect anything at the time and Henry was very courteous and helpful all day."

"Yes, you've mentioned that. Jack King isn't leveling with me, and I'd bet on it, but I don't know why."

Tony reached for his phone again and dialed Rob.

"Howdy, partner," he greeted Rob. "We've gotten ourselves into a bit of a pickle and we could use some help. Would you round up the posse and head this way as soon as possible?"

Tony picked up his beer and slid the coaster over to the edge of the table so he could read it.

"Leave the captain behind to mind the ship and call me back when you get close to the Royal Crown Pub on the other side of the bay."

While they waited for Rob and the crew of the Dolphin Diver, Tony explained his plan to Carley.

"When the troops arrive, I'm going to have them wait outside the door. You and I will casually get up and make our exit and then they will spill in here and stage a fight right in the doorway. By the time this guy gets out onto the street, we will be long gone in the cab Rob will leave waiting for us out front."

"What if he has friends outside? Won't they see us drive off and follow us back to the ship?"

"Perhaps, but that's a chance we'll have to take. And we can defend ourselves on the ship. That's not so easy out here in public."

Tony's cell phone rang and he answered it. After explaining his plan to Rob, he flagged down the waitress and handed her a fifty dollar bill to cover their five dollar tab. He and Carley then slipped out of the booth and made a bee line straight for the door. Caught off guard, the other man tried to get the attention of the same waitress, but she completely ignored him, as Tony had requested. They were out the door in a flash and Rob, Rigo and Nickolas Banks squeezed in right behind them pretending to be in an argument. As Tony pulled the taxi door shut, he could hear their voices beginning to escalate.

When Tony and Carley reached the top of the gang plank, the captain was waiting with his sawed-off shotgun cradled in his arms.

"I don't think we're going to need that," smiled Tony. "But thanks for the thought!"

"And the lads?" asked the captain. "What have you done with the lads?"

"Ah, well, they're busy providing some much-needed cover so we could make our getaway, Captain. They should be along very shortly."

Carley slid open the salon door and stepped inside.

"What is all this!" she yelled.

The salon was decorated with crepe paper streamers and the ceiling was covered with balloons. A keg of beer was chilling in the galley sink and a large cake sat on the serving counter. The tables were covered with paper table clothes and set with brightly colored plastic plates, cups and utensils. In the galley, Cesar Acosta was busy preparing a fresh veggie platter and sporting a cone-shaped birthday hat.

Carley spun and glared at Tony but he raised his hands in mock surrender.

"It wasn't me! This was all Cesar's idea and all his doing!"

"Is this why you suggested going into town?" she demanded. "And all that fuss about being followed—was that all part of this, too?"

"Okay, I'll admit that I knew Cesar was planning something, but I had no idea what. I figured going ashore would be a good diversion, but this has nothing to do with that guy in the bar. He really was following us, I swear."

While Tony was still pleading his defense, Rob, Rigo and Nickolas scampered up the gang plank and joined the group.

"Did you lose him?" asked Tony, turning his back on Carley and her protest.

"Yes, I think so," smiled Rob. "The driver of our cab put out the word not to pick him up, so he's probably still standing on the sidewalk in front of the restaurant."

"Did you recognize him from yesterday?"

"Not his face, but I'm pretty sure I've heard that voice before."

"What was that?" asked Carley, joining the conversation. "Did you say you recognized his voice?"

Rob nodded.

"He was desperately trying to get the waitress' attention so he could pay his tab and I'm pretty sure I heard that voice on the boat with us yesterday. I think it was the voice behind the newspaper."

Chapter 21

Tony wanted to question Rob further about the strange man on the inter-island ferry boat but the rest of the crew was anxious to get the party started, so he decided to let it slide and talk to Rob in private on the way to the ferry in the morning.

Cesar had done a remarkable job of throwing together a party in just a few hours. In addition to the decorations and the large, decorated cake, he had procured two large platters of fresh fruit to accompany the vegetable platter he had prepared himself. A boom box was playing Caribbean music in the background and Carley was happier than Tony had seen her since the day she was invited to join the crew of the Dolphin Diver.

About an hour into the celebration Tony was standing near the dockside entrance of the salon when he spotted a pizza truck pulling up next to the ship. He hiked down the gang plank and met the driver as he was trying to convince the security guard that he had a delivery for the Dolphin Diver.

Tony paid the driver and turned to the guard. He considered inviting him to join the crew but instead he just lifted the lid of the top box and nodded.

"I won't suggest you abandon your post, but I do insist you have a piece of pizza."

Tony lugged the four, extra-large pies back up the gang plank and when Cesar saw him enter the salon with the boxes, he came to meet him.

"Hey, I was going to get that," he protested.

"Nothing doing! In fact, I want to reimburse you for all this. You shouldn't be covering the expenses for a crew party."

Cesar leaned closer to Tony and whispered, "You pay us way too much, you know. The duty is easy, the company is good and the salary is about twice what it should be. This one's on me."

Tony smiled and handed Cesar the stack of pizza boxes.

"As you wish, but the pizzas are on *me*."

There was more than enough food to go around and Rob even managed to coax Captain Braydon off the bridge long enough to have a slice of pizza and a beer.

By 9:00 p.m. everyone was stuffed and some had consumed more than enough alcohol but no one wanted to be the first to leave Carley's good-bye party. Sensing what was happening, Rob clanged a knife against the side of a glass to get everyone's attention. When the room was quiet, he began.

"As you all know, tonight is Carley's last night as member of our crew and I, for one, would like to tell her that we are going to miss her good company and her good cooking! A toast to Carley Quinn and a safe trip back to Belize!"

Everyone raised their glasses in Carley's honor and gave her three loud cheers. By the end of the final salute, her eyes were misty and so were a few other eyes in the room.

"Speech!" yelled Tony from across the room. Speech!"

"Wow, this has been a really great evening, you guys," she smiled. "I feel like we've all become really good friends during the past month and I can't tell you how much I appreciate you allowing me to be a part of the crew. All of you have been so kind I just…"

She choked up so Tony started a round of applause to let her off the hook. He crossed the room, put his arm around her shoulder and addressed the others.

"Most of you don't know my real back story, and that's probably for the best, but Carley took me in off the street—literally—and gave me a place to stay with no questions asked and no strings attached. I had been on the run for a while and by the time I found my way to the Belize City waterfront I was out of options. If she hadn't found me, I don't know what I would have done.

"Fortunately, she gave me food and shelter and introduced me to Rob, who helped me reclaim my life. I owe them both a lot, but it all began with Carley's unselfish act of kindness to a complete stranger. We're all going to miss you, lady, and none more than me."

By this time Carley was openly sobbing so Tony ushered her out onto the rear deck for some air. Inside, the rest of the crew began to disband and head for their rooms. When Tony and Carley turned back around, the salon was completely empty.

"This was really nice," she said, trying to smile. "You know, this is the first party anyone has thrown for me in a long, long time. Thank you, Tony."

"I wish I could take the credit, but this was all Cesar's doing. His idea, his planning and he even insisted on paying for it out of his own pocket, although he would not want you to know that. They're going to miss you, kid."

"And what about you, Tony?"

"Yes, like I said in there, I'm going to miss you the most. Rob has become a good friend and he's a fantastic businessman, but you're the kind of friend I can confide in—tell things to that I wouldn't tell anyone else. I'm going to miss that. Are you sure I can't talk you into coming along as far as the Bahamas?"

"Yes, I'm sure. I've made up my mind, I've purchased the tickets and the crew has thrown me a farewell party. I couldn't change my mind now, even if I wanted to!"

Carley laughed at her own comment and then looked up at Tony.

"But let's go downstairs and make sure, okay?"

***

Erick Mueller had remained in the shadows near the ferry dock all afternoon visually scanning the face of every person who passed through the central plaza. It was now 7:00 p.m. and there was still no sign of Tony Nicoletti. As impossible as it seemed, Mueller was now beginning to doubt his own theory that Nicoletti would, sooner or later, return to the house he had shared with Jill Harris.

As he contemplated his next move, two local constables watched him from across the plaza.

"Are you sure that's him?" asked the first.

"Positive," replied the second. "We'd better call this in."

Using a portable radio clipped to his belt, he contacted the local station and reported Mueller's position.

There was a long pause while the dispatcher contacted the team on stakeout at the house. When the dispatcher returned, his voice sounded confused.

"Our team on the hill insists that he has not entered the property. We don't know where he's been for the last two days, but without an eye witness we can't arrest him for entering the crime scene. Continue to monitor him and keep us posted."

"Actually, he's getting on the ferry right now," reported the second man. "Shall we tag along?"

"No, I'll alert the St. Thomas division. He's their problem now."

Knowing that he wouldn't be on the tiny island of St. John forever, Mueller had wisely purchased a round trip ticket when he had come over on Tuesday, so he was able to avoid being out in the open at the tiny ticket booth. He simply waited for a group of people to pass near his location and then he fell into step with them as they boarded the ferry. He smiled as he took a seat, sure that no one on St. John would know he had ever been there.

When he arrived at his hotel, he stopped at the front desk to check for any messages, but there weren't any so he went to his room and ordered dinner from room service. He hadn't eaten since morning and he was starved. While he waited for the meal to arrive, he started a list of things to do in the morning. At the top of the list, in capital letters, he wrote, "CALL EDWARDS!" It wasn't a call he looked forward to, but he was out of ideas and the local U.S. Customs office was still holding his passport, so he was going to need more help from his boss.

***

In spite of the previous night's party, every single member of the crew was up early to see Rob and Carley off. Rob would be back in less than thirty-six hours, but they wouldn't see Carley again until the Dolphin Diver returned to its home port in Belize City—and no one knew when that would be.

Carrying Carley's overstuffed duffle bag and another bag she had picked up in Road Town, Tony followed the two travelers down the gang plank and out to the waiting taxi. When Tony piled into the back seat with Carley, she looked surprised.

"I'm only going as far as the ferry dock, because of, well, you know," he frowned, referring to his fake documents.

"Well, I appreciate the gesture," smiled Carley. "For a minute there, I thought you had changed your mind about continuing the voyage!"

"I have to do this, Carley, but afterwards, well, we'll see."

Turning his attention momentarily to Rob he asked about the mysterious "voice behind the newspaper" he and Carley had heard on the boat back from St. John.

"Yes, I'm pretty sure it was the same person," explained Rob. "That would mean that we probably picked up a tail on St. John but I sure didn't see anything suspicious."

"Other than this Henry guy you mentioned," added Tony. "And I'll get to the bottom of that before you return from Miami. But if he was already with you, why waste the resources to put a man on the boat? After all, where else could you have been going except here?"

"And I still don't believe that Henry is working for the other side," said Carley. "He just didn't strike me as the type of guy who would be sneaking around behind peoples' backs. Now your friend Jack King, on the other hand, looks like one slippery character."

"That's exactly what I'm going to get to the bottom of," replied Tony. "He's always been a little strange, but yesterday he was just plain lying to me."

The taxi rolled to a stop and Rob glanced at his watch.

"We only have about five minutes, so we should get Carley's stuff loaded."

Tony asked the driver to wait and carried the duffle bag to the boat. Rob took her second suitcase and his own carry-on, leaving Carley with just her small purse and backpack.

After a long hug, Carley broke away and kissed Tony on the cheek.

"See you soon, right?"

"I promise kiddo. Just as soon as possible."

Rob and Carley climbed aboard with the other passengers and Tony stood on the small pier until the boat was out of sight.

Slowly, he climbed back into the taxi and nodded to the driver.

"Back to my ship, please, but can you stop at a liquor store on the way?"

Once he was back on the Dolphin Diver, Tony sought out Cesar. He found him on the dive platform inspecting and filling tanks in preparation for Sunday's departure.

"I know I said I wanted to do that last dive today, but I'm not feeling much like it right now and I don't think I'd be able to concentrate. How about if we put it off until we get to the Bahamas?"

"It's your call, boss. If you aren't able to focus one hundred percent, you definitely shouldn't be making this dive. Maybe if you're feeling better later we can take the Zodic out again and go through some emergency procedures in shallow water. We could even do that tomorrow, if you like."

"Okay, we'll see how it goes. I have some things to take care of this afternoon and I might have to make a quick trip over to St. Thomas tomorrow, but we'll see."

From the dive platform, Tony made his way forward to the bridge.

"Tony!" greeted the surprised Captain. "I didn't expect to see you back here for hours."

"Well, I only went as far as the Road Town pier. I decided not to push my luck with U.S. Customs this close to our departure."

"I see," replied the Captain. "I must admit, I got used to having her around. I still don't believe it's any way to run a ship, but I did get used to her."

"I knew you would! And speaking of Carley, do we have a replacement for her yet?"

"Yes, at Rob's request I made some arrangements yesterday. We'll be taking on a local sailor who has experience as both a cook and an engineer so we'll have some backup for young Rigo. He's due to come aboard tomorrow morning so you and Rob can meet him before we actually sign him on."

"Perfect! I'm going to check Carley's room in a few minutes to make sure she didn't leave anything behind and then I guess we have a single room available. I'll let you figure out how to do room assignments, as long as you don't kick me out of my single!"

"No worries, Tony. So tell me what to expect when we get to the Bahamas. Will we be proceeding directly to the dive site or will we be stopping at Andros Island first?"

"I believe the message said I was to attend a meeting at someplace called the Guardian Blue Hole and I believe that's on Andros Island, so I guess we'll be stopping along the way. However, it may be a quick stop. This Guardian Blue Hole appears to be very close to the coastline, so maybe I'll just run in with the Zodiac, attend my meeting and then we can motor on to South Bimini."

"We'll need to check in with the Bahamian immigration authorities somewhere, and if you're going ashore at the blue hole, we should notify the officials on Andros since that will be our first landfall."

"That works for me, but it could all change before we get there. I'm going to go down and check out that room and then I have some paperwork to take care of. I'll be in my room if you need me."

Tony sat on the edge of what had been Carley's bed and stared at the empty closet on the opposite wall. He had checked the room thoroughly and found nothing. She had left the room spotless, as if she'd never been there and he realized that he missed her already. He had tried to change her mind about leaving, but she was determined and nothing he had said seemed to make any difference, even after they had spent the last two nights together.

The ring of his cell phone startled him back to the present.

"Tony, this is Anne. I apologize for calling this number, but Rob won't be arriving for another two hours and I thought you'd want to know about this as soon as possible. Your Learjet pilot is alive and well."

"What?" replied Tony. "That's great news, Anne. I assume you heard from Susan, then?"

"Yes, she just called. Fitz called her from the plane as he was making his approach into the Key West Naval Air Station. He figured the military would be all over him once he landed and he wanted to make sure Susan knew he was back."

"Back from where? Did he say where he and the plane had been?"

"He told her he had been held in Cuba but that's all the time he had to explain because he was getting close to his final approach."

"That's really, really good news, Anne, and thank you for letting me know. What a relief!"

"I'll try to get more information as soon as Susan talks to him again. And I'll have Rob call you as soon as his flight gets in."

Tony took one more look round Carley's room and then crossed the hall to his own room. The news about Fitz' safe return temporarily lifted his spirits and he smiled as he sat down at his small desk and fired up his laptop to do a little research.

Fitz had told Susan he had been "held in Cuba" so that's where Tony started. He doubted that there were many airports in Cuba, capable of accommodating a Learjet because of its requirement for a six thousand foot long, paved runway. He was surprised to learn that, according to the CIA's online *World Factbook*, Cuba had 136 airstrips and twenty-three of them could easily accept the NWIDI Learjet. As he scanned the list on his screen, he quickly eliminated Guantanamo Bay Naval Air Station and Havana's Jose Marti International as places kidnappers probably would stay away from, but that still left twenty-one possibilities!

With the short list still open on his desktop, he opened Google Earth to look for some of the names he was unfamiliar with. His eyes dropped to the very bottom of the list— Varadero—and he punched in the coordinates from the list. He was surprised to see that this airport was only about sixty miles east of Havana and had an eleven thousand foot paved runway that was one hundred forty-eight feet wide! Additional research revealed that Varadero was the second largest and second busiest airport in Cuba and it apparently existed to serve a nearby resort area which catered to European travelers.

Tony leaned back in his chair and clasped his hands behind his neck. Here was an airport capable of handling Boeing 747 Jumbo jets and yet it only had one terminal, a small cafeteria and 3 small souvenir shops. He had no reason to believe this was where Fitz had been held, but this place definitely warranted further investigation!

***

Erick Mueller had slept like a baby. After being on a high state of mental alert for nearly forty eight straight hours, he had finally been able to relax in the hotel bed and he was surprised when he awoke and saw that it was already 8:30 a.m. After a long shower, he called room service to order breakfast.

"I'm sorry, sir, but I can't charge anything to your room at this time. Will this be cash?"

"What?" demanded Mueller. "Why can't you charge to my room?"

"I'm not given that type of information, sir. All I know is that the computer won't accept any charges. However,

I'm sure the front desk can explain the situation to you. Would you like me to transfer you?"

"No, I'll go down and talk to them personally, because there must be some mistake."

"Very well, sir. And what about breakfast?"

"I'll stop at the restaurant after I straighten out your front desk. Cancel this order."

Fuming at the inconvenience, Mueller slammed the phone down and got dressed. Ten minutes later he was at the front desk demanding to know what was wrong with his account.

The clerk pulled his file out of a metal container behind the counter and examined it briefly.

"Let me get the manager, Mr. Mueller. He can explain this better than I can."

A minute later a middle-aged man dressed in a suit appeared and approached the counter.

"Mr. Mueller, my name is Clarence Watson and I'm the hotel's General Manager. Sir, I'm terribly sorry, but we tried to run your card this morning to settle the week's charges and it was declined. I'm afraid we'll need to get another card from you or ask you to settle your bill in cash. And we'll need another card in order to extend your stay beyond today."

"That's impossible! The card I used to check in is a U.S. Government credit card and it has a *very* high credit limit."

"The problem isn't the limit, Mr. Mueller. The account has been suspended. In fact if we had the card in our possession, we would be obliged to destroy it rather than returning it to you. I'm sorry, sir, but those are our instructions."

"That can't be right!" shouted Mueller. "I travel all over the world and this has never happened before."

"I understand, and I'm truly sorry for the inconvenience. Perhaps there's a mistake at the bank that issued the card. I suggest you call them and see if you can get the situation resolved, but in the mean time, I need to know how you would like to settle your account. Including last night's room service, your current balance is seven hundred five dollars and thirty-nine cents."

Mueller pulled his personal Mastercard out of his wallet and slapped it down on the counter.

"I'm going to get to the bottom of this very soon, so clear my balance but do not put any new charges on this card. If I find out this is all a screw-up on the hotel's part, I'll be checking out today!"

"Very well, sir. Just let me run this card and I'll let you be on your way. Check out time is 11:00 a.m. but I will gladly extend you a late checkout until 1:00 p.m. at no charge to give you a little extra time."

The manager busied himself while the credit card machine processed the transaction and when it beeped, he smiled.

"All done, Mr. Mueller, and again, I apologize for the inconvenience. Please let me know about your future plans, as we are expecting a full house tonight."

Mueller put the card back in his wallet and checked the bill compartment. He had a twenty, two fives and three ones—enough for breakfast, but that was about it. And the hotel had probably come close to maxing out his Mastercard, so he opted to get a light breakfast to go and take it back to his room. He didn't know how she had done it, but he was sure the local U.S. Customs supervisor, who clearly had it in for him, was somehow behind this.

When he tried to call the number on the back of his government credit card, he discovered that the hotel had his phone blocked for everything except local calls.

"Jerks!" he said out loud, knowing that they were probably just being cautious.

Reaching for his cell phone, he dialed the number again and, when prompted, he entered his sixteen-digit credit card number.

"I'm sorry, that is an invalid number," said the automated voice at the other end. "Please try again."

He tried it three more times before finally navigating his way through the menus to a live customer service representative.

"I'm sorry, sir, but our records indicate that a hold has been placed on that account."

"By whose authority!" shouted Mueller. "I'm stuck out here in the middle of nowhere with no funds!"

"I don't have access to specific names, sir, but I can tell you that it was not due to being over limit. My records indicate that the hold was placed by the account owner, not by the issuing bank. I suggest you contact the company responsible for this account and talk to them."

Realizing that he wasn't going to get anywhere with a third-party credit card servicing company, he abruptly ended the call and dialed Buzz Edwards' cell number. It rang several times before switching to voice mail. Next he tried the office number where he and Edwards "officially" worked. The phone was answered by a stranger who introduced himself as "Agent Oliver."

"Where's Sandy?" he asked.

"This is Agent Oliver, how may I help you?" replied the monotone voice.

Suspecting that he had somehow dialed the wrong number, Mueller hung up without saying another word. Instead of retrying the office number, he dialed the personal cell of one of his co-workers in the office.

"Yes?" answered Jackson, softly.

"Hey, it's Mueller. What's going on back there? I need to talk to Edwards because my company card has been suspended and I'm in the field."

"He never came in this morning, Erik, and right now there are FBI agents going through everything in the office. They burst in here about an hour ago and told us no one was allowed to leave the room until further notice. Listen, I have to hang up because they're headed my way. I wouldn't call back here unless you want to get sucked into whatever is going on. Good luck, Erik, wherever you are!"

With that, the called ended, leaving Mueller dumbfounded. Why would the FBI be in the offices of an agency of the Department of Defense? Clearly this was bigger than his run-in with a local Customs agent – something serious was going down! And where was Edwards?

Mueller called the number on the back of his personal card and heard the automated message say, "Your remaining balance is one hundred ninety-four dollars."

That wasn't even enough to get him back to Washington, D.C.!

Chapter 22

Tony saved some links to information about the Juan Gualberto Gómez Airport, as the Varadero facility was officially called, and shut down his laptop. Rumblings from his stomach convinced him it was time to go up to the galley and see what he could throw together for lunch. As he entered the salon, he spotted the back of a person with shoulder-length hair and he stopped dead in his tracks.

"Carley?" he shouted.

"Sorry, mate," replied the middle-aged man as he turned around, "but I think she already left the ship. I'm Terry and I'll be taking over the galley duties, I hope."

Tony laughed so hard he almost fell over, putting the other man on the defensive.

"I don't think it's all *that* funny, mate."

No, no, I'm not laughing at you, I'm laughing at me," managed Tony, trying to catch his breath. "Just for a second, when I thought you were Carley... well, never mind. Pleased to meet you, Terry. My name is Tony and I'm sort of the cruise director for the time being. I thought you weren't going to arrive until tomorrow."

"Tony! I've certainly heard a lot about you. I'm not officially here until tomorrow, and even then only if you decide to hire me, but when I heard that your current cook had left the island and that you plan to sail early Sunday morning, I decided I'd offer my services for today, even if I don't get the job."

"How did you get past security?" asked Tony with a frown.

"Oh, your Captain Braydon vouched for me. He's just gone forward to the bridge for a minute. Would you like some lunch?"

"Uh, yes, actually that's what I came up here for in the first place. But I can do it."

"Nonsense! I'm here and I need to familiarize myself with the setup anyway, so let me see what I can rustle up."

He opened the door of the large commercial refrigerator and scanned the contents. "How about a roast beef sandwich, some fresh potato salad and a tall glass of iced tea?"

Still a little taken aback by the assertiveness of the stranger, Tony nodded. "That would be great. I'll be right back."

Tony charged to the bridge but before he could say anything, the Captain greeted him.

"Good afternoon! Have you met the new cook?"

"I've met the stranger rummaging around in our galley, if that's who you mean," responded Tony. "I thought Rob and I were going to make the final decision."

"You are," smiled the Captain, "but that's tomorrow and that's for a permanent position on the crew. In the mean time, I have provisions arriving this afternoon and I needed some help getting them stowed away so I hired him by the hour. I thought it would give you two a chance to get acquainted. If he doesn't meet with your approval, we can save time tomorrow by interviewing someone else. We don't have a lot of time to fill this position, you know."

Satisfied, but not entirely happy about the situation, Tony returned to the salon just as the new cook was setting a plate on the nearest table. He had already arranged an assortment of condiments on a red and white checkered table cloth. Next to the plate a folded linen napkin held silverware.

"Enjoy!" beamed the man as he waved to the table and returned to his work in the galley.

Tony took one bite of the potato salad and waved the man back while he was still chewing.

"Where did this come from?" he demanded.

"I brought it with me. I made it fresh this morning. Do you like it?"

"This is the best potato salad I've ever had. You're hired!"

***

Erik Mueller sat at the small hotel room desk and pondered his situation. He didn't know what was going on back in Washington, D.C., but the presence of FBI agents in the office definitely wasn't a good sign. He couldn't raise Buzz Edwards, his immediate supervisor, on his personal cell phone and he hadn't showed up for work that morning, either. Both were very uncharacteristic of the man Mueller had known for many years. What's more, the local U.S. Customs office was holding his passport and his agency credit card had been suspended, leaving him fifteen hundred miles from home with practically no funds.

"Time to improvise!" he said to himself as he began to pack his belongings.

His first order of business would be to check out of the hotel before they tried to charge his personal credit card again. Unfortunately, that would leave him without a base of operations, but the last thing he needed right now was to have the hotel call the St. Thomas police because he couldn't pay his bill.

His second order of business would be to find a way off the island and back to the U.S. mainland. With limited funds and no passport, catching the next flight out wasn't an option but he might be able to talk his way aboard a merchant vessel if he returned to the docks where he had purchased the black market handgun his first night on St. Thomas. And if that didn't pan out, he remembered reading a book once about a guy who had stowed away on the Queen Mary and traveled from Brazil to the United States. Since the St. Thomas docks hosted several cruise ships every day this seemed like a viable backup plan. He might be short on money, but he was never without resources!

He stopped at the front desk to drop off his room key and announce loudly that he was checking out and then he headed for the hotel's front door. Carrying his suitcase in one hand and his brief case in the other, he marched down the stairs, feeling an odd sense of freedom. At the bottom of the short flight of steps, he was met by two men in suits who appeared out of nowhere.

"Erik Mueller, you are under arrest for acts of terrorism against the United States of America."

Within seconds, Mueller was disarmed, handcuffed and stuffed into the back seat of a waiting sedan.

***

After lunch, Tony chatted with the new cook while the other man put away arriving provisions. Terry, whose last name turned out to be Hedges, had begun his career at sea as a seventeen year old in England. A chance trip to the British Virgin Islands on a supply ship had introduced him to the beauty of the Caribbean and as soon as his tour of duty was up, he had resigned and made his way to Tortola on his own. These days, he only accepted positions that kept him in the tropics, which, of course, Tony's mission to the Bahamas would do.

Satisfied that Hedges would fit in with the rest of the crew, he left the man to his work and returned to his cabin. While his laptop was booting up, he called Jack King, the tavern owner on St. Thomas.

"Jack, it's Tony Nicoletti here. Listen, I just got off the phone with my friends Rob and Carley and they're convinced that someone is following them around down there and your man Henry seems to be their prime suspect. What's going on, man? I thought we were friends."

"Hey, Tony, I was hoping you would call! Before we talk about Henry, I have some good news for you. This Erik Mueller character you've been worrying about is off the streets, as of an hour ago."

"What? Are you sure?"

"Positive. I just learned that the FBI took him into custody in front of his hotel and he's already on a private jet back to the U.S. But get this—he was arrested on terrorism charges! Apparently he's in cahoots with some international organization called the Six."

"Never of heard of them," replied Tony. "But how do you know all this?"

"Let's just say that I have my sources and leave it at that. Now what's this about Henry? "

Tony re-described the events of the past two days, beginning with the island-long car chase and working his way back to Henry's introduction to Rob and Carley at King's tavern.

"I don't know what to tell you, pal. Henry is a straight shooter—that's why I asked him to accompany your friends. I assure you he's not connected with any bad guys and if your friends were actually followed Henry didn't have anything to do with it."

"They *were* followed, Jack, I'm sure about that. If it wasn't Henry or some of his friends, then who was it?"

"Well, there were at least two FBI agents here on St. Thomas until they apprehended this Mueller guy. Maybe they were tailing your friends because they were inquiring about Mueller. Could that be the connection?"

Tony thought about that for a minute.

"You could be on to something, Jack! But I'm not letting Henry off the hook that easy. If I find out he's involved…"

"Listen," interrupted King, "if you're so concerned about Henry, why don't you just come over and I'll introduce him. I think once you get to know him you'll agree that he's harmless."

"I can't do that right now. Like I told you before, I'm tied up on the mainland for a while."

"Yea, *right!*" replied King. "You forgot to turn on caller ID blocking, buddy. I know you're calling me from a BVI cell phone. Jump on a boat and come on over—I'll even pay you that twenty dollars you claim I owe you!"

With that the line went dead and Tony dropped his cell phone onto his bed.

"What an idiot!" he said out loud.

His moment of carelessness had given away his approximate position to a man he was losing trust in by the minute. And knowledge that Tony was in the British Virgin Islands would immediately tie him to Rob and Carley, who had probably already been traced to the Dolphin Diver.

Of course, it was possible that whoever followed Rob and Carley had been working for Mueller and he was now out of the picture, according to Jack King. Maybe things weren't so bad after all. If Tony could just stay out of sight for another thirty-six hours he would be at sea and off everybody's radar screens.

And the Mueller situation brought up another interesting possibility. If Mueller really had been working for Edwards, as Tony suspected, what had become of Edwards? Had the FBI picked him up, too? And if so, what did that mean for the NWIDI team? Were they also on an FBI watch list due to their association with Edwards?

Tony's head was spinning with questions when his cell phone rang. Picking it up between thumb and forefinger like it was a hot potato he turned it so he could see the display.

"Carley!" he shouted into the phone. "Where are you?"

"Hi! I'm sitting in a departure lounge at Miami International waiting for my flight to Belize but as I was going through my purse I discovered that I still have the cell phone Rob gave me in BVI. Should I just take it back home with me?"

"Yes, I guess so. In fact, I wish you had mine in your purse, too. I just called Jack King and forgot to block caller ID, so now he knows where I am."

"Oh, no! You have to press star-six-seven before every call, Tony. I thought we went over that!"

"Yes, we did, but I had a senior moment and forgot. However, on the plus side, Jack told me that Mueller was just picked up by the FBI and he's already been flown back to the mainland. And get this—they arrested him on terrorism charges."

"Well, that should make you feel better. Mueller certainly won't be looking for you anymore, so that portion of your mission is complete. What about that Edwards guy?"

"No word, but I have to believe he's in big trouble, too. I may get to the Bahamas and discover that there's no one left to hide Frank's secret from."

"And where, exactly, are you headed? Suppose a girl had a change of heart and decided to catch up with the Dolphin Diver—where would she do that?"

"Really? Are you actually considering that? That would be great, but I have to warn you that I already hired your replacement just based on his homemade potato salad."

"You may have hired a new cook, mister, but I doubt if you hired a replacement for *me*. I'm sure I can find *something* to keep me busy. Anyway, where is your first port of call?"

"Well, that's a tough one, because I don't know what's available for marinas on Andros that can handle a vessel as big as the Dolphin Diver. However, I want to snoop around the place we stayed when the team was there and that's near the Andros Town Airport. Do you really think you might do that?"

"I don't know, but the longer I sit here, the more I think about it. It might be nice to take a couple of days off to see something in Miami other than the airport and then fly on over to the Bahamas. No promises, though, okay?"

"No promises. Are Rob and Anne still on schedule to return to BVI tomorrow?"

"As far as I know. Oh, hey, I heard about your pilot. Great news and I bet he'll have a bizarre story to tell. This NWIDI team of yours is starting to sound pretty interesting. Uh-oh! They're making some sort of announcement about my flight so I need to go. I'll talk to you later."

"Okay, bye. And maybe I'll *see* you later, Kido. Be safe."

Tony ended the call and flopped back onto his bunk smiling. All in all, it hadn't been a bad day and it was only a little past noon. In fact, it hadn't been a bad few days, really. He had survived a dive to well past two hundred feet and he had literally talked to a dolphin. His arch nemesis, Erik Mueller, was in custody and maybe Buzz Edwards was there, too. And he'd eaten the best potato salad on earth. It didn't get much better than this!

A series of loud thumps on the deck above his cabin suggested that supplies were starting to arrive, so Tony decided to head up and see if he could lend a hand. He was surprised by the size of the still-growing stack of boxes and burlap sacks in the middle of the salon.

"Are we really going to eat this much?" he asked Hedges.

"Yes, sir, that and more! And Andros is not a good place to purchase provisions, so the Captain is smart to stock up here on all the non-perishable items. There is virtually nothing produced up there, so the cost is much higher."

"So you have some experience with Andros?" asked Tony as he helped the man transfer boxes from the delivery man's hand-operated pallet jack to the galley area.

"I've been there a few of times, yes. It's quite a diving area, if I remember correctly. Your young divemaster should be very happy in the western Bahamas."

"Well, I hope so. He's finally going to get to do some real work for the first time on this voyage. Actually, our first stop is going to be a place called the Guardian Blue Hole. Do you know it?"

"Not from personal experience, but I've heard of it. It's the source of many legends among the locals. Do you know how it got its name?"

"I have no idea," replied Tony as he continued to shuffle boxes. "But I'd love to hear the story."

"First of all, there are two entrances—large fresh-water pools, actually—to the complex and from the surface it doesn't look like much. For years and years an old barracuda lived in the pool considered the main entrance and they called this big guy 'the Guardian.' When tourism started becoming a major economic factor, the government decided to give all the odd geological features intriguing names and the Guardian Blue Hole was born. But it wasn't explored with scuba equipment until years later. That was when they discovered the vast extent of the complex."

"I've heard that it's a half-mile long and some four hundred feet deep," puffed Tony as he moved the last box and sat down at one of the tables.

"That sounds about right," nodded Hedges, as he took a seat across from Tony. "And that's just the part that's been explored. There are some tunnels too small for a diver to squeeze through and other places that are simply too far from the entrances to allow safe diving. And then there are the spheres."

"The what?"

"The locals claim that metallic spheres about the size of a basketball are often seen in the two large vertical caves located near the secondary entrance. In fact, since the old barracuda died, they've taken to calling *them* the Guardians."

Tony was suddenly all ears. Could these be the same spheres Frank had mentioned seeing?

"Have you ever seen any of these spheres?"

"Me? No, I'm not much of a diver and I'm certainly not qualified for cave diving in these blue holes. But I fancy local lore and that's why I know about this place. Wherever I travel, I try to learn as much as I can about the local legends and compare them to stories I've heard from other places. It's amazing how many of them repeat from place to place but Andros has some really unique ones. In addition to the original Guardian and the new high-tech guardians, there are two mythical creatures supposedly unique to Andros Island: The Chickcharney and the Lusca. The Chickcharney is a furry and feathered three-foot tall creature with one red eye and three-toed claws. The Lusca is a giant half-octopus, half-shark creature that supposedly swallows whole boats."

"Are you kidding me? These things actually exist in the lore of Andros Island?"

"Oh, yes," insisted Hedges. "When I ran across the last two I did some digging and talked to a number of island elders. The stories are all passed down verbally, of course, but there are many people who believe these creatures roam the island's interior. Vast areas of the island are still unexplored, you know."

"How, in this day and age, can there be any unexplored territory left?" Tony asked. "Especially on such a small island less than one hundred miles from the U.S. mainland? It just doesn't seem possible!"

"I know, but it's true. Most of the locals won't venture into the interior and the tree canopy hides the ground from satellites and airplanes. So back to the Guardian Blue hole for a minute—why are you going there?"

Tony thought about his answer before speaking because this man was practically a stranger and hadn't signed any of the non-disclosure paperwork that Rob had asked the other crewmembers to sign.

"I can't really go into details with you yet, but I can tell you that our help was recently requested in a very bizarre message and the GPS coordinates for the Guardian Blue Hole were specifically listed as the meeting place."

"This is already shaping up to be an interesting trip and we haven't even left the dock!" laughed Hedges. "But, seriously, if you intend to dive there you need to study every diagram and drawing you can find about the place because it's a very dangerous site. Not only are the caves flooded with water, but they are also below the island itself, so there are no escape routes to the surface. You either come back out one of the two known entrances or you don't come out at all."

"I'll keep that in mind," frowned Tony. "Maybe I should go check in with our divemaster and make sure the equipment is ready for this."

Tony left the new cook in the galley and headed out the back door of the salon to the aft deck. He looked down onto the dive deck but didn't see Cesar Acosta anywhere so he went below and knocked on the man's cabin door.

When Cesar opened the door, Tony handed him the printouts he had made earlier.

"Have you seen these?" he asked. "Our new cook was just telling me about this Guardian Blue Hole place where we're supposed to meet with someone."

Cesar glanced at the sheets of paper and then opened his door all the way and pointed to his laptop.

"I was just going over some similar charts. I don't mean to be rude, Tony, but I don't think you are ready for a dive in this place. There's just too much that can go wrong in tight, underwater spaces."

"Well, let's wait until we arrive to make that decision. I don't even know who I'm supposed to meet with and nobody would schedule a meeting *inside* the blue hole. Somebody must have messed up the coordinates. Or maybe the translation was off."

"Maybe," nodded Cesar. "The hole is land-locked, but not by much. It's only about twenty-five meters from the shoreline. Maybe the hole was just picked as a reference point. However, if anyone has to go down inside the cave system, it has to be me—and me alone."

"Like I said, let's wait until we get there before we make any decisions. According to Hedges, Andros is a pretty weird place. Have you talked to him about it?"

"No," replied Acosta. "But I will before we get there. I don't like weird when it comes to dive sites."

Tony left Cesar to his charts and headed back to his own cabin but before he reached the door his cell phone rang. This time he checked the Caller ID display before answering the call.

"Rob! How's Anne? How's Miami?"

"Both are doing well," replied Rob. "We'll be back in St. Thomas about 5:10 p.m. tomorrow afternoon. I know that's getting pretty close to your pre-departure curfew, but it's the earliest flight we could get. How are things going there?"

"Pretty well. I've just been discussing this Guardian Blue Hole with our new cook – that's the place that showed up in the dolphin's message."

"Our new what? Anyway, that's actually the reason I'm calling. If you remember, the end of the message contained an undistinguishable word just before the character string you identified as Frank's Air Force Serial Number. Well, the lab thinks they've figured it out. It either says "The Guardian" or "the Guardians.""

Chapter 23

Tony was speechless for so long Rob thought the connection had been lost.

"Tony? Tony, are you still there?"

"Yes, I'm here. Are you sure the message contains the word 'Guardians' and not something else?"

"Positive, why?"

"Our new cook just told me that the Guardian Blue Hole originally got its name from an old barracuda that lived in the pool that serves as the main entrance…"

"Well I doubt if the message was from a barracuda!" interrupted Rob with a laugh.

"No, probably not," continued Tony, "but now they use the term to describe the metallic spheres often seen in two of the main caves. They call them the Guardians."

This time the long pause was on Rob's end.

"Are you kidding me?" he finally responded. "They've actually seen metallic spheres at this site? Didn't you tell me once that your friend Frank reported seeing metallic spheres on a dive near Andros?"

"Yes he did," replied Tony. "Is it even remotely possible that the message we received via 'dolphin mail' originated with these spheres? This is beginning to sound like something out of a science fiction movie! You're positive there can't be any mistake with the translation device, right?"

"Positive, Tony. All our project dolphins, including Emma, are really excited about the new device and now they want to work twenty-four hours a day. The staff has to force them to take a break for the sake of the humans on the team. Using the rudimentary sign language they had already developed, our scientific team managed to convey to Emma and the others that the message was delivered to you by dolphins and they went nuts. They listened to the recording over and over at various speeds and frequencies and finally, as a group, they agreed that the missing word was either Guardian or Guardians.

"That reminds me, the team is preparing a prototype to send to us and they need to know where to ship it. It won't be ready for a couple of days, so we should probably have it sent to Andros. Any idea where?"

"Yes, have them send it to my attention at the Bay Club Resort in Andros Town. I'll call up there today and let them know we'll be arriving in a few days and I'll ask them to hold any packages that arrive for me."

"Bay Club, Andros Town—got it! Have you heard anything from Carley?"

"As a matter of fact, I have!" replied Tony. "She called from the departure lounge in Miami and it almost sounded like she was having second thoughts about going back to Belize. I wouldn't be the least bit surprised if we ran into her at the Bay Club, too."

"Don't bet on it, my friend. She was back and forth about that very subject all the way from St. Thomas to Miami. She's a very confused lady right now and I think her decision could go either way. Anne is waiting for me, so I'll probably talk to you later and we'll both see you tomorrow afternoon. Anne is dying to see the Dolphin Diver, by the way."

"We'll make sure the honeymoon suite is ready," laughed Tony. "See you tomorrow."

Tony glanced at his watch. It was almost 4:00 p.m. and he was sleepy but there were more provisions arriving, so he made his way to the port side to sign for the delivery. When he looked up from the driver's clipboard, something caught his attention at the end of the pier.

"Terry is inside and he'll help you with these—just tell him I've already signed."

With one eye on the end of the pier, Tony made his way down the gang plank and approached the guard who had been serving them every afternoon since their arrival.

"Have you noticed anything strange while you've been on duty?" asked Tony. "Anything suspicious or out of the ordinary?"

"No, sir, I don't believe so. There have been a lot of deliveries today, but one of your men mentioned that you are sailing tomorrow, so that's not unusual."

"What about away from the ship? Say, on the pier or in the immediate area?"

The guard glanced around and shook his head.

"No, sir, not that I can think of. Why, is something wrong?"

Tony could hear a sense of concern in the other man's voice.

"No, not wrong, but maybe unusual. I'd like you to keep an eye on that warehouse at the end of the pier, but don't be obvious about it. My mind might be playing tricks on me, so I'd like a second opinion."

"What am I looking for?" asked the guard as he stole a glance at the spot Tony had indicated.

"Ah, if I told you that then I'd bias your observation. Just keep an eye out for me and check back in before your shift is over, okay? My name is Tony and I'll be onboard."

"Yes, sir!" replied the guard, feeling suddenly important. "Yes, sir!"

As Tony walked back up the gang plank, he made a conscious effort not to look in the direction of the warehouse he had pointed out to the guard. He continued on up to the lookout station, retrieved the large spotting binoculars and then returned to the salon where he took up a position on the bench seat that ran most of the way across the back of the boat. He propped the binoculars on the back of the seat and slowly panned the dock where the Dolphin Diver's pier attached. He had been at it for several minutes before he finally saw what he was waiting for—the heavy, wooden sliding door on the front of the warehouse was open just slightly, exposing a narrow crack. The sun was low in the sky off the bow of the ship and shining brightly on the front of the warehouse. Tony waited and watched and soon his patience was rewarded with a glint of light from inside the crack. Someone was watching the ship, either with binoculars or with the telephoto lens of a camera!

Tony went forward to the bridge to find Captain Braydon, but First Mate Nickolas Banks was on watch.

"I think the Captain is in his quarters, if you need to see him."

"No, that's okay. He might be sleeping and I wouldn't want to disturb him. I just wanted to let him know that I'm going ashore for a while."

"I'll pass the word," replied Banks. "Can he reach you on your cell?"

"Yes, my cell," replied Tony, patting his pockets for the phone. "I must have left it in my room, but I'll go get it before I take off."

In his room, Tony threw together a backpack containing a smaller pair of binoculars, a small flashlight, a black hooded sweatshirt, a pair of black sweat pants and a few other miscellaneous items. He quietly closed and locked the door to his room and made his way down the hall to his private storeroom that had been locked since before the Dolphin Diver left Belize. Inside, he chose an automatic pistol and two additional clips of ammunition. He also selected a black web belt and holster and a nasty looking knife in a sheath that he could fasten to his leg. He exited his private arsenal, locked the door and double-checked it.

On the dive platform he quietly slid into his wetsuit and transferred the contents of the backpack into a diver's dry bag. He selected the same rebreather he had used on his deep dive with Cesar but this time he was going to take advantage of another one of the unit's qualities—the fact that it made no bubbles and no noise. Tony checked the unit's computer to make sure the gas bottles were fully charged and then silently slipped below the surface.

The visibility in the marina was poor due to all the pollution from the anchored boats but Tony had a keen sense of direction and he soon reached the edge of the dock at the shoreline. Before surfacing, he swam to his right, under the ramp that attached the floating pier to the dock. Invisible to anyone above, he removed the rebreather and strapped it to one of the metal braces. He removed his mask, fins and wetsuit and tied them to the rebreather with a length of cord from the dry bag. He crawled up onto some rocks along the shore and hunkered down to wait for sunset.

As the last rays of the sun disappeared, darkness fell over the Road Town harbor. Above him, Tony could hear the sounds of the waterfront and if he leaned far enough to his right, he could look out along the length of the pier and see the back half of the Dolphin Diver. Lights from the salon suggested that the new cook was probably serving dinner to the crew. Just the thought of that made Tony hungry, but he had more important business to take care of tonight.

He pulled on the black sweatpants and hooded shirt and added a black skull cap to complete the outfit. He fastened the web belt and holster around his waist and secured the automatic handgun. A rectangular pouch on the belt held the two extra clips and his flashlight. Finally, he strapped the knife to his right calf, under the sweat pants.

He crouched and listened for several minutes to get a sense of what was happening above him. Somewhere he could hear a small group of men laughing but his senses told him they were walking away from his location. When the dock had been quiet for some time, Tony crept out from underneath the ramp and raised his head just high enough to be able to see up and down the cement dock. He was almost directly across from the suspicious warehouse and in the dim light he could see that the door was still open about six inches.

Lowering himself back down, he moved horizontally along the dock until he felt he couldn't be seen from the door. Again, he peeked up over the edge of the dock. No one was in sight, so he scrambled over the edge and raced across the width of the dock to the building on the other side. He hid himself in the doorway of a dark waterfront business and waited to make sure he hadn't attracted any attention. When no one stirred, he stuck his head out far enough to evaluate his position and formulate a plan.

He could see that the doorway he was hiding in was in the building immediately adjacent to the warehouse and that the two structures were separated by a narrow, dark alley.

He launched himself out of the doorway and into the alley in a flash, his neoprene dive boots making his footsteps inaudible.

About ten yards down the alley, Tony came to a set of dilapidated wooden steps that led to a second-floor entrance into the warehouse. It had probably been an office at one time, but the stairs looked like they hadn't been used in a long time. He continued along the side of the building looking for a better option, but there were no other doors or windows on this side of the building so he returned to the staircase.

He took his first step gingerly, half expecting the step to break—or at least creak—and arouse the occupants of the warehouse. The step held, so he lifted his left leg off the ground and placed it on the edge of the second step. This time there was a slight creak and he froze. In his younger days he would have already been at the top but the years were catching up with him and he was no longer the nimble Army Ranger that had survived the jungles of Southeast Asia during the closing months of the Vietnam War.

Keeping his feet on the extreme edges of the steps to avoid breaking any boards, he slowly made his way up the staircase. At the top, he paused on the small landing and examined the door. Removing the knife from its sheath on his leg, he picked at the lock but it didn't budge. With the blade of the knife, he pried the molding away from the casing until he could touch the lock's bolt with the point. Keeping pressure on the door with his foot, he worked the bolt back until the door swung open, exposing a small, dark room.

Cautiously, he stepped into the room and swung the door almost closed, leaving it ajar just enough so the latch wouldn't lock him into the room. After his eyes adjusted to the darkness, he scanned the room. There appeared to be some old furniture piled randomly about the room but its days as an office were clearly over.

Tony carefully made his way across the room to a door on the other side. He tried the knob and found that it turned so he slowly opened the door just enough to peek out. The door opened onto a catwalk that ran along the side of the large, two-story warehouse. Below, he could hear the sound of voices but he couldn't make out what was being said and he couldn't see anyone because the interior was totally dark.

He closed the door and chambered a round in the automatic. With the gun in his right hand, he opened the door again and stepped out onto the catwalk just as the interior of the warehouse burst into fluorescent light—someone had flipped on the main switch!

He jumped back through the door, closed it and took cover behind one of the old desks, half expecting a hail of gunfire to rip the wall to shreds. Instead, he heard only silence. As he crouched, ready to open fire on anyone who entered the room, he noticed that the light at the bottom of the door suddenly went dark and then he heard a door slam at the rear of the building. Voices fading into the distance suggested that whoever had been watching the Dolphin Diver had given up— at least for tonight.

After waiting several minutes, Tony was satisfied that he was alone in the building so he returned to the door, stepped out onto the catwalk and scanned the dark interior. He made his way along the catwalk to the front of the building, where a narrow stairway took him down to the ground floor. The large sliding door was now closed and locked from the inside but there appeared to be some equipment just inside the door so he made his way over to it. Using his small flashlight, he discovered a tripod—minus its camera—and two crates that had obviously been used as makeshift chairs. So somebody *was* spying on the Dolphin Diver!

For the next hour, Tony methodically searched the entire ground floor of the dirty warehouse looking for clues. He was about to give up when he opened a drawer under a work bench near the back of the structure and found something very interesting—a relatively clean newspaper. Holding his light in his mouth, he unfolded the paper and examined the front page. It was a copy of the Virgin Islands Daily News dated Wednesday, May 7th—two days ago. When he pulled the paper out of the drawer something had rattled back into the darkness, so he directed his light into the drawer and found some even *more* interesting objects: a syringe, a small glass vial containing a clear fluid and a sheet of paper folded into quarters. He laid the newspaper, the syringe and the vial side by side on the counter and unfolded the sheet of paper. He gasped as he recognized the picture of someone he knew very well—Carley Quinn!

"They've been after *her* the whole time!" he blurted out without thinking.

And suddenly, a lot of unusual events started to make sense. The man they had encountered in the tavern the day before wasn't following Tony; he was actually following Carley. The man on the St. John ferry who had hidden behind a newspaper—probably this very same newspaper—had no interest in Rob; he was following Carley. And the boat that had followed them out of Belize City hadn't been shadowing the Dolphin Diver because of its research secrets; it had been keeping tabs on Carley!

Tony picked up the vial and examined it closely. The words "Sodium Amytal" were hand printed in small letters on the otherwise blank label. He had heard of sodium pentothal before and he suspected this vial contained something similar. He put the picture and the vial in his ammo pouch and destroyed the syringe by jamming the needle into the work bench until it broke off. Then he carefully wrapped it in the newspaper, placed it back into the drawer and closed it. He didn't know who was behind this, but someone was going to pay!

Tony exited the building the same way he had entered, making sure to close and lock the doors exactly as he had found them. Once outside, he replaced the molding before descending to the alley. A quick dash across the dock put him back under the ramp where he repacked his dry bag, wiggled into his wet suit and put his arms through the straps of the rebreather. As he entered the water, he noticed that the Dolphin Diver was dark except for a few running lights that were left on all night for safety. When he reached the stern of the boat, he removed his fins and quietly climbed out of the water using the dive ladder.

"Need a hand, sailor?" asked the stern voice of Captain Braydon.

For the next thirty minutes Tony tried to justify his solo clandestine operation to the angry Captain. He made little progress until he showed the older man the vial he had recovered from the warehouse.

"This is a very powerful sedative often used as a truth serum," he frowned. "Whoever is watching us from that warehouse isn't just following Carley, they meant to kidnap her. One dose of this stuff would put her out for ten or twelve hours—long enough to get her back to Belize, I suspect."

"Or Guatemala," mumbled Tony. "In the morning I'm going back down there and I'm going to put an end to this."

"You most certainly are *not!*" replied the Captain. "The last thing you need is to be locked up by the local police carrying false documents. I'll handle this. But you should alert Carley about what you found. If they're looking for her here, they will surely be waiting for her back in Belize City. She could be walking into a trap this very moment."

Without saying another word, Tony ran through the salon and down to his room. Even though he had promised Nickolas that he would take his cell phone ashore, he had intentionally left it on his desk when he packed his dry bag for the away mission.

The phone rang once and then immediately transferred to Carley's voice-mail, indicating that it was either busy or turned off. He tried again, with the same results. To calm himself, he dressed and unpacked his dry bag. A third call to Carley yielded the same results.

Glancing at his watch, Tony guessed that it was only 9:00 p.m. in Miami, so he chanced a call to Rob.

"Have you heard from Carley?" he asked as soon as the phone was answered.

"No, Tony, I haven't, but you don't sound too good. What's the matter?"

Tony repeated the story he had just told the Captain and added the Captain's suggestion that she might be walking into a trap when she lands in Belize.

"I'll see what I can find out," offered Rob. "But you are the one who told me that she was considering rejoining the boat in the Bahamas. Maybe she didn't even get on a plane to Belize. If she decided to stay in Miami for a few days, she would have disappeared into the crowds by now and she should be relatively safe. I assume you've tried her cell phone, right?"

"Yes, of course. It transfers to voice mail on the first ring, but I'll keep trying."

"Okay, and in the mean time I'll call the airport and see what I can find out. They may not be willing to give me any information, but I know she was originally scheduled on an American Airlines flight, so I'll start with them. I'll call you back when I hear something."

Tony retried Carley's cell phone every half hour until Rob finally called him about midnight.

"I think you can relax, Tony. I have been able to confirm that Carley was not on any of today's flights to Belize so she must have decided to stay in Miami. If that's the case, I'm betting she will give you a call tomorrow to let you know she decided to stay."

"Well, that's a bit of a relief but I'd really like to let her know the situation so she stays alert and safe. Maybe she could even hook up with you guys and fly back here instead of roaming around Miami. I'll keep trying her phone, but she hasn't answered all night so I imagine it's turned off."

"Probably so. What about the guys who are watching the ship?"

"Well, the Captain wants me to stay out of it because of my fake documents, but if he doesn't come up with some answers first thing in the morning then I'm going down there and getting my own answers. I still have that vial of stuff they were going to use on Carley and I'll jam it down somebody's throat—broken glass and all—if I have to!"

Chapter 24

Tony awoke Saturday morning to the smell of bacon and cinnamon toast. Carley's cooking had been good, but this new guy was off the hook! He showered and dressed quickly before calling Carley's cell phone one more time but it continued to switch to voice mail after the first ring. He clipped his phone to his belt in case she called and raced upstairs.

"Where's the Captain?" he asked no one in particular.

"I believe he's gone ashore," answered the new cook. "Are you ready for breakfast?"

"Yeah, sure, but make it light because I may be doing some heavy lifting this morning."

"In that case, you'd better sit down and try Terry's buckwheat pancakes," said Cesar Acosta. "And what's the idea of going diving without letting me know?"

"You heard about that, huh? Sorry, but that job fell under the heading of ship's security, not diving. Did you hear what I found?"

"The Captain said that somebody has been watching the ship and that it appeared they were about to grab Carley," nodded Cesar. "I wonder how they missed the fact that she left the boat yesterday morning."

"You know, I thought about that until the wee hours this morning," replied Tony as he dug into the stack of pancakes that had been placed before him. "I just happened to be inside that warehouse when they left last night, and they sounded pretty casual about the whole thing. I didn't see them, mind you, but it sounded like they just closed the front door and called it a day. They must have been so confident that Carley was on the ship that they didn't see any need for round the clock surveillance. We left for the ferry about 6:45 a.m. so maybe they don't get to work that early."

Just then, the Captain stepped through the port door of the salon.

"Well?" demanded Tony. "What did you find out?"

"The police have the place staked out and they will notify us as soon as they make an arrest. At that point, they may want to talk to you but I've already told them about the syringe and the vial you found. It turns out that sodium amytal is a controlled substance in the British Virgin Islands, so they will face charges for possession, if nothing else. Oh, and the police insisted on keeping the vial. I think they are checking it for fingerprints."

"That's fine, but I want to talk to those guys! I want to know what their connection to Carley is and I want to know if there are more of them out there."

"All in good time, Tony. All in good time. For now I suggest that everybody give their duty stations a final once-over to make sure everything is ready for tomorrow's departure. I know Cesar has a rebreather to refill and Rigo is standing by for a fuel delivery in an hour or two. Has everything else arrived and been stowed?"

The crew members all nodded their heads and then disbursed. Tony retrieved the large spotting binoculars from the salon couch and caught Cesar's eye.

"Let me put these back where they belong and then I'll help you with that rebreather. I need to learn how to refill them, anyway."

Once he was up on the roof he couldn't help climbing up into the lookout chair and scanning the waterfront with the binoculars. He smiled as he saw men stationed on the roofs of both adjacent buildings. Maybe it was best to leave this to the professionals!

On the dive platform, Cesar showed Tony how to swap out the various gas cylinders that made up the rebreather pack. A large cabinet attached to the back of the vessel held a supply of each different kind.

"So, how do you refill these canisters that we've used?" asked Tony.

"We don't, at least not onboard. We can fill regular air tanks but it takes special equipment to fill the oxygen and nitrox canisters. We just store any empties and replace them the next time we're in port. But the good news is that they last a long time under normal conditions. For example, the oxygen bottle from your little adventure last night is still at 99% capacity."

"Good to know," nodded Tony. "Listen, I apologize again for keeping you out of the loop, but I had no idea what I might run into and I went in there armed. That's not a position I want to put my crew members into unless it's absolutely necessary."

"And I appreciate that, but what if that rebreather had been down for maintenance? You could have had a serious accident or been killed!"

"Cesar, give me a little credit, okay. I was never more than fifteen feet below the surface and I only went from here to…"

Tony had started to point towards the dock when he saw movement on the roof of the building to the left of the warehouse.

"It's going down right now! Come on!"

Both men climbed up onto the rear deck and stormed the salon, only to be met by the Captain on his way aft from the bridge.

"They've called off the stake out, if that's what you're so excited about," smiled the Captain. "Apparently they already had the men in custody as a result of an incident that took place early this morning. They have a positive fingerprint match."

"An incident?"

"Yes. About 2:00 a.m. this morning a disturbance was reported at one of the cheap waterfront hotels around on the other side of the bay. When the police arrived, two very drunk men were beating the daylights out of each other in the parking lot behind the hotel. The police broke up the fight and arrested them both. It turns out that they were sharing a hotel room and it was full of illegal drugs and weapons. They are going away for a long, long time."

"I want to talk to them!" demanded Tony.

"Well, that's not going to happen. They claim they don't speak any English, for starters, but they have also been connected to a Central American drug cartel. Your lady friend isn't in the drug trafficking business, is she?"

"Not that I'm aware of! Cesar can translate for me, but I need to talk to them. I need to find out if there are others looking for Carley."

"Tony, these guys are associated with an international cartel—you must assume others will step in to take their places now that these two are off the street. The real question is why a cartel is looking for Carley, and these guys won't have that answer. They will just have orders to pick her up. Due to the charges against these two, they are being held in a high-security facility and there's no way you are going to get in there. I asked, but it's just not going to happen."

"Then we have to find her and make sure this cartel doesn't grab her."

"That's already being handled. I gave the police the picture you brought back last night and they've already broadcast it to every law enforcement agency in the Caribbean. It's also been sent to agencies in Florida. When Carley surfaces someone will find her and take her into protective custody. Everything that can be done has already been done. Just be patient."

Tony finally accepted that he was not in control of this situation and gave up the argument. Cesar talked him into returning to the dive platform to take his mind off the situation and soon Tony was back to normal. The two divers puttered and chatted until the bell rang indicating that lunch was ready.

Terry Hedges' lunch meal had been another big hit with the crew and Tony was stuffed. All the provisions had been stowed away and there wasn't much left for him to do to prepare for tomorrow morning's departure so he decided it might be a good time to grab a quick nap. As he lay back on his bunk, his mind went back to his conversation with Rob the day before and he thought about the message from the dolphins that contained the word 'Guardians.' He couldn't wait to get to Andros and find out what this big meeting was all about—or who the other attendees would be!

He awoke to a rapping on his cabin door.

"Who is it?" he shouted. "And what time is it?"

"It's Nickolas Banks, Tony, and it's about 3:00 p.m. Could you come upstairs, please? There's someone here insisting that he talk to an Anthony Nicoletti and I'm afraid the Captain is going to shoot him if he doesn't leave."

Tony had been napping for almost an hour and he was very groggy but when he heard the name Nicoletti he threw his feet over the side of the bed and was up in a flash. No one aboard the Dolphin Diver knew that his real last name was Nicoletti except Rob Jefferies and Rob was in Miami!

When he reached the gang plank, the Captain had his sawed-off shotgun leveled at a man in a dark suit who was standing on the pier. The guard, who would normally be protecting the foot of the gang plank, had taken cover behind a dumpster about twenty feet up the pier.

"Captain!" shouted Tony, "there's no need for that. What's going on here?"

"That fool down there insists he's coming aboard and I was just about to show him why he's not," replied the Captain. "He insists on talking to somebody named Nicoletti and he doesn't seem to want to take 'No!' for an answer."

"Let me talk to him, Captain. Maybe I can figure out what's going on. But please, let's don't shoot anybody just yet."

The Captain grumbled, but yielded to Tony's suggestion and lowered the gun.

After checking to be sure that none of the other crew members had taken up arms, he made his way down the gang plank and stopped just inches from the stranger.

"What do you want?" he demanded.

"I want you, Mr. Nicoletti. I'm Special Agent Danwell and I'm here to escort you back to Washington, D.C."

"Is that right, Special Agent Danwell? Well, my name is Wykes and I have no intention of going anywhere with you so why don't you just high-tail it back to wherever you came from before I let the Captain fill you with buckshot?"

"Mr. Nicoletti, before your Captain fires on a federal agent, I think you should read this."

The man pulled a folded sheet of paper out of his inside jacket pocket and handed it to Tony. As he read the letter, he started to smile but the smile had slipped away by the time he reached the end.

"Where did you get this?"

"Dr. Barnes personally handed it to me, sir. He was pretty sure you wouldn't come along without some convincing, so he gave us letters that include facts he was sure would demonstrate their authenticity. A similar letter is being delivered to Linda McBride and her husband. And the Fitzgeralds are already in D.C."

"But I can't leave the ship now," insisted Tony. "We're leaving for the Bahamas tomorrow morning and I have a very important meeting there."

"This ship may be going to the Bahamas tomorrow, Mr. Nicoletti, but you are going to Washington, D.C. by order of the President of the United States and we are leaving today. I can give you an hour to collect your things and say your good-byes, but I must caution you not to divulge any of the details I have just shared with you. Now shall we go aboard and get you packed?"

Tony reread the page again, and frowned. If what Jim had said in the letter was true, the implications were staggering. Apparently, his research with the triangles had produced answers much more important than anyone anticipated and Edwards was turning out to be much more of a villain than anyone, including Tony, had ever imagined. Among other things, Jim briefly explained how he had unwillingly traded the triangles for the exact GPS coordinates of the Dolphin Diver. The closing paragraph of the letter was totally unrelated to the rest of the content, but instead described in detail an incident that had occurred on the last NWIDI mission—an incident that only Jim could have known about. And he had signed the letter 'Special Advisor to the President!'

"I'm only going along with this because there's no doubt that Jim dictated this letter. But if I find out he was coerced into providing this information, you will be a very sorry man, Special Agent Danwell. *Very* sorry!"

Tony led the way up the gang plank and stepped onto the ship. The Captain was standing his ground on the left, Cesar Acosta had positioned himself on the other side, Nickolas Banks was blocking the entrance into the salon and Tony could see Rigo Mejia in the lookout chair, undoubtedly with one hand on the high-powered rifle.

"A very loyal crew," commented Danwell, "but please tell them all to stand down. I am not without my own resources, and I won't hesitate to sink this boat while it's still tied to the pier if I have to."

Danwell nodded to the opposite side of the ship and as the crew of the Dolphin Diver turned they saw the small but heavily armed U.S. Coast Guard vessel that had just moved into position in the middle of the harbor.

"The Coast Guard has no authority here," insisted Tony. "This is British territory."

"The Coast Guard often works closely with the local authorities and that vessel is here to convey you back to St. Thomas where a Navy plane is waiting to take you to Washington as quickly as possible, Mr. Nicoletti. However, I won't hesitate to order it to fire on your ship if necessary."

"Why do you keep calling him Mr. Nicoletti?" asked Cesar. "His name is Tony Wykes."

Danwell smiled and nodded at Tony. "I'll let you handle that one."

Tony turned to face his crewmates.

"Nicoletti is actually my real name and this guy is here to escort me back to Washington, D.C. for a very important meeting with some old friends. I know the Dolphin Diver is scheduled to leave port tomorrow morning and it's very important that you stick to our original schedule. This business in Washington shouldn't take too long and I'll catch up with you in the Bahamas. By then I'll be able to give you more details, but for now I need you to trust me and press on. I'll be gone before Rob returns from Miami, so please tell him I'll call and explain everything at my earliest opportunity."

With that, Tony stepped into the salon and headed for the stairs to the lower deck with Special Agent Danwell following close behind.

"That was all a lie, wasn't it?" asked Tony, as he unlocked the door to his cabin. "I won't be seeing them in the Bahamas."

"No, sir, I don't believe you will."

THE END

Epilogue
(Sunday, May 11, 2008)

When Tony was escorted into the "holding room" at the Naval Research Laboratory, in Washington, D.C., the scowl that had been on his face for the past several hours suddenly melted. To his right, seated at a long, folding table sat Linda McBride, Javier Reyes and the former NWIDI flight crew, Susan and Fitz Fitzgerald. When he spotted the Fitzgerald's dog, Sandstrom, in the corner of the large room with a little girl, he looked at Fitz and said, "I see you still have that mutt!"

He joined the others at the table and they immediately began catching up on the events of the past five years. Tony soon learned that the little girl was Mariana, Linda's and Javier's three-year-old daughter. Several minutes later, the door opened again and Jim Barnes stepped into the room.

"Hey, there he is!" shouted Tony. "What's the big idea of interrupting my nap to drag me all the way back to the U.S.?"

Jim tried to smile, but he wasn't looking forward to the news he was going to have to break to his friends about being captives of their own government. After handshakes and back pats all around, he sat down at one end of the table and sighed.

"Listen, guys, I don't know how much you've been able to share with each other, but I have some news that you should probably hear sooner rather than later. Do you all remember Buzz Edwards?"

"You bet I do," replied Tony without waiting for anyone else to speak. "He had me locked up in that underground facility in Cancun from the day after Linda's wedding until about six weeks ago and I've been after him ever since. I almost had him, too, but a couple of days ago he slipped through my fingers and disappeared."

"What was that?" exclaimed a shocked Linda. "Are you saying you were held prisoner for more than five years?"

"Well, maybe 'prisoner' is a bit too strong, because I wasn't actually in a cell, but I wasn't allowed to leave the facility beneath the airport, either. I know every square inch of that place and I planned my escape for years, but the opportunity didn't present itself until a rainy Sunday night last March when the security system went on the blink and gave me a chance to get away."

"Incredible," replied Jim. "Well, your friend Edwards is in charge of an international terrorist group known as 'the Six' and he's used us—all of us—as pawns to further his plans."

"Yes, we were just talking about that," nodded Linda. "Javier and I have been intercepting coded messages from an Asian group for weeks now. We've leaked many of them to the press, in an effort to disrupt some of their plans."

"No kidding?" smiled Jim. "So, independently, we've all been causing him grief. Good! That makes me feel a little better. The reason he disappeared from your radar, Tony, is because an associate of mine here at NRL finally connected him to a crime that would have resulted in his arrest. We also identified the other key members of his organization and now they've all gone into hiding. We don't know where yet, but we think it's a facility similar to the one where you were held."

"Really!" remarked Tony. "Judging by the power you seem to wield here, I'm guessing you've faired a little better than me. What have you been up to since the wedding?"

Jim gave them a five minute recap of his time at AUTEC, his meeting with the strange Professor Schmidt in Germany and his most recent experiences at NRL. Except for expressing his outrage at being controlled and manipulated by the U.S. Navy, he glossed over a lot of the details and instead focused on what he and his team had learned about the aliens known as *the Teachers*.

He described his theory that *the Teachers* had been intervening into the affairs of mankind for a long, long time in an effort to save the species and he described his own experience with them, including how they had somehow entered his top secret lab and retrieved the triangles but left in their place the previously unknown locations of Linda, Javier and Tony.

"Did you ever decode the messages on the triangles?" asked Linda.

"No," frowned Jim, "but we now believe they contain incoming messages—information very important to *the Teachers* that was lost for thousands of years."

Jim related the first-hand experiences of Professor Schmidt, Sophie Hoffman and German intelligence agent Max Becker when they visited the "Other Side" and were questioned about the missing triangles.

"Wow, the 'Other Side,' huh?" said Tony. "I need to check that place out! Can you get me an invitation or a ticket or whatever it takes to get in?"

Before Jim could answer, a Marine assigned to guard the makeshift shelter in the basement of the NRL administration building stuck his head in the door and signaled for Jim. When he returned to the table, Jim pointed to a telephone on a small stand on the far side of the room.

"We have a call. I'll put it on the speaker phone, but please keep the chatter down."

Jim pressed the button and said, "Good morning, Mr. President."

"Good morning, Jim, and good morning to all of you. I understand that your old group is reunited except for your fallen comrade Frank Morton. I won't take much of your time, but I promised Jim I would get back to him as soon as my advisors and I had agreed on a new plan and we've just accomplished that.

"The six of you seem to have a knack for uncovering bizarre facts in an incredibly efficient manner. You've learned more about the Six—and done more to thwart their activities—than the entire U.S. Intelligence community. Jim knows more about *the Teachers* than we would have learned in a hundred years and he's even been directly approached by them.

"So here's the deal, folks. Your government would like to ask you to step up one more time and accept a very special assignment. We would like you, as a group, to make contact with these *Teachers* and establish a working dialog with them. We would like you, in effect, to become our ambassadors. Learn about them, understand them and gain their trust. And more importantly, get them to trust us. We have good reason to believe that the Six will stop at nothing to disrupt *the Teachers'* plans but we don't even know what those plans are or how they affect us."

"So you want us to be spies for you?" challenged Jim.

"Not at all, Jim," replied the President. "Tell them up front what your motives are. Tell them that your mission is to get them to agree, on their own terms, to a meeting with us. I don't expect or want you to be dishonest with them in any way. I don't know if you're a Star Trek fan or not, but we'd like you to be our 'away team' with *the Teachers*. You will, of course, have access to any resources you might need and we've even come up with a pretty decent place for you to hang out that will be a lot more comfortable than your current location. You'll even have access to the outdoors!"

"And what if we decline your offer, Mr. President?" asked Tony. "Not that we would, but I'm just curious."

"Jim can provide more details, but I suggest you all take a long look around and ask yourselves if you want to be confined to a windowless, underground environment such as your current location. I suspect you'll need to discuss this as a group before giving me a final answer, so take an hour or so and talk about it. The only thing I should warn you about is that this is an 'all or nothing' decision. Either you all agree to the new project or you all stay where you are for an indefinite period of time—at least until we bring down the Six."

"How do we get our decision to you, Mr. President?" asked Jim.

"Call Captain Stukey and let him know because if you decline he will need to arrange additional sleeping quarters there at NRL. Good-bye, ladies and gentleman. I wish you the best whatever you decide."

A click in the speaker signaled that the President had dropped off the line. Jim punched the speakerphone button on his end and then turned to face the group at the table.

"I can't believe it!" he shouted. "They're blackmailing us again!"

"What are you talking about?" asked a puzzled Tony. "We have an opportunity to be the first official emissary to an alien culture and you're complaining? As an anthropologist, I would think you would be ecstatic about this opportunity."

"Yes," echoed Linda. "This is ten times better than the finds in the Yucatan or on Yonaguni. It's even better than the discovery of the triangles because you get to interact with living beings instead of smelly metallic relics."

"But they are playing us again, don't you see? Once we've made contact and gained the aliens' trust, they will steam roller right over us and proceed with whatever agenda they already have cooked up. I'm not going to be their patsy again!"

"Well then we will take measures to guarantee that doesn't happen," said Tony.

"Like what?"

"Well, I don't know, off the top of my head, but we can figure it out as we go. If we know what's coming, we should be able to prevent it."

"Or we develop our own agenda," added Linda. "We decide how much information to share and we control the situation through our knowledge. Come on Jim, you can't possibly want to walk away from an opportunity like this. This isn't just the chance of a lifetime this is one chance in the history of human civilization. I vote to accept the President's offer."

The other four members of the NWIDI team all spoke at once, supporting Linda's vote.

Jim frowned but nodded.

"Okay, I'll go along with the group, but with some serious reservations. I can't help wondering how Frank would vote if he were here right now. I'm not sure he'd be so quick to jump into bed with the same government that's used us over and over."

Jim passed out some sheets of paper he'd been clutching since entering the room.

"These are menus from the cafeteria upstairs. I know it's been a while since some of you have eaten, so circle anything you want. Without credentials you can't roam around the building, but I can have it sent down here. While you're deciding, I'll go call the Captain and give him our answer."

Jim made the call and then returned to collect the sheets. As he was handing them to the guard outside the door, he noticed that there were seven sheets instead of six so he flashed through them. The very last piece of paper wasn't a menu at all, but instead contained a simple, handwritten note. As his eyes scanned the four short lines, he gasped out loud.

R.J. Archer

Read the entire Parallel Ops series:

The Scientists (ISBN 978-0977910946)
From their secret laboratory, scientists work to protect alien artifacts from powerful international terrorists.

The Informants (ISBN 978-0977910960)
While on the run from international terrorists, a young couple stumbles upon a dark secret in the mountains of Mexico's Baja.

The Guardians (ISBN 978-0977910984)
From their floating base in the Caribbean, a multi-national team struggles to protect a secret hidden deep beneath the sea.

The first three novels in this series take place at exactly the same time and may be read in parallel—a chapter from each book before moving on to the next chapter. They may also be read in series, the normal way.

The Teachers (coming in 2013)
Sorry, but details about the exciting conclusion to the *Parallel Ops* series cannot be revealed at this time.

What Fans Say About the Series

"Parallel Ops is a series that weaves different story lines together into one cohesive plot. If the first three in the series are any indication, the last one will be great."
Jon Hudson

For more information about this series, please join us at
www.ParallelOps.com

www.ingramcontent.com/pod-product-compliance
Lightning Source LLC
Chambersburg PA
CBHW060527260626
47161CB00003B/789